A HAN OF R

Kamala Markandaya

ORIENT PAPERBACKS
A Divison of Vision Books Pvt. Ltd.
New Delhi • Mumbai • Hyderabad

ISBN 81-222-0135-0

1st Orient Paperbacks Editon 1985

A Handful of Rice

© Kamala Markandaya, 1966

Cover design by Vision Studio

Published by
Orient Paperbacks
(A division of Vision Books Pvt. Ltd.)
Madarsa Road, Kashmere Gate, Delhi-110 006

Printed in India at
Rashtriya Rachna Printers, Delhi-110 092

Cover Printed at
Ravindra Printing Press, Delhi-110 006

A Handful of Rice

In this extremely fascinating novel Kamala Markandaya
has succeeded in producing a work of art which is
compulsively readable and gratifying in a most complete
way. It depicts the hard struggle of life in a modern city
and its demoralisation. Ravi, son of a peasant, joins in the
general exodus to the city, and, floating through the
indifferent streets, lands into the underworld of petty
criminals. He falls in love with pretty Nalini, and marries
her against all odds. She tries to change his way of life,
but fate conspires against him... and the story moves to a
memorable and a haunting climax.

Kamala Markandaya was born and brought up in South
India. She attended various schools there and later went on
to Madras University. She has worked as a journalist and
writer in both England and India. Her first novel, the
classic *Nectar in a Sieve*, was published in 1954 and has
been translated into fifteen languages. Her other widely
acclaimed novels include *A Silence of Desire* and *The
Possession*. Kamala Markandaya is married and has a
grown daughter.

*"Certainly makes absorbing and enjoyable reading ... the
author has successfully and virtually captured the mores, the
spirit and, above all, the lingo obtaining in the streets and by-
lanes of India."*

Indian Express

*"Shades of Pearl Buck haunt the descriptions, situations and
the characters."*

Tribune

Chapter 1

THE policeman was watching him. He let go of the railing and walked as steadily as he could to the unlit turning in the road and waited. When he walked on the policeman followed; he had big boots on: probably a sergeant.

'Hey, you!'

'Me?'

'What's your name?'

'That's my business.'

The heavy experienced hand spun him round; his arm was held and twisted behind his back, he knew he was helpless.

'Answer.'

'Ravi. Ravishankar.'

'Ravishankar. You're drunk. Where did you get it?'

Another twist. The pain made him furious.

'You bastard,' he said, and bent his head. The khaki cloth was strong, but it ripped under his teeth, his sharp white buck teeth. He felt the flesh split, and it was, momentarily, as voluptuous as a climax.

He ran, heard the man's sharp yelp, and gloated. Big boots was after him, very hard and purposeful; but the feet inside were Indian, unused to running in boots. He, Ravi, on the other hand, though barefoot was drunk, which evened the odds. Well, he was not so drunk that he could not shake off his official tail. Abruptly he stopped, looked for a turning, doubled back on his tracks. The street must have lain parallel, the pounding boots sounded very close as they passed, unseen. The sound died. He leant against a wall, waiting. The silence continued. Night had saved him, the darkness to which he was used, and the fact that there were no people about. People, he thought. People were everywhere, swarming like ants. They weren't necessarily against you, or for you: they were simply there and if there was a chance they became a mob and followed, bellowing: got in the way, until some poor devil like himself was trapped. He spat his disgust.

'Hey, you!'

He whirled round. Set high in the wall was a small window with a rusty grille in front, wooden shutters behind. The louvers were open; he could just see a pair of eyes through the slits.

'Clear out, do you hear? Waking respectable people up in the middle of the night! Clear out, double quick.'

'Why?' He leant more comfortably against the wall. 'I'm doing no harm. Just resting.'

'Just resting, are you. Well, you can't rest here. Go find a *chatram*. I'll give you just one minute.'

'No.'

'Then I'll call the police. The police, my lad. They'll soon get you moving.'

The police. He began to laugh softly, looking up at the terrified eyes glimmering palely behind the wooden shutters.

'And how will you send for them? You will have to come out first and I'll hack you into little pieces before you've taken one step, you poor old fool.'

He slid down, rocking with laughter, until his head touched the rough ground. Above him the shutters squeaked, the stiff vanes were being forced to slant down at an extreme angle so that the eyes could squint down at him. He laughed again; it came out like a girl's giggle.

'You lout,' the voice said. 'You no-good lout, you're drunk.'

Rage filled him. He levered himself up slowly.

'Drunk, am I,' he said distinctly. 'I'm not only drunk, I'm starving, I tell you.'

Waves of giddiness assailed him. It would have been better not to have remembered that, he thought, and he lowered his head and waited; but the sickness would not pass and he began to retch, gross heaving spasms that wrenched his stomach, though nothing came up.

'Go away,' the voice said.

The heaving subsided. Furious anger mounted strongly in him again. He thrust his face close to the grating.

'Listen,' he said. 'I'm hungry, I want a meal. You let me in, do you hear? I'll give you one minute.'

'Go away.' The voice quavered—either an old man or a weak man, a man without men behind him.

6

He stretched his hands up to the grille and grasped the cross-bar triumphantly, sweetly conscious of his strength.

'One minute,' he said, 'then I'm coming in and it'll be the worse for you.'

Silence. He tightened his grip and wrenched, and the bar broke, spattering rusty grit on him.

'You see?'

'All right, all right, I'm coming.' The voice mumbled nervously.

He reached up and broke another bar, for good measure, while he waited.

'Please don't do any more damage.'

This time bolts rattled in earnest. The wooden door creaked and opened. Inside stood the man, cowering. He had thrown a shawl around his shoulders and lighted a hurricane lantern; the light trembled with him.

'What do you want?'

'Food, I told you,' he said impatiently. 'And be quick.'

The light retreated, returned. There was bread, buttermilk, a small sweet-potato. He ate, keeping one hand on the rusty broken-off bar. The man watched, both eyes on him, hardly daring to blink. The old fool, Ravi thought, the bar wouldn't have cracked a saucer, let alone a skull. Anyhow, did he really look such a thug? He finished, blotting up the last crumbs with a wet thumb; wondered whether he should call for more, just to savour the feeling of power, but decided he was full.

'Is that all?' The voice still quavered and shook.

'Yes,' he said, and changed his mind. 'No,' he said, peremptorily. He felt commanding, conscious of dominion: this was what *they* felt like, the people who said 'Hey, you!', who gave orders and expected you to jump to it, who had money, who had power, who did the pushing around. Well, tonight he would do the pushing.

'A bed,' he said. 'I'm staying the night. And make it soft—just anything won't do.'

His host stood wavering, reluctant, aghast.

'Go on, get moving.'

He spoke sharply, saw the instant reaction, and exulted. This was what life should be like: this was what he wanted his life to be like: and he tested and savoured the revelation, vouchsafed for the span of one night. In the morning—well, he knew that in the morning his brief reign would be over. The old fool would come into his own again, shed his coward's mantle and become a man of strength—the householder, the ratepayer, the outraged citizen entitled to raise a hue and cry against vagrants like himself. It was only in the jungle, by night, that they were equal.

By morning he intended to be gone.

There was a mat, a mattress, a pillow, a shawl—luxury. He was reeling and log-heavy with sleep. He pulled the bedding over to the door and spread it. The old man was watching him. For a moment he hesitated, then he shrugged. If he did, he did, that was all. There was no avoiding that risk.

'No monkey tricks,' he said with concentrated ferocity, curled himself up and slept.

Chapter 2

WHEN he woke in the morning he found that he could not move. A bicycle chain was fastened round his ankles, its free length clamped under a big stone mortar; and his arms had been crossed and bound in a woman's cotton sari which in turn was tied to a tin trunk. The mortar he could not shift, but when he heaved the trunk moved, allowing his torso limited play. It also roused his guard, a fat, middle-aged woman who sat near by, half-fearful, half-ferocious, a rolling-pin clutched in her hand.

'Don't you dare move, do you hear?' Her voice was very shrill.

He was partially sitting up. The position was insupportable, he had to move. Instantly she began hitting him. The blows fell indiscriminately—back, shoulders, head. Too late, he tried to avert his face: the blow caught his temple, splitting an eyebrow and almost stunning him. Blood began to drip, a warm trickle down his face, vivid scarlet on the white cloth imprisoning his arms. He stared at the spreading stain, stupidly. Was this really happening to him, Ravi, bound like a criminal, beaten as if he were a mad dog? Pain and bewilderment combined; he lowered his head into his arms, so that the woman should neither see him bleed nor weep.

8

'My God, what have you done to him!' The man had returned. His face was mottled and discoloured with shock.

'I didn't mean to...I swear it. I thought he was trying to escape—'

'Never mind what you thought! Water, quickly.'

The woman brought water, a towel, rags to staunch the flow. The man released him, fears forgotten in horror of bloodshed, grunting and straining as he shifted the heavy imprisoning weights, his meagre frame bent with the effort.

'Here, hold up your head. It'll help to stop the bleeding.'

He did so, obediently, thankfully abrogating his responsibilities to their will. She bathed his eyes, his temple, the cut eyebrow, dried the wound and bound it. The man unbuttoned his shirt, his hands moved over Ravi's back, pressing and probing.

'No bones broken, thank God.'

'The cut is quite shallow too. Thank God.'

They stared at him, awkwardly, waiting for him to—well, what the hell did they expect him to do, walk out with a bloody bandage on and his head swimming like a shoal of fish? He said, bitterly, 'What did you have to hit me like that for?'

'What did you expect, breaking in like a ruffian?'

'I was hungry,' he said sullenly. 'I hadn't eaten—'

'But you were drunk.'

He looked at the old man, hating him, but the hate guttered away like a cheap candle, dissolving into drab listlessness. He shrugged. 'So would you be,' he said, 'if all you had was one rupee between you and kingdom come.'

'You could have bought a meal,' the old man said accusingly, 'instead of boozing. A rupee buys a very reasonable meal.'

'Yes, and what then?' He roused himself. 'I *didn't* want to buy reason, I *don't* want to buy reason, what I wanted to buy was something quite different, something that would stop me thinking about tomorrow because the more I think of it the sicker I get—sick, sick of it!'

'One must!' The old man was shocked, the shock overriding even his agitation in the face of violence. 'A young man like you —you must think of the future!'

'What future?' he sneered. 'It's bad enough getting through the day, without dragging that in!'

'You mustn't talk like that.' Now the woman was starting on him.

'Why shouldn't I?' he shouted. 'You know nothing about me, nothing about how I feel or why I feel it!'

They took no notice of him. They were no longer even afraid of him. Where was his power of the night? Reduce everything to the jungle, he thought, and *then* see—see who is the beater, and who the beaten-down. He lay back, his head throbbing. He was alone. The man had gone to the tap in the courtyard to wash, he could hear the water splashing, purling along the runnels that skirted the sides. The woman had gone too. She had washed first, and was now clattering about in the kitchen. *They*, he thought, had taken up their ordinary lives again, the routine of it, the order, leaving him to—to do what? Hey you! he wanted to shout, but he could not: you had to get in the habit of it first, he thought, and you didn't acquire the habit until you were on the up-and-up, not down and out like himself. The shouting came after the summit. Ah, the summit! it was almost a physical sensation, the craving to be there.

He got up and went to the kitchen and stood in the doorway because he could not get in, it was so small. A blackened range ran along one wall, with firewood and charcoal stacked at the end. At the other stood the woman, fanning a slow fire over which a brass vessel simmered.

'What do you want?' She didn't even stop fanning.

'I ought to be going,' he mumbled.

'Either come in or go away, will you?' she said over her shoulder. 'I can't see what I'm doing.'

He turned sideways and flattened himself in the opening, so that he should not obstruct the light.

'I'm going now,' he spoke more loudly.

'No, no, no,' she said, 'everything's nearly ready. You mustn't start the morning on an empty stomach.'

'It won't be the first time.' He said it as a matter of fact, without self-pity, but it stopped her in what she was doing, the back she had turned on him was straight and attentive.

'Never mind about other mornings,' she said at last, and set to work again.

He stood watching. She was younger than he had at first

thought: perhaps forty, but flabby from too much flesh. He could see the veins standing out on her arms as she lifted the heavy vessel off the fire and he went to help but she waved him away. 'I can manage.'

She took off the lid and a cloud of white steam rose, bringing familiar and tempting smells to his nostrils. He peered into the steamer, knowing exactly what he would see: three *idlies*, composed in clover pattern in the steamer, each wrapped in butter muslin, well-risen, rounded and pure white. His mouth began to water.

'Here you are.'

There were two for him on a square of plantain leaf, with ghee, pickle, a tumblerful of coffee.

If I had a wife, he thought as he ate, she would cook for me, it would be like this every day ... but what had he to offer to get himself a wife? ... I'll buy her a little house, small but nice, he thought as he finished, and some nice new shiny aluminium cooking vessels, these brass things are too heavy, old-fashioned ... and with a job one can save say a quarter of one's wage—

'How are you feeling?'

'Oh. I'm all right.'

'Head ache?'

'Well, it was a bit of a clout.'

Without any warning her indignation exploded. 'What right have you to criticize? Didn't you deserve what you got? Perhaps a few more blows and you would really have learnt your lesson!'

She was about to strike him again, he thought, the bitch! He said, furiously, 'I've got a good mind to complain to the police about you.'

'The police!' She was gasping with anger. 'Yes, that's just what we should have done, gone straight to the police, it's not worth taking pity on you and your like.' She turned to her husband. 'Come on, we can still go, it's not too late by any means. They'll have you under lock and key—'

They would, he thought dully; he didn't stand a chance, especially if that bastard of a sergeant was there and his luck was such that he would be. He didn't stand a chance even if he was innocent, and he wasn't innocent, even he knew that.

'It was only a joke,' he said uncomfortably, swallowing his anger.

'We don't understand jokes like that in this house.'

He had finished everything, the last crumb, the last drop of coffee. He folded the four corners of his leaf inwards, picked up the parcel fastidiously, between finger and thumb, took it out into the street and flung it into the open gutter where cows were nosing. Then he came back, washed his face and hands and the tumbler he had drunk from, poured water over his feet and finally stood before her.

'I'm going now.'

She looked up. Her anger had simmered down to indignation.

'Behaving like that,' she said, 'a decent boy like you!'

He went out. Decent? When had he last been decent? Not since he had left that arid dump in the village which his mother, and indeed their neighbours, lyingly labelled 'a decent home'. What had been decent about it? When he tried to be honest he knew that what was decent about it was its honesty. They did not lie, they did not cheat, they did not steal. But then in that small struggling farming community what was there to steal? As far back as he could see they had all lived between bouts of genteel and acute poverty—the kind in which the weakest went to the wall, the old ones and the babies, dying of tuberculosis, dysentery, the 'falling fever', 'recurrent fever', and any other names for what was basically, simply, nothing but starvation. The pattern must have gone on a long time, for generations, because nobody objected, nobody protested, they just kept going, on and on, and were thankful that they were able to.

And yet, somewhere, a leaven must have been at work, a restlessness, a discontent in the towns whose spores had spread even as far as the villages so that suddenly it was not good enough and first one home and then another began to lose its sons, young men like him who felt, obscurely, that it was not right for them and— this with conviction—that it would be utterly wrong for their children.

Where now? He whittled it down, as he had learnt to do, from a contemplation of the future to the next actual hour. He could go and work in the coffee shop, earn himself the few coppers he needed to tide him through the day. Or he could rout up some of the gang for a game of dice which they played against chits that mortgaged the next day's earnings. Or he could go and hang around the docks, where there might be a small job going. Then he remembered his head. It felt better, almost well, but he could hardly be expected to do anything with his head swathed like this. Anyhow, who expected him to? No one, he had no one. Well, there was only one thing to do—rest. He began to walk—at last with some vague sense of purpose.

They had made the station their headquarters for the time being—he and one or two others. It made a good base, rent-free, where they could be sure of meeting one another, where one or other could be trusted to keep watch over their pitch and their possessions, removing themselves at speed whenever the railway *banchots* came along to carry on the war against just such as they.

At this time of day it was not difficult to get in. The crush grille was open, and the ticket-collector sat comatose on his hard, high wooden stool, his clippers in his hand. A quick look round, then he was past the sleeper, on to the platform, past the refreshment rooms and into the waiting-room—all without trouble.

'Yah, Damodar!' He padded in silently and pounced on his friend. Instantly Damodar was in flight, a quick practised flight that he cut short abruptly, sourly.

'You and your silly tricks. Is it funny to frighten people? You could easily give them a heart attack—why, what have you done to your head?'

'I've been hitting it against a wall,' Ravi said, flippantly, and turned his eyes to the two on the near-by bench. Damodar nodded and got up. They took their possessions and sat in a far corner, lowering their voices against people who might or might not be like themselves.

'Was it the police?'

'No,' said Ravi. 'A woman. She thought I was about to do her.'

'Were you?'

'No, no,' said Ravi impatiently. 'You should have seen her, the bitch. But she gave me a good meal. *Idlies*, with *spoonfuls* of ghee.'

'What for?'

'For not robbing them, I suppose.'

Damodar's eyes grew reflective. 'Sounds like a good racket.'

'What does?'

'Getting paid for not doing something.'

Ravi shrugged. 'I didn't plan it that way. It just happened.'

'How?'

'Well, I was drunk,' said Ravi, 'and the old man got my back up, otherwise I would never have broken in.'

'How *did* you?'

'The window was pretty low,' said Ravi, 'and the bars—well, I'm not a weed you know, I wasn't going to be defeated by a few bars, I wrenched at them—'

'Don't boast.'

'Anyhow, that *is* how I got in! Go and ask them if you like.'

'Where's the house?'

'Oh. Near George Town.'

'In it?'

'No, near. One of those streets that run—' he stopped.

'Near the brewery?'

'Why do you want to know?'

'Want to keep a good thing to yourself, do you?' said Damodar, and beneath the teasing Ravi felt the steel.

'All I got was a meal,' he said. 'It just happened that way, I tell you! I wouldn't—I mean those people, they weren't too bad, I wouldn't want—'

'Who said I was going to do anything?' Damodar slapped his stomach, which was lean and curved inward. 'All I want is a meal —a nice hot home-cooked meal, not bazaar muck—but if you don't want anyone on easy street except yourself—'

'It's not that!'

'—I suppose I better start shifting for myself.'

'Where are you going?' Ravi asked nervously.

'The coffee shop. That's probably my best bet.'

'I'll come too.'

'What for? You don't want to work when you don't need to!'

'You can have my share,' Ravi offered.

Damodar grinned broadly and slapped him on the back. 'Ai, you have got a soft conscience! But you're a decent one, I'll say that for you: a decent one.'

14

In the night Ravi grew uneasy again. They took it in turns to sleep, but even when it was his turn he could not. Curled up on a bench, his head resting on his bedroll, he watched Damodar, dozing on guard duty beside the swing doors of the waiting-room, and wondered whether he had not said too much. Really, he would not like any harm to come to the couple who had—not exactly coddled him, but they had not thrown him to the wolves either. Supposing Damodar—? Damodar who knew the brewery, who knew all the bootleggers in town, who knew the town like the back of his hand—it would not take *him* long to pinpoint the house with the broken grating. And his friend wasn't like him, a country youth newly up from a village. Damodar was a city slicker, born and bred in the streets of the city, with city standards that were not exactly different from his own but tougher, more elastic, so that Ravi was never sure exactly how far they would stretch. Usually it did not concern him. He knew that life was a battle in which the weak always went under; he accepted the fact that the man who did not do all he could to keep on top was a fool. He would never fault Damodar on that score. It was simply that he had some way to go yet in toughening his own fibre, flabby from all those homilies on decency.

In his corner Damodar yawned and stretched and came shambling over.

'Up, lazy.'

'It's not my turn yet.'

'It is.'

'How do you know?'

'Clock in my head.'

It was true, Damodar did have a time-keeping brain. His own had broken down. The clock that in the country woke him with precision, told him the time of day, here refused to work, or buzzed fitfully, giving wrong information. One day, when he had money to spare, he would buy himself a clock—an alarm with a soft repeating chime and a luminous dial—

'Come on.'

'All *right*. I'm coming.' He grumbled, but he was glad to be up; it was a tedious affair, pretending to sleep when he could not. Damodar had no such block. In two minutes he was snoring gently, his thin body careless of the hard wooden bench.

15

Chapter 3

BY morning Ravi had capitulated. He woke Damodar first, shaking him to make sure he was fully awake, and then he slipped out, leaving him to his own devices. There was nothing unusual in this: they worked in partnership only when it suited them: and today it did not suit him at all.

From the station to George Town was a fair trek, but one he could ordinarily take in his stride. Today, however, his steps lagged, and although he tried to put it down to his battered head he knew it was because he was hopelessly unsure of what to do. Warn the couple to watch out? They would only suspect a trap, and anyway, how long could they maintain this vigilance—days, months?—it was clearly impossible. Offer his services as unpaid night watchman? He smiled faintly: there was a foreseeable certain end to that: himself in the cells. Well, he would see when he got there.

Meanwhile getting there was proving difficult, for try as he might he could not remember the location of the street in relation to George Town. George Town itself he knew and knew well. It skirted the docks, was its unproclaimed clearing house, and into the maze of streets that penetrated inland poured the products of a thriving industry, the world's underground trade. Here he had seen the wine butts coming in, from Porto Novo and Pondicherry and round the Cape from as afar off as Mahé and Goa; and hemp, opium, bhang, hashish—all the deadly disguises of the beautiful poppy off-loaded under the noses of the Customs men from junks that had wallowed in from Rangoon and Singapore and even, it was rumoured, from the China ports.

It was the first territory he had got to know, and it was Damodar who had initiated him, who had told him of the pickings to be had by those who did. What he had found out for himself was that initiation and novitiate were still not enough, for the pickings here glittered and were not for small fry like himself. One day he would take the next step: graduate upwards,

16

or was it deeper into the maze . . . and then, ah yes, then he could live, really begin to live.

Meanwhile they waited in the wings, and sometimes he (more often Damodar) was approached by a remittance-man, guarded in speech to the point of incomprehensibility, or offered the overspill from a liquor or drug peddling job. Some things were troublesome, but flogging duty-free spirits was easy. There were handsome profits to be made here, and out of this came a handsome cut for himself. More important were the contacts he made, the middle-men he met, the places he discovered—tea-houses, lodging-houses, warehouses with irreproachable mercantile façades from which a blessed oblivion could be bought. It was from one of these that he had reeled, the night the policeman had been watching, and he remembered he had clutched at railings—quite suddenly the shutter in his brain slid back, he knew exactly what the railings looked like, where they were, the street up which he had run, the wall he had leant against. He laughed to himself. It was easy, once you got your mind moving, only you had to give it a hefty shove or two first.

He rode his confidence all the way to the house and there sud-denly it bolted, leaving him on his own to negotiate difficult ground. What next? He stared nervously at the window set high in the wall. It was the same one all right: there were the two bars still missing, the brown wooden shutters behind. These were open, but there was no way of seeing in unless he stood on some-thing, or jumped up and down. There was nothing to stand on. He began to jump, and instantly the busy street stopped minding its own business. People! He swallowed his anger, walked away, down the street, up another, and came back again. The shutters were still open, the door closed. It was a heavy door, studded with round brass nails that were sunk and rusted into the wood, and it had a brass handle, also rusted and black, in the shape of a snake curled nose-tip to tail. He didn't remember this handle—the night had been too dark, or his senses too fuddled. He put his hand on it and a voice said, 'What are you doing?'

He leapt back. He felt the shock travelling up his arm, exactly as if the snake had come alive and bitten his hand.

'It's you,' said the woman, 'again. Up to no good. Hanging round just waiting for a chance—'

In a moment, he thought, she would be hollering and if the police came—he could be as innocent as a new-born babe, he thought, and it wouldn't make one blind bit of difference, they would take her word against his to hang him.

'No, no, no,' he said rapidly, revitalized by hard thinking that produced an inspired explanation, 'You've got it wrong. I wasn't going to—to do anything, I was just wondering if I could put the bars back for you seeing it was I who did the damage.'

'You're lying.'

At least she wasn't yet shouting, that was a good sign. He stole a shrewd look at her. Yes, he was right. Her face was undecided, nowhere as harsh as her words.

'Ah, madam,' he said, 'if I could lie to you I would lie to my own mother.'

'I expect you do.'

'Madam, believe me . . .' He drooped in her doorway, defeated, pathetic. He had, he knew, a soft face—'dolly', they called him sometimes, or 'softie', or 'baby-face'. It could occasionally be useful, although more usually it generated a vast irritation.

'Are you sure you can make a good job of it? It'll save me having to send for someone.'

Bitches, he thought, all of them: greedy for free labour, grudging a rupee to some poor devil in the bazaar who would have been glad of the money. He made his face brighten.

'Yes, easy. Make you sleep sounder in the night when I've done.'

The point was, he could relax too. He almost laughed: tell her *that*, and she would be instantly, unshakeably convinced he was a liar.

'Well, come in then.' She moved her great bulk at last. 'I suppose you'll need some tools.'

She went away, shouting to some girl to bring something. God, he thought, what lungs, what a voice. He looked about him. It was a small house, but not so small that he would have minded owning it. The room he was in was small too—perhaps twelve feet square. This was where he had broken in, where he had been battered . . . it looked very different at this time of day. In one corner bedding rolls were neatly stacked, one on top of the other —*eight* of them, he thought incredulously, where had these other people been buried that night? He had been luckier than he realized to escape further injury. Against a farther wall, where most light fell, stood a Singer sewing-machine, surrounded by bobbins and reels, ribbons and tape, festoons of material. So the old man was a tailor—a craft that was neither exciting nor lucrative. His interest dwindled. From within he could hear women's voices, two, three, then a man's voice joined in. Really, the place was swarming . . .

'Here you are.' A girl came in with a box of tools. 'My mother said to give you these.'

Her mother! He was astounded. She was young, pretty. Her hair hung down in a thick glossy plait to below her narrow waist. How could such mothers have such daughters?

'And don't be all day about it, do you hear?' Mother had come in behind daughter. 'I want it finished before my husband returns, he can't work if there's dust flying about—'

'At once,' he said. 'I'd best take these out first, they're no good to you . . . see?' The old rusty bars came out with ease. He crumbled one for effect, then cleared up the dust and brushed out the sockets.

'I think six bars should be enough,' he said, 'I'll measure up . . . yes, six bars, two-foot lengths—'

He waited. She took no notice. What was she waiting for—for him to ask for money? crawl on his belly simply because she had it and he hadn't? Well, she could think again.

'What are you waiting for?'

'It'll cost four-five rupees,' he said weakly. 'If you could—'

'If I did that would be the last I saw of your face and my money,' she said. She was glaring at him.

No feelings, he thought, as if you had no feelings either. They'd shred you to pieces right in front of you as if you weren't there, the feeling part of you. And that went for all of them, the big memsahibs down to the would-be memsahibs, petty little squirts like this one who was a petty tailor's wife: all of them, who called themselves respectable and bamboozled you into falling down in worship. He turned away abruptly.

'Don't go.'

He wrenched at the snake handle, was out on the street.

'Come back!'

19

She ran after him and grabbed his shirt-tails. He stood still, terribly afraid they would tear. It was his only shirt.

'Well?' They were both back in the house.

'Here you are.'

She thrust a five-rupee note into his hand. The purse was close to her person, a cloth affair tucked in at her waist. He wanted to thrust it back, but he conquered the impulse: he could not afford to be all that high and mighty. One day: not now. Besides, there was the girl, she of the gentle voice and beautiful hair who had not said anything, who was obviously too cowed by her mother to do so. But she had stood apart, apart from her mother, and she had the grace to look ashamed.

By the time he reached the blacksmith the money had begun to burn a hole in his pocket. There was a lot he could buy for five rupees, things that he needed over and above basic props like food which was all that his earnings ever ran to before his energies expired. Besides, people like that old sow deserved to be bilked: it was what they expected of you so you gave it to them. Why deny them the satisfaction of having been right? Then he thought again. After all, she *had* changed her mind, she *had* given him the money. Moreover there was Damodar, his eye on easy money—Damodar, who made him vaguely uneasy although they were partners. Not that even Damodar could do much, with that horde that seemed to be encamped in the house—but suppose they were asleep? At night most ordinary people were asleep, and Damodar moved like a cat, he could pick Ravi's pocket without waking him. Well then, would bars restrain him? He tried to say no; but in his heart he knew they would. Noise, the thought of a hue and cry, put them off many an enterprise... and not even Damodar could remove the stout bars he intended putting up without a good deal of noise, enough to wake the whole street. Well, he thought, the thing had more or less decided itself for him.

At the threshold of the smithy he hesitated again, fingering the note in his pocket. There was so much that he needed, that he went without day after bloody day.

'Ah, Ravi!' The blacksmith turned, momentarily putting aside his bellows. 'Changed your mind and come to work for me, have you?'

'I'll let you know,' said Ravi, 'when I decide I want to die at forty.'

Kannan chuckled. He was a short, thick-set man with a barrel chest and muscles that bulged, who did not look like dying at forty, which was five years off. But they were reputed to, thought Ravi, and no wonder with all the heat and coal dust in your lungs, and those deadly filings flying about getting in your hair and eyes. Kannan had lost an eye that way—at least it was still there but it looked greyish and putrid somehow, like a decayed shellfish, and it had shrunk, so that the lids around it were horribly puckered. He should have been wearing goggles of course, as they did compulsorily in factories nowadays . . . but Kannan said these things were expensive, and anyhow it had all happened years ago.

Ravi did not mind: but there were some lilies, sahibs and memsahibs mainly, who could not bear to look at that sightless eye—as if a man could help these accidents that twisted and warped him. Kannan took the same view. He had a quickened extended understanding so that not only did he not bawl out cripples and beggars, but he was not too hard on people, like Ravi for instance, whom the well-ordered, well-heeled sectors of the world called drifters, loafers or delinquents. Ravi liked Kannan, worked for him off and on, would have worked for him on a regular basis but for the fact that the smithy simply would not support two. The repeated offer of a job, the continued refusal, was in the nature of a joke between them, a secret tilt at crooked attitudes under virtuous cloaks that found unemployment and idleness indistinguishable.

'Now you haven't just come to keep me company, have you?' said Kannan, between clangs of his hammer.

'No,' said Ravi, who never indulged in circumlocution with Kannan. 'I came to see if you had any rods—iron rods to bar a window, two-foot lengths . . .'

'Expect I have—I'll have a look in a minute.'

'No hurry,' said Ravi courteously. 'When you're ready.'

He squatted down comfortably, a safe distance from anvil and hammer. He liked being in the smithy, the look of bright coal, the smell of horse and hay that the little jutka ponies left behind them. He liked the horse-shoes hanging on the wall, he admired the skill and precision that went into their making, and if he could have ordered the world to his will he would have ensured that a value

21

was set upon them less despicable in terms of money than the prevailing one.

'Ravi, give it a blow will you? there's a good chap.'

Ravi took up the bellows and began to work it. The coal glowed like a small inferno. It was special high-grade stuff, Kannan said; it had to be to produce this smelting heat, a heat in which iron could be bent and flattened and fashioned at will.

'Ready now.'

Kannan advanced, bearing in tongs the short heavy strip of metal that he held to the fire, playing it over the surface until the grey grew radiant. A quick twist into shape and on to the anvil ... ah, what skill, Ravi thought, what a skilled deployment of strength! He leant forward in admiration as the hammer blows fell, swift, disciplined, exactly where Kannan intended.

'Finish off, will you, Ravi?'

Ravi began filing the rough edges, soothed by the rasp, the smooth powdery feel of the metal when he had finished. Four horse-shoes, a set of four finely-fashioned shoes with the four square holes for the nails that would bolt them on to the living hoof ... it was with a sense of satisfaction that he strung them together and hung them up.

By now he had forgotten what he had come for.

'Here, will these do?'

'What for?'

'A window, you *said* ...'

'That's right.' Ravi returned to himself. 'You don't suppose I want to batter someone over the head with them, do you?'

'Who knows?' Kannan considered him judicially. 'On the whole, no—although someone's taken a bash at you.'

'Oh, that,' said Ravi, 'that just happened. Bit of a mistake really.' He began to examine the bars—he did not want to talk about *that* affair.

'All right?'

'Yes, fine. I'll need six ..?' he picked out the rods. 'What do you want for them?'

'Nothing, lad. They're spare, don't even know where they came from.'

'You must,' Ravi urged. 'It isn't my money. The old sow paid up—had to, in a way. Here, look!'

22

'You keep it.' Kannan waved the note away. 'It'll keep you out of mischief.'

Ravi bound the rods together and hoisted the bundle on to his shoulder. 'Well, thanks.'

'It's nothing.' Kannan turned again to his forge. He banged away, hoping, although it was not his business, that Ravi would not use the bars on human beings. On the whole he thought not; but you could never be sure about youngsters nowadays, they seemed to be driven by devils sterner than those his generation had known.

Chapter 4

RAVI was jubilant as he loped through the town. He would tell the old bitch it had cost four rupees, give her one rupee change, and be in pocket to the nice tune of four rupees. After all she expected to be rooked: he might as well oblige, give her the pleasure of having been right, although of course she wouldn't know that.

But *he* knew: he knew she had been right. Well then he wouldn't, he thought with a kind of sick determination, he wouldn't prove her right. His resentment against her rose like a wall.

When he got back the house seemed to him to be swarming with people—he almost backed out again in distaste. From within came the sound of a good many voices, women predominating, and in the front room with the gaping window three men and a boy were crammed round the sewing-machine, seated in a sea of billowing material, although only one of them seemed to be really working.

'What do you want?' They all looked at him.

'It's all right.' This was the old man he had cowed, no longer a trembling hulk but a householder in full authority. 'A workman to fix the window. My wife sent for him.'

'Jayamma's workman.' There was a murmur—reverent, it

seemed to Ravi. And no wonder, he said to himself. He could well imagine others finding her formidable—those who hadn't the courage to stand up to her. He braced himself to meet her.

'There you are at last!' Jayamma's voice was shrill. 'Didn't I say be quick? Now the dust will get in everything—all these fine new clothes . . .'

'I'll put up a screen,' he said sarcastically, 'and work behind that.'

'Yes, do.' Sarcasm was lost in the capacious quality of her self-absorption, her total immersion in her own affairs. 'We don't want anything soiled, do you hear?'

He turned his back on her and set to work. It did not take long —would have been quicker still if he had not had to sally forth for the bag of cement which he had forgotten. He had scarcely put down his trowel when Jayamma appeared. She had been in a dozen times to look already.

'All done?'

'Yes, and here's your change. Four-fifty.' He counted it into her palm. 'That's fifty paisa for the cement and nothing for the bars,' he said pointedly. She did not take notice; merely put the money away and waited for him to go. How like her, how like *them*, he thought, filled with a great contempt. She suspected the bars were stolen, but rather than ask, rather than miss the chance of something for nothing she was prepared to hold her tongue.

He was about to leave when the girl came in. All the time he worked he had been hoping for a glimpse of her, this young beauty whose looks made a man's day as her mother's marred it: it was just his luck, he thought, that she should appear now, when there was no further excuse for lingering.

'Well, I'll be going.'

'Wait a minute.' Jayamma (belatedly, he thought sourly) was actually opening her money purse. 'Here you are. A little something for your trouble.'

He looked down in astonishment at the coin coyly slipped into his palm. It was twenty-five naye paisa—a quarter of a rupee.

'Thank you,' he said. 'Are you sure you can spare it? I'll take good care to see I don't spend it all at once.'

This time at least he had got under her skin—*skin*, he thought,

My god, it's not skin, what it is is *hide*, what they get after years and years of toughening up, of not looking, of not caring to look, of glazing their eyes when they do. But this time he had pierced it, hide or skin whatever it was. She was staring at him, glaring at him, moving her mouth around and shaping words although no sound came. It was almost funny, he thought, and at that moment the girl giggled. It was a small giggle, but it was not a nervous one, a reaction to an imminent explosion from the older woman. She was really amused—amused with him, on his side: for the first time in as long as he could remember a decent girl was on his side. He stole a glance at her, and was nearly thrown into a fit of laughter himself. She had drawn her sari over the lower part of her face like a yashmak, and over this her eyes peered, round and swimming with tears of smothered laughter. What a girl, he thought. Take a girl like that, and half a man's troubles would be over.

He was in high good humour almost before the door banged behind him.

Chapter 5

IN the days that followed Ravi thought about her a lot—this girl with the bright eyes and the thick, glossy hair, who could transform a man's life. He would have liked to meet her—properly, not as a labouring coolie in her father's house; to talk to her as an equal, to get to know her, as other young men came to know young girls, within the approving, carefully conducted circle of mutual friends and family relationships.

But how? He took painful stock of himself. He had no family, and without them who would arrange it? He had left his family, a long time ago—three years was it?—as his brothers had done, as all the young men he knew had done or wanted to do, joining the exodus to the cities because their villages had nothing to offer them. The cities had nothing either, although they did not discover this until they arrived: but it held out before them like an incandescent carrot the hope that one day, some day, there would be something.

His own father had half-believed in it, in this shining legend of riches in the city—and not only because he had to, there being nothing in the village for the sons of a small rack-rent tenant farmer like himself, but because the vision had burned so long in his brain during years of fear and exhaustion that it had become enshrined there as a relic of truth.

And his mother? She had watched, powerless, unable even to comment, as bereft of knowledge as her husband but unwilling to substitute visions and legends for it. One after another they had been forced out, and had gone: three sons, her daughter, her son-in-law, all in turn had boarded the train that bore them away to the city.

In fact, thought Ravi, she had always known they would go, had always accepted that there was no counterweight she or the village could apply to thwart the drawing power of the vast magnet dangled by the city, for he could remember her, even when they were quite small children, withdrawing into a closed misery of her own each time the steam-engine and its three coaches came clanking in. It came once a day, barely paused—for the village was not even a station but only a Halt—and in a few minutes was gone, vanished beyond the horizon for another whole cycle of night and day. But the lines remained, double lines of steel bolted on to sleepers that moved both ways into the distance like an articulated animal; remained, and became a presence in their lives.

They brooded on it: his mother with a kind of paralysed fear that to the day of her death never expressed itself; he and his brothers with an increasing, heightening excitement that almost threatened to consume them before the actual day of departure. And what had happened to that excitement? At any other time he would have spat his disgust, rid his mouth of the taste of it and turned to dicing, drinking—anything that would disable his mind. Now he examined it carefully, minutely. What *had* happened? Somewhere between that bright beginning and now the vital fluid had drained away, leaving a sludge that sometimes made it difficult for him to shift his feet in the morning.

If there had been a job, he thought, it might have been different: but there was no job. The city was full of graduates—the colleges turned them out in their thousands each year—looking for employment, so what chance had he, with his meagre elementary-school learning? His father had been proud of this learning, had insisted on it as a key to the power of earning which was the broad base of a man's pride, had taken his whip to his whimpering sons to drive them to it. But he had been wrong. The key opened no doors: it closed them, for his education did not allow Ravi to compete against the gaunt, shabby-genteel young graduates who hung around the streets, while it had taken from him the ability to work with his hands except in an amateur capacity.

So what did that leave him with? The analysis was hurting now, probing regions so raw that he usually kept them well shielded. He could read, he could write—not only the vernacular but English—English because that had been the language of the overlords when he was a boy, and if you aimed anywhere higher than the rut you were in, learning it was one of the routes. He was young, able-bodied, healthy. He had a certain quickness of hand and eye and mind which gave him a fractional advantage in his dealings with men. With these assets then, which added up sizeably, was it still true to say that in this city of hundreds of thousands of inhabitants, each with a hundred needs, there was no job for him between coolie and clerk?

Ravi wanted to stop thinking, but he could not. He laid his throbbing head on his arms while the inquiry went on. Somewhere, certainly, there was such a job. It was the drag round the streets, and the searching, and the wait and the frustration and bearing the pinpricks that the haughty rich always had in plenty for the poor, which he had not been able to endure.

Then Damodar had come along, with his introductions to a whole gang of young men like himself, and his passport to a world shot with glitter and excitement: a world that revived the incandescent glow the city had once kindled; and suddenly the terror and the loneliness were gone, lifted from the load whose other components were hunger, the lassitude of hunger, and the terror of losing his identity in an indifferent city which was akin to death. Of course much of this world, this dazzling world, lay in the future: but every kind of fear and privation became bearable in the light of its bright promise.

Yes, Damodar had helped; but would Damodar be able to help him in his relations with this girl? Would any of his friends? He almost smiled. Produce any of that set, he thought grimly, and he might as well write finis to this chapter of his dreams.

'Ai, Ravi! What's the matter, girl trouble?'

It wasn't only that of course: but he could not go into all the details of his discontent. He nodded silently.

'No need to fret, man!' Damodar banged him encouragingly on the back. 'She'll come round in the end. They all do.'

'Not this one.' Ravi spoke out of his depression. 'She's—different.'

'When we're smitten we all think that.' Damodar laughed. 'Believe me, my dear Ravi, girls are all the same. I know them.'

Ravi knew, too, the sort of girls Damodar knew: bazaar girls who were two a penny, who joked with you with unseemly camaraderie, who scarcely bothered to draw the cloth of their saris over their breasts; or who were to be seen riding in rickshaws at night on the Marina between Mylapore and the Fort, hidden behind grimy white drapes in perverted semblance of the habit of a nun. That sort of girl was not for him—never, never! He almost trembled, contrasting them with the chaste young beauty who had crossed his path.

'Come on, man,' Damodar urged, 'out with it.'

'Well,' said Ravi weakly, 'there's not much to tell,' and then a little to his surprise he found himself recounting what had happened, leaving out only the address, the actual locale, from a deeply-grounded nervousness of Damodar.

'And then what happened,' asked Damodar, listening carefully, 'after she took your side, I mean. Finish the story.'

'But that's it,' said Ravi, feeling he had welshed on his friend. 'She giggled, I came away, that's all.'

Damodar let out a long, low whistle of amazement. 'You mean you actually had her on your side, and you simply let it go at that?'

'What else could I do?' Ravi spoke resentfully. It was all very well for Damodar, who kept different company, who had forgotten the difficulties of getting to know a respectable girl without the solid background of family—and especially after you had quarrelled with her mother! But even Damodar was silent, and Ravi went on, boldly. 'What would *you* have done?'

There was another silence. 'You'll have to propitiate her,' said Damodar at last. 'The mother, I mean.'

'Oh yes,' said Ravi sarcastically. 'I'll take her some garlands, and perhaps a sari or two. What does it matter if I don't eat for some months?'

Damodar pondered. 'Has she any brothers?'

'I don't know.'

'Making friends with them would help.'

'I don't *know*, I tell you.'

'Or you could help her father.'

'To do what?'

'Whatever *he* does.'

'He's a tailor.'

'Oh well.' Damodar splayed his hands in defeat; and then suddenly, in between horse-play and genuine concern, he grew still.

Ravi looked up, surprised: 'What is it?'

'There's the warehouse,' said Damodar thoughtfully. His eyes had narrowed, giving him the look of a wary cat. Ravi knew the look and shivered; it meant business, and although he partnered Damodar, followed where he led, seldom had misgivings, yet he never escaped this preliminary spurt of panic.

He never showed it, never risked the blistering scorn that he knew underlay Damodar's easy jovialities. And Damodar for his part trod carefully, never forcing the pace, allowing novices to step gingerly over a borderline at which they had earlier baulked, willing to sacrifice a plum or two rather than lose a recruit.

The warehouse was more than a plum, it was a whole orchard. Damodar, Ravi knew, had been itching to have a crack at it, had desisted only because he knew he could never do it on his own. A large tin shed, it lay within sight and hailing distance of the docks and, indeed, was periodically floodlit by a powerful beam from the lighthouse beyond; but few took notice of what seemed a dump for empty sacks and battered petrol tins, or looked beyond the untidy squatters' shacks that further disfigured it. Fewer still knew that it was in effect a bonded warehouse although the goods in bond had never come under Customs scrutiny, or suspected that the complex system of rate-fixing and exaction of dues was operated by a ring at least as efficient and well-organized as any of the more respectable commercial houses.

Ravi had been inside once, in the early days, and had come away bemused by what he was shown, the vast collection of silks and satins, bolts of brocade and velvet that lined the shelves from floor to ceiling. Later there were other visits, after he had proved he could keep his mouth shut—visits during which his suspicions hardened that what he saw concealed a good deal of what he was not meant to see. But even this visible truth seemed rich enough to him, as gradually he came to appreciate the wealth that was locked up here in this finery, in these French chiffons, Genoese velvets, Honiton lace, imported to satisfy the whims of conditioned women who could have been served as well by Benares or Bangalore, but who believed that a foreign label conferred a certain cachet, a little indefinable something that set them above the common herd. Commercial interests would have catered for their needs: but in these post-British days there were bans, quotas, import restrictions imposed by a government more interested in fostering national industry than in pandering to the rich. So the black marketeers took over.

Even here, Ravi discovered, there were circles within circles, the full ramifications of which he did not yet know fully. He knew, however, Damodar's ring: the small operators who lived off the backs of the large operators, although the reprisals against those caught were so ferocious that Damodar had great difficulty in gathering henchmen for his bolder schemes. As he himself savagely said, he was limited by the timidity of his followers.

'There's the warehouse,' Damodar repeated. He watched Ravi, coldly willing him to acquiesce.

'Yes.' Ravi shrugged, throwing off the pressure he could feel being exerted on him. 'I don't see the connection.'

'Don't you?' Damodar leered. 'Or don't you want to? What I'm saying is take him a bolt or two, brocade, what you will, and you'll have the old man eating out of your hand.'

It was true enough, Ravi knew. With material like that to offer, a tailor could choose his memsahib and fix his price, instead of the other way round. No questions would be asked, for fear of cutting off the supply; and there was little risk, for it was entirely beyond official scope to crack down on every petty trader hawking forbidden goods. On the point of acceptance, Ravi hesitated, felt tempted, then hung back again. He had no particular scruple about lifting goods from the warehouse. After all, as he told himself, it was not exactly stealing, for they should not have been there in the first place; and taking it further back, why shouldn't people bring into the country what they wanted? If it was wrong, it was a paper thing, nothing to do with morals as he now practised them; but it was pertinent in the context of those respectable connections for which he intended making a determined bid. Furthermore, the proposal frightened him. Tweaking the nose of the law was one thing, operating against one's kind entirely another: unsavoury, and frightening. He said:

'We couldn't do it.'

'Why not?' Damodar's voice was edged.

'There's the watchman.' He forced himself to go on. 'Two of them, night and day.'

'Easy,' Damodar rubbed thumb and finger together in the universal gesture betokening bribery. 'Grease their palms.'

'With what?'

'With the proceeds.'

'It's dangerous.'

'Isn't life?'

Ravi was suddenly very weary. He would do it for her, he told himself sullenly: for her sake, not his. Anyhow, what did it matter: what mattered now, at this moment of time through which he was living, was not to have to hold out against Damodar any longer. And Damodar was right, he saw that: life was hazardous in all its aspects, and was it to be reckoned more so here because the danger was blatant and obvious, than in a village where it was hidden in duller, more insidious forms? There were, after all, man-traps everywhere.

'All right?'

'Yes.'

'Good man! Now listen. The night-watchman comes on at—'

Damodar's voice had lost its serrated edge, he was brisk and friendly again as he detailed plans which, Ravi realized fleetingly before he was borne away on the other's enthusiasm, must have been worked out months before on the certainty of his cooperation.

31

Chapter 6

By the time the rolls of material were under his arm Ravi had forgotten the rigours of the night that had produced them. All he could think of was that at last he had a passport that would get him into the house he wished to enter. He walked boldly up to the door and knocked.

'What is it?'

Jayamma stood widely in the doorway, hands on her hips. How uncouth she was, he thought, barring his way as if he were an interloping· pi-dog, speaking in that brassy voice ill-suited to a woman! He said, civilly, 'I've got a few things here ... I think your husband might be interested.'

'What sort of things?'

'Cloth—material ...' he began to stammer. 'I thought you— your husband might be interested.'

'My husband has gone out.'

'Apu said he wouldn't be long.' The girl was peeping over her mother's shoulder—trying, Ravi thought with a surge of pleasure, to help him. His confidence returned.

'I can wait,' he said, and deftly avoiding Jayamma stepped in.

It was the first step that counted: this had been one of his father's maxims, automatically rejected along with scores of others. Now, however, Ravi endorsed it, for here he was, as a result of that first step, ensconced in a house to which he would never otherwise have gained entry. Acceptance, of course, was another matter: but he could see it coming as he worked at it assiduously, collecting and delivering for Apu, running errands for Jayamma, never saying no to whatever task he was set to do. Already there were signs that the older. woman was softening. Nowadays, if he came early, she would bring him an *apam*, with some of her own home-made pickle, or if it were evening a tumblerful of coffee. The old man, too—roughly from the time his loving greedy fingers had felt the rich, heavy textures of Ravi's offering—appeared to be revising his earlier unfavourable impression. He spoke to him now as to the son of an equal, some other worthy tradesman: and once or twice Ravi had felt himself being thoughtfully studied, as if the old man were considering absorbing him into the busy hive of his industry.

It was, Ravi knew, within his power to do so: for despite appearances it was Apu who ran the business, who took the decisions, who held the household together. Jayamma, large and vocal, carried the appurtenances of strength: it was her mouse-like husband who exercised it. Ruminating on it Ravi sometimes felt affronted, indignant almost, that this shrivelled-up nonentity, whom he had seen by night cowering and cringing before him, should by day order him about here and there. At these times he would wrap the jungle around him for comfort . . . ah yes, the jungle, its darkness, its lawlessness, where a man's strength and courage alone gave him mastery . . . live by jungle law, and then see who survived!

Mostly, however, he did not resent Apu. Indeed, as the days went by his respect for the old man grew, at least one ingredient of which was a kind of reverence for the fact—incredible it seemed to Ravi—that he had fathered Nalini.

Nalini, his girl. He said it to himself sweetly, roundly, secretly, and it filled him with a delicious sense of pleasure. Nalini, the girl who could make a man feel like a man even outside the jungle of his choosing, the girl for whom he was ready to repudiate all in his life that was unworthy. And what this was, he realized clearly, was precisely what would have alienated his own respectable family: his dubious activities on the fringes of the law in the dubious company of Damodar. But whereas the standards of his family filled him with contempt—for what had it taught them except an excessive endurance, and what had it brought them except perpetual poverty!—he accepted them as entirely necessary for this girl. Nor did the split in his thinking trouble him. One varied one's criteria to circumstance, as any fool knew: and how a man reacted to the strictures of his father was entirely different from the returns he willingly made to his girl.

For her, he resolved, everything would be different, he would be different. No act of his should sully the wholesome quality he discerned in her, a kind of vulnerable purity that he wanted to enclose and guard, feeling himself cleansed and enriched by it. Even so he did not close with the past, cast no moral stricture on what he had done, saw no wrong in it. It was simply part of the battle of life: and, equally simply, now it had ceased to be good enough.

His girl. He said it to himself again, softly, and felt a gentle glow diffuse itself throughout his body. Yet in what way was she his girl? He came to her house as often as he could, slaved for her mother, worked for her father, bore with the whims of the hangers-on in the household, neglected his own distinctly precarious finances—for what? For the few words he was able to exchange with her in between, if he was lucky. Sometimes there was not even this: sometimes after a whole day's endurance all he had for his comfort was the sound of her, the swish of her sari as she whisked about the place at her mother's bidding, or a glimpse of her sitting cross-legged like an inaccessible goddess in one of the inner rooms. Except once, when someone had forgotten to close the door that led to the tiny open courtyard beyond, and he had seen her sitting on a small wooden plank near the tap in the centre, soft and flushed from her bath, dressed in a pink mull sari with her hair loose about her shoulders. It was like a curtain, her hair: a shining silk curtain that rippled and shimmered as the ivory comb worked down from root to tip. He hardly dared to breathe, he was so taken by the beauty of it, her grace, the lovely movement of head and rounded arm that curved and lifted her uncovered breast.

But this was only once, a single isolated moment of distilled pleasure.

Mostly, otherwise, it was frustration: frustration and people, too many people for one house, whose presence made it almost impossible for him to communicate with the girl. Cousin, nephew, in-law—a whole host had attached itself to the household and, as far as he could make out, lived off the old man. Day in, day out—except for occasions of free food and merriment like a marriage or a naming ceremony when they departed in a body leaving the house empty as it had been on his first entry. Otherwise they ate here, they slept here. It was with envy and a great longing that in the mornings Ravi saw the tottering pile of bedding-rolls, for he would have given anything to share the same roof with Nalini as they unthinkingly did. Jealousy, too, was interwoven in his feelings, jealousy that tenuous links of blood or marriage should allow these others a familiarity with Nalini that he, the outsider, was denied. From an amalgam of his emotions sprang a contempt for them of which he was hardly conscious until an ill-chosen remark of Varma, the nephew, gave it form and an uncompromising name.

'Well if it isn't our friend Ravi again,' said Varma facetiously, 'propping up the wall as usual.'

It happened to be true, this particular morning. Ravi had come looking for work, and been told there was none. He was lounging against the wall, having nothing better to do. It lent a keener edge to his voice.

'At least,' he said, 'I don't get paid for doing nothing.'

'What do you mean?' Varma's voice was haughty, that of a householder with entrenched rights addressing a disfranchised squatter.

'I mean I'm not a parasite,' said Ravi explicitly.

'Something of a leech though, aren't you?' Varma was annoyed, but not unduly perturbed. And why should he be, thought Ravi; as a relative his security was established, no family would boot a relative into the street.

'I shall know soon enough if I am,' he rejoined. 'When it's time for me to go—I'll go.'

Varma smiled. It was a superior smile, as if he knew better—and indeed so did Ravi, for there was hardly a household that did not have its hanger-on whom, once in, it was virtually impossible to dislodge. All the same he knew he was not in that class, whereas Varma undoubtedly was. He turned away contemptuously.

This prickly exchange had taken place in the street, outside the house, and the door had been closed. Nevertheless their voices must have carried, or at any rate the overtones, for without any precise indications Ravi became aware that Apu was aware of the situation, and had come down on his side. He did nothing about it —simply let it go, and watched. Meanwhile the hope Ravi had unwisely allowed to quicken, that he would be speedily promoted from leech to regular, painfully died.

Then one day out of the blue on his way to the fitting of an important customer Apu invited Ravi to accompany him. Ravi obeyed with alacrity—indeed, it had been more of a command than an invitation, observing which Jayamma had prudently refrained from insisting that he finish her work first, which was trimming the oil lamps against electricity failures that nearly every night plunged them into darkness.

They went out together, Ravi carrying the brocade gown over his arm, its rich stiff folds enclosed in starched muslin against creasing, the old man with his box and bundle that held everything conceivably necessary for his craft. Apu never said much—he left speech mostly to his wife. Now they walked in silence until they were some distance from the house—for the whole object of the exercise was privacy—and then he said, not even slackening his pace:

'Do you still earn your living like a ruffian?'

Ravi gaped. It was not a promising start.

'Why, no,' he stammered. 'That night I—I must have been drunk—'

'You were.'

'I don't know what came over me,' said Ravi desperately, 'I don't make a habit of—of that kind of thing, you know.'

'Good.'

'I—I fell into bad ways.' It was the truth, but Ravi offered it tentatively, watching the old man narrowly for his reaction. Confession was all very well, but you never knew which visage the two-faced goddess would turn on you—forgiveness, or condemnation and banishment. 'But that's all over,' he said.

'Is it?'

'Yes,' said Ravi earnestly. 'Over and done with. It was just a phase.'

'Was it?'

'Yes.' Ravi persevered, though he found the dry monosyllabic questions unnerving. 'I'm going straight now.'

'Then how do you live?'

Live? Ravi hadn't thought about it for some time, his mind had been engaged in other matters. Now that he did he realized that he existed on one meal a day and Jayamma's bounty, plus the few coins he earned from coffee-shop and Apu's household.

'Oh, I get by,' he said awkwardly. 'It's a little difficult, of course, but—'

'Nothing saved up, I suppose.'

'No.' Ravi was slightly shocked. Saving was something his father had done, uselessly stacking one anna on another and in the end the pile had not saved them from anything, not even the sight of his mother's prolonged dying for want of decent food and medicine. No, he did not believe in saving, nor did any of his gang. When a deal came their way, after they had done a job, they spent it all, gloriously, in one day if possible. That was the way to know life, however briefly: to taste what it could be like, to understand what it was about, before the final pall descended.

The old man said nothing. He kept on walking, taking short, precise steps that brought his sandals up sharply against his bare soles, his legs working like pistons. Ravi kept pace with him, uneasy, wanting to ask the point of the inquisition, but quelled by Apu's seniority, his authority as head of the family and controller of the household—the patriarchal authority he had by his own decree refused on his flight to the city, though he found himself unable to resist it now.

They were in Nungambakkam, nearing the end of their long walk, before the old man broke the silence. It was quiet here, with large cool detached houses, and dancing patches of shade from spreading tamarind trees and gulmohur such as never lined the streets where they lived, and in the shade an occasional slab of stone or a concrete bench where people could sit.

'Let us rest.'

Ravi was glad to do so. It was a dry, hot day, and his arm ached from the stiff, stilted way he was obliged to carry the precious brocade dress. He sank down gratefully on the low stone slab.

'Careful with that dress! You're crushing it—quick, up!'

Ravi shot up, extending his arm like an iron rod in front of him as before.

'No need to stand,' Apu gazed at him distastefully. 'Just be careful, boy, a little less clumsy if you can!'

Ravi sat down again, gingerly, the accursed dress held against his body as if he were some ghastly female impersonator. Did it really matter, he thought indignantly, if the dress showed a crease? Would the wearer melt away, be consumed by shame? He gave the cloth a surreptitious, angry tweak.

'It is important not to lose a customer.' Apu, thought Ravi

disgustedly, missed nothing. His rheumy old eyes, which ran so that you would hardly believe he could see through the fluid, saw much more than was good for others.

'Clothes,' the old man went on, 'Rich clothes are not important to you and me, nor can we afford to think about them for ourselves. But goodwill is, the goodwill of our customers. Unless you understand that, understand and act on it, you cannot be of any use to me.'

'I do understand!' Ravi gulped. Here he was, on the point of getting a proper foothold in the house, and he had almost thrown his chances away by one careless move. 'I do realize that the customer comes first. It was just that—that—'

'You are young.' Apu shut him up. 'Patience, care, craftsmanship—all these are things you will have to learn. The question is, are you willing to make a start.'

'Do you mean go into business with you . . . in partnership?' Excitement bubbled up in Ravi.

'As an apprentice.'

'I'm willing.' Despite the come-down, Ravi managed to sound fervently grateful, as indeed he would have been but for higher expectations. 'More than willing. Any time you say. Anything you want me to do, I'll do.'

'I've noticed that. I've been watching you. I don't like doing things in a hurry, you know, but I'm getting old . . . one begins to feel very much alone when one is old.'

Alone? with that army encamped in the house? Ravi glanced at the old man cautiously.

'Ah, yes, that mob.' The old man flicked disparaging fingers. 'They don't count. There's Varma. You ever seen him work? He eats and sleeps and talks—why, to hear him talk you'd think he was a jagirdhar, not my nephew at all. He thinks so too, that's why *he* can't work. Then there's my son-in-law. He's got a shop, it's been losing money for years, he doesn't even go near it now, but ask him to do something and that's where he has to go, at once, urgently. And then there's that cripple.' Apu stared at Ravi owlishly. Ravi had the feeling he was not really seeing him at all, or even talking to him, but rather listing the ills that were eating into him simply because once started he could not stop. 'He can't help being a cripple, I suppose. So he sits all day long nursing that shrunken claw as if God hadn't given him one sound hand to be getting on with. Idlers, I tell you, idlers all. Ché!'

'Ché!' echoed Ravi dutifully. He shook his head in sympathy and wondered when Apu would come to the point.

'Jackals,' the old man said, 'waiting for me to die. No, I have no use for them. What I need is a man, someone to carry on when I'm gone, someone who would learn from me in a spirit of humility as you might.'

'I would,' said Ravi fervently. Apu did not hear him. He brooded and went on, bitterly: 'A man needs sons . . . I have none, only daughters.'

Ravi almost ceased to listen. He clamped an expression of grave concern on his face and thought that really he could not be bothered to involve himself in an old man's woes. Moreover he had heard it all before, or something very like it. A man needs sons, his father had said. Well, he had had them and much good they had done him for in the end they had all quit, leaving him to scratch around alone on his barren acre bewailing the sorrows they had brought him. Sons or daughters, it came to the same thing, thought Ravi, so long as all you had to offer them was empty hands and an appeal to their filial piety. Now for his children, when he had them, he would do better than that, he would see to it that—

'So that's settled.'

Ravi started. 'Yes,' he said. He had no idea what settlement had been reached, but fortunately for him his brain had recorded the talk, and going confusedly back he realized that he had been accepted as a tailor's apprentice.

Secretly, he did not think very much of it, this petty craft of stitching clothes. He did not deny, of course, that it was an honest, respectable calling: but there were two special yard-sticks he applied to it, of both of which it fell sickeningly short. Firstly there was the seed his father, out of his own extremity, had implanted in him: that better things were due to a man who could read and write, better things than working with his hands for a pittance, things, for instance, like working in a Government office for one hundred rupees per mensem (after all, had he not been the brightest pupil in his class at school?) and a pension when he retired.

Secondly, he knew to the last degree of intensity the ribald light in which Damodar and his friends would view his worthy calling as they compared it with the glitter, the excitement, the languid gentlemanly days and pulsing hopeful nights, and, finally, the prizes that lay round the corner of their choice of living.

Ravi sighed, deeply, secretly, with a profound sense of sacrifice. Ah, Nalini, he thought, Nalini. She was worth it, worth anything, even worth giving up the sweet life for. He put it all on her, forgetting the trinity of hunger, drink and misery that had been intermittent companion to his sweet life, and which had forced his entry into Apu's ménage in the first place.

Chapter 7

RAVI had sisters, and so he knew the strict watch that was kept on young unmarried girls in their community, in all communities except shameless ones like the European, or, so they said, the American, or even, though only occasionally, among Indian Christian converts who copied their ways as well as their religion. Nevertheless it irked him unbearably to see how assiduously Jayamma glued herself to her daughter whenever he was present and unoccupied. This in itself did not happen often, for Apu was a hard taskmaster, and he saw to it that his assistant's hands were kept busy with tacking and basting and hemming—routine detail whose perfection he insisted was basic to good tailoring—until Ravi's inexpert fingers were peppered with holes from the fine sharp needles they used.

And yet, maddening though he found Jayamma, the moral standing of the whole household—not least that of Nalini—would have fallen in Ravi's eyes had such vigilance not been exercised. Between abiding by this inculcated ideal, and coping with its practical difficulties without benefit of family and friends, Ravi's spirits, despite the propitious first steps he had taken, sank abysmally low.

One day, desperately, he took time off and went out to the

corner shop and returned with bottles of Orange Krush and Kola for Nalini and her mother. It was a sweltering hot day, the gifts were gratefully received, and Jayamma unbent so far as to say he was a thoughtful lad.

'I don't know why it is,' she sighed, 'but nowadays we never seem to buy these things. It must be because we are getting old.' She said 'we', but gestured towards industrious Apu, her middle-aged face mischievously alight and contracting out from this imputation of age.

'Old and sensible,' Apu grunted. 'Nothing but coloured water with bubbles in it, fit only to amuse children.'

'Cool and pleasant, all the same,' murmured Nalini, 'especially on such a hot day.' Her slim hands clasped the cool glass of the bottle, the soft flesh tinted a deep rose by the Kola.

'If one goes to the stall,' he ventured, 'one can drink it really cold. Ice-cold.'

'Full of riff-raff pushing and shoving, that's the trouble,' said Jayamma. 'They hang around there all day long, good-for-nothings.'

'No, no,' said Ravi earnestly. 'Not at this time of day,' he amended hastily, seeing her gall rise. 'Later it gets crowded of course, but just now it's quite empty.'

'How far is it?'

'Five minutes. Not that.'

'Too far for me in this broiling sun.' Jayamma took up her palmyra-leaf fan and waved it languidly in front of her perspiring face. 'You take the girl.'

Ravi nearly gasped. He knew that if he had made the suggestion he would have had his head bitten off for his pains. It must be, he thought, one of his lucky days.

Lucky days continued. Jayamma was too indolent to stir in the afternoon, Nalini's sister Thangam was preoccupied with her baby, and Nalini liked her Kola ice-cold. They became regular customers at the stall, whose owner went to great lengths to produce the coldest Kolas for them, delving deep into his ice-box and bringing out bottles rimed with frost, wet sawdust clinging to their sides, and coloured marbles clattering brightly in their necks.

From Kolas they went on to ice-fruit. Ravi tempted her, ruthlessly, overpraising their merits to secure the extra ten minutes he coveted of her exclusive company which the longer walk to the ice-fruit vendor entailed.

Nalini came docilely. She walked gracefully beside him, the glass bangles on her delicate wrists tinkling as she shielded her eyes from the worst of the sun. There was something utterly delightful to him in that sound, something utterly feminine, the distilled essence of all that was sweet and desirable in a woman. He stole another look: indeed he could hardly take his eyes from her, and was struck anew by the beauty of her profile, framed in the soft muslin folds of the sari she had drawn over her head. What a lovely face, he thought, what a lovely woman. If, by some extreme, improbable chance she were to become his wife, what would he not do for her, what could he not achieve!

'You are very beautiful,' he said, huskily, and trembled in case he had affronted her. But she only cast her eyes down and said nothing, so he knew she was not offended. He also knew, and exulted over the knowledge, that the balance of their relationship had altered, the overflow of his cup seeping into hers and making her tremulously, sexually conscious of him.

There was a small cluster of people around the ice-fruit stand, mostly children without the money to buy, who stood transfixed like small worshippers in front of the row of coloured syrup bottles.

Each ice-fruit cost fifteen naye paise. Ravi paid with a bad grace. He felt the price was inflated, because he happened to be accompanied by a girl in whose presence no man of sensibility would want to haggle; or if not inflated it was certainly outrageous, for what was there to it but a little crushed ice? One could go into the business oneself, and make a fortune! Payment had to be made in advance. He handed over the coins in a sour silence, ignoring the vendor's well-meant remarks, and they watched while the man scraped out a spoonful, packed it round a stick with his bare hands and poured a thick, heavily rose-scented, rose-coloured syrup on to the ice-crystal mass. But his annoyance vanished before Nalini's child-like pleasure.

'All right?'

'It's very nice.' She smiled, showing small white teeth. The syrup had made her lips and the tip of her tongue a bright pink.

'What shall we do now?' She licked away delicately but steadily; soon there was nothing but stick left.

'Go back, I suppose.' He did not want to, but more than that he did not want Jayamma's vigilance aroused again. Moreover there was the old man, grudging the time he was away, marking off the minutes against him in that sweated workshop he ran. It certainly would not do to upset him—not now, not when there was so much at stake.

They walked back together in silence, not touching but acutely aware of one another, Nalini with her sari drawn about her closely, but not always able to prevent the thin material billowing against him, Ravi filled with the desire to sing every time it did so. And then all too plainly they were over the threshold, with Jayamma blotched and yawning from her midday sleep wanting to know where on earth they had got to, and Apu with armfuls of chiffon for Ravi to hem, and the fretful baby wailing, and the Singer flashing its needle and thrumming away like a maniac, hum-click-clack-click until the very floor quivered, and the hanger-on relatives squatting on the floor. God, if I were Apu I'd turf them out, thought Ravi, watching with irritation their indolent comings and goings, the frequent recourse they had to the mud-pot of water that stood in a corner.

The weeks went by, the ice-fruit walks became routine: not less pleasurable by any means, but suggesting that extensions and improvements might be feasible. Greatly daring, believing his star to be still in the ascendant, Ravi broached the question of taking Nalini to the cinema. *Shakuntala* was showing, a nice classic picture without any modern forward nonsense to which the parents might object, would she not like to see it? The cinema was a stone's-throw away—practically on the doorstep, he stressed, trying to create the impression that it was virtually an extension to the house, making the presence of a chaperone unnecessary, even ludicrous. But his day seemed doomed for it was Jayamma who accepted, jumping in before Nalini could even open her mouth. He should have got her alone, asked her then, thought Ravi, gritting his teeth. But when was Nalini ever alone?

They went in a threesome and sat in the cheap seats, six rows away from the screen, Jayamma vivacious and excited like a young woman, Nalini sedate to make up for her mother's lack of dignity. She sat in the middle: Ravi, determined not to be beaten on every point, had engineered this after some thinly disguised scuffling, so that he did not have to ford the mother when he wanted to reach the daughter.

The arrangement pleased Ravi. If he leaned back Jayamma was hidden, he could even pretend she was not there: and meanwhile here was Nalini, his girl, close beside him. She sat upright, dressed in her best shot-silk sari, orange and green with a narrow mango border and an orange blouse to match. Her hair was braided and coiled, and circled with jasmine flowers and rosemary—he had seen her that afternoon, twining the florets together. When she moved he could smell their fragrance, wafted up strongly on the slight current of air; and if he moved he could touch her, their seats were so jammed together. He did so, trembling, and felt her arm soft and warm against his shoulder. A tremor went through him again. He kept still, holding his breath: to his joy she was very still too, and he imagined he could feel the same tension that electrified him coursing through her body.

In the interval they went out, their progress impeded by empty soda-water bottles and discarded chaplis whose owners had curled up their vulnerable toes on their chairs. Outside was nearly as crowded as in, but less stuffy. Moreover there was Jayamma's fan, which she seldom moved without in the hot weather. She had wielded it even in the cinema: the stiff palmyra had caught the heads in front a glancing blow or two. Ravi had heard the rasping sounds and had shrivelled inside, mentally dissociating himself from the barbarian; but to his relief no altercation had followed. Jayamma's manner, even in the dark, had presumably been sufficiently quelling.

'Beedi-cigarette-soda-saar?'

'No!'

He cursed. One came to the cinema and it was like going to Moore Market, from the number of things that were sold. They had already been offered tea, coffee, Kola, monkey nuts, ice-cream, pakora and karabandi.

So far neither Jayamma nor Nalini had shown any inclination to join in the general orgy of eating and drinking; but he was deadly afraid in case they should. What with Kolas, ice-fruit, and three seats in the cinema, he had nothing but small change left in his pocket, and there was still a week to go before he drew his next month's wage. Not that he grudged Nalini anything, of course, but—

'Nalini, aren't you thirsty? I am. My mouth feels as dry as a ditch. Ravi, could you get us—'

Trust her, he thought. Just trust her!

'What would you like?' He did his best to be civil.

'Anything will do, anything cool.'

'Nothing for me,' Nalini said.

Now there was life for you, thought Ravi grimly as he went in search of the required drink: forcing you into something you didn't want to do, and holding back on what might have given you a little pleasure. Why couldn't Nalini have been indebted to him, instead of that simpering nanny-goat of a mother? Still, it showed that she had sense and sensibility, this beautiful girl of his who knew how to accept gracefully, while never initiating impossible demands of her own.

He had to wait, the vendor was besieged. Where, he wondered, did so many people get so much money from? Other people's finances were an abiding, absorbing mystery to him. He was toying with the idea of saying that drinks had been sold out—speculating, rather, whether he could get away with this—when he heard the sound of splashing and laughter filled his breast. Water, of course: she had asked for something cool, and something cool she should have—from the hydrant that the management provided in compliance with fire regulations rather than for the convenience of its patrons—who had nevertheless wholly appropriated it. They jostled and pushed, and held their dhotis clear of the muddy bog they had created, and cupped their hands and drank.

A cup . . . Ravi looked around, determined not to be defeated by this small detail. Then he thrust through the crowd to where, huddled against a wall, the tea-boy crouched over a bucket, washing cups in tea-coloured water.

Ravi laughed again, secretly. After the training this city had given him, after Damodar's careful grooming, whipping a cup was child's play. A few minutes waiting and then . . . it was done, he felt the thick smooth glaze of the cup and exulted in the successful exercise of a skill long neglected. Well, he thought, no one could say those early days were wasted: the painfully acquired cunning was still there, carefully—and it seemed imperishably— stored inside him until he cared to use it. Not that he would, of course: no, never again, he was done with dishonesty because of Nalini. Lifting a cup was different: wasn't it an empty one, and anyhow wasn't it going to be returned the moment it was done with?

By the time he got back the interval was over, bells were ringing. Jayamma had to gulp her water, hardly noticing what sort of liquid it was, so that Ravi felt robbed of his triumph over her, petty though he knew it to be.

'Come along, come along,' she urged, dabbing with her sari at the water trickling down her chin. 'What are you dithering about for? We don't want to miss any of the picture!'

Ravi did not want to either, but there was the cup to be disposed of first.

'I'll follow you,' he said awkwardly. 'Excuse me.'

At last it was done. He groped his way inside, and subsided thankfully into his seat, only to discover that Jayamma was now sitting in the middle.

Chapter 8

WHENEVER he thought about it, which he preferred not to do, life seemed to Ravi to be nothing but frustration. If he took Nalini out, it was only briefly, just long enough to conduct her to the stall and back, just long enough to whet his appetite. Cinemas— monthly events, for his wage never ran to more—followed the wearying pattern set at the beginning, with Jayamma for ever in tow, or what was worse, trailing Thangam and the baby, whose crying completely destroyed his pleasure in the film. In the house he had to bear with, even be obsequious to, in-law and nephew who quarrelled and idled while he worked, his fingers pricked to pieces, at a trade both alien and uncongenial to him.

Then one day something really awful happened. They had gone

to watch a procession, he and Nalini and Jayamma. Jayamma, apart from the need to safeguard her daughter, liked being taken. She could not very well go by herself, her relatives were markedly reluctant, and her husband, a good deal older than herself, preferred staying at home to jostling in a crowd. On their way back, while they were still all three in the jolly mood processions engendered, Jayamma said, pleasantly, 'Let us go to your quarters, Ravi. It will make a nice change.'

His quarters! Ravi was violently shocked. He had no quarters. He worked for Apu from eight in the morning until six or seven in the evening, and then it was a matter of chance where he slept. A bench in the park, an empty six-by-two space in a doorway, the veranda of an empty house, the pavement, all in turn had served to bed down on. For the last several weeks, too tired to poke around, it had been the pavement, the familiar stretch of it outside the coffee-shop where he had once worked. Since he had left the railway station, the coffee-house and its pavement frontage had become a second home to him.

The pavement! How could he tell anyone that, least of all his prospective mother-in-law? He had got used to it, it was nothing to him, but he could tell exactly how respectable people would react.

'No, it is impossible,' he said in great agitation. 'I have an aunt staying.'

'No matter,' said Jayamma, still amiably. 'We ought to meet some members of your family, so far we have not seen anyone.'

'She is not well,' said Ravi. 'She has been ailing for some days, and doesn't like being disturbed.'

'I don't think it would disturb her.' Jayamma frowned. 'It would only be a short visit, I am sure she would be glad to see another woman.'

'Another time,' said Ravi. 'Really, she only wants to lie and sleep ... I don't want to upset her, she is well-to-do and likes her own way, you know.'

Jayamma understood this. It was sensible for a young man to humour an ailing aunt, especially if he had expectations from her. Fleetingly she wondered why, if Ravi had well-to-do relatives, he had broken into their house for a meal, giving them all such a fright: but she put it down to his drinking and other bad habits which young men so easily fell into nowadays.

'Very well,' she said, allowing herself to be dissuaded. 'But tell your aunt to visit us when she is better.'

Afterwards, when he was a little calmer and could think, Ravi took this as a good sign. Unless Jayamma wished for a closer relationship, or at least did not dismiss it as unthinkable, she would never have wanted to meet one of his family. That she had done so meant he was to be lifted out of the limbo that he now occupied, not quite a relative and not quite a servant.

The prospect pleased him, and at the same time it raised horrifying problems. He would have to get quarters of some kind, even if it was only a small shared room. Pavement sleepers belonged to another category, another species even, that had nothing to do with respectable people. Respectable people would not mix with them, indeed were hardly aware of them. The good-for-nothing labels that Jayamma freely applied to loitering youths were never used for the huddled shapes they passed at night on their way home from some outing. She merely went round, or stepped over them with her sari bunched up in her hand in the same way as she walked over puddles in the street when it had been raining.

But how? The city was so crowded, rents so high, that even men with decent incomes searched for years, squashing themselves and their families on to whichever relative had managed to secure foothold in some house. It was a little easier for single men, but even sharing a room would cost ten or twelve rupees a month, too big a slice to take out of the twenty he earned. Besides, who would he share with? His friends, his set, believed in free living; they would slap their thighs and jeer if he told them his plan: say he was going soft, becoming respectable, and hadn't they always called him a doll? Nothing would be achieved except his own mortification, and anyhow hadn't he finished with that crowd?

Apart from somewhere to live, he had to find someone to put forward his claims, a go-between, some interested party in whom he could confide, and who would act as matchmaker. The big question was who, and the answer was no one, there was no one here. In his village things were very different. Women came and went, and one always knew which girls had come of age, which young men were looking for brides, and when the time was ripe there was never any shortage of emissaries, you never had to look for one because they were always there, experienced women who went determinedly back and forth until the marriage was arranged. Yes, there it would have been different, he would have had no problems at all. Ravi sighed for his village, a thing which he did not often do; and was unhappy.

That night as he lay on his mat on the pavement, his arms folded under his head, gazing up at a sky brilliant with stars, peace suddenly descended on Ravi. He would write to his father. This natural thought had not occurred to him before because when he left his village he had hoped to be done with the old life for ever.

It still sickened him, that life: the misery and the squalor, the ailing babies who cried all night long, the way one was always poor and everyone one knew was always poor too, the desire—the constant nibbling desire—to have a second helping of food, a cup of coffee every morning, a shirt without holes, a shawl made of pure wool to keep out the cold of a monsoon dawn; and to know that one never would.

They always *knew*: knew that things would never be any better, knew they were lucky to stand still, for the only other way was downward. It was this knowing the worst, the hopelessness of it, plus the way people accepted their lot and even thanked God it was no worse—thanked God!—that sickened him. Just thinking of it, even now, made him want to spew.

So he had got out, the very first moment he could, before he too got stuck like them, like flies on fly-paper, while his own belief was still intact. And this belief was that life could be sweet, that it was meant to be sweet, that if it was not it should be made so. Tight-wound coils of feeling inside him insisted on this, rebelling against wholesale acceptance of life as a culture for the breeding of suffering with a wild energy that sometimes made him want to break and tear whatever upheld it, and sometimes actually, physically ill with rage.

It was these rages that had driven him out in the end; and when he went he had meant to cut himself off for good. But there was nothing irrevocable about this, no boats had been burnt: unlike some others, he had left with a prudent minimum of denunciation and declamation, so that theoretically he still had access to his village and family. But he shrank from the actuality —quite apart from having to find the train fare. Far better, he thought, to summon them here, where the work was to be done.

So he wrote, giving Apu's address as his own for what else could he do? and a month later, by which time he had bitten his nails down to the quick, came a postcard from his father—who in turn had had to look for his train fare, in addition to finding a reader of his son's letter, and a writer for his own—to say that, as requested, he would gladly see about negotiating the marriage, and that he would be arriving in due time.

This Ravi interpreted, rightly, as presaging another long delay. Fortunately for him he used it in looking for accommodation for his father, eventually striking a bargain with the coffee-shop proprietor who had a small private room for his richer customers, seldom used after ten at night, which he was willing to allow the old man to sleep in. But for this he would have been seriously incommoded, for one afternoon, some months later, without warning, he found his father standing on the doorstep.

Actually it was Thangam who heard the nervous knocks and opened the door. She did not quite understand what he said—his speech was slow and rustic, and somewhat impeded by the sight of an obviously married young woman—but from the strong resemblance she gathered who it was and ran in to tell Ravi.

'Your father!' she cried, her big healthy face beaming. 'You must be so happy!'

But Ravi was less happy. Negotiating a marriage was a delicate affair, his sense of what was fitting cried out against this crude dumping of one's father on one's unsuspecting father-in-law's doorstep. Fortunately the position was not irretrievable. Apu had gone out with Jayamma and Nalini, and as usual the rest of the household had sunk with relief into slumber. Swearing Thangam to secrecy Ravi bounded out, got hold of a passing jutka, bundled his father into it and sprang in himself.

It was afterwards, jogging along to the coffee-shop that Ravi became acutely conscious of the embarrassment that stress and urgency had suppressed. Here, opposite him, sat his father: his *father*, the man from whose loins he had sprung: and instead of closeness it was even worse than sitting next to a total stranger, with whom at least he would have had no difficulty in exchanging a few idle words. On a lesser level, what about all those promises to keep in touch he had dutifully made and never kept—until now when he needed help? What must his father think of him? Ravi felt his cheeks burning. And what debilitated him still further was the conviction that he would never be able to discuss the matter in which he needed help so urgently with this worse-than-stranger who was his father.

Fortunately for him the older man suffered no such inhibitions. They sat opposite each other on sacking in the narrow, covered jutka, their legs drawn up, their knees colliding every time the carriage lurched, and although Ravi shrank at each touch he kept his head and managed to conceal these unnatural feelings, and even listened dutifully while Ram spoke of the village, his land, his ills, his loneliness, and his son's sense in deciding to marry and settle down.

'Otherwise one is led astray,' he said, peering closely into Ravi's face. 'When the blood runs hot who is to blame a young man?'

Ravi said nothing. He braced his back against the sides of the jutka and held himself in, hoping his father would not pursue this line.

'In a big town like this there are so many temptations,' Ram went on. 'Temptations which fortunately do not-come one's way in a village.' He sighed deeply, and the jutka-driver, sitting six inches in front of them, turned round and sighed in sympathy, saying there were indeed many pitfalls in a town, traps specially set to seduce your men away from right into wrong.

Town, town, town, thought Ravi, chafing in silence. They gathered every evil they could think of and laid it at the feet of a town, as if they were making an offering to some black god. He felt he knew why: because they had nowhere else to spill the blame. But his father? who knew the evils of another kind which infested their village? What right had he to slander any town? It was hopeless, he decided: a hopeless case; and the gulf widened between parent and son.

'Now if his mother were alive,' Ravi's father said, warming to the sympathetic audience in front, 'but poor soul, she passed away some years ago, how happy she would be!'

'No doubt, no doubt,' said the jutka-driver, shaking his head in agreement.

'Such a nice girl, my son says,' the old man pursued. 'Pretty, modest, virtuous—she is virtuous is she not?'

'Of course!' said Ravi furiously, and suddenly had no difficulty in finding words. 'She comes of a most respectable family, a family that is very highly spoken of I can tell you.'

'I only asked,' his father said humbly. 'They do say that young girls in towns—'

'*What* do they say of young girls in towns?'

'Only that they are—' the old man stopped again, and gestured and winked in a way that Ravi found horrible. From having little feeling for his father he began to detest him.

'That they are what?' he asked. His mouth was dry from anger, but he knew he must curb his tongue and he did.

'A little bolder than ours,' said Ram, and he spoke as humbly as before. 'But they say so many things, who am I to say if they are true, I who have never known a town?'

At this point, luckily, they reached the coffee-shop, for Ravi could feel his temper swelling inside him. He felt he could not sustain his courteous front much longer. His father, on the other hand, was calmness itself. He might have been made of wood, thought Ravi, for all the awareness he showed of the turbulences he had generated in his flesh-and-blood heir.

He returned in under the half hour, having expended more precious money on jutka fare in order to do so—money well spent, in his judgment, since it had enabled him to get back before Apu and so avoid yet another of his lengthy lectures.

Thangam was nursing the baby. She pulled her sari over her breast and the baby's head and said, 'Why has your father come?'

'On business.' Ravi busied himself with some hemming.

'What business?'

'How do I know? Some personal business,' said Ravi, and to his annoyance felt his face kindling again.

'Oh, so master doesn't know his own father's business,' said Thangam. 'Well, well.'

Ravi refused to be drawn. There was a silence. The baby had

stopped suckling and could be seen struggling under the folds of the sari. Thangam extracted it and laid it on her lap while she pulled and pushed herself into shape again.

'We could tell him, couldn't we,' she addressed the yawning infant. 'My jewel, my precious, we could guess, couldn't we.'

'Go on then, guess,' said the goaded Ravi.

But Thangam shook her head. Her lips were curved and smiling in a faintly lascivious way, and her eyes were round and knowing. Ravi knew the look: it was very common on the eve of betrothals, and he had often guffawed when seeing it. It was the irritation it caused that he had never before taken into consideration.

Chapter 9

THEREAFTER things proceeded at a speed which left Ravi in a kind of permanent daze, unsure in all that was happening of what was real and what a part of those dreams which were a fair-sized slice of his life.

This haste was due mainly to Ravi's father, lost and uneasy in the bustling city, afraid of foreclosure on his land, yet another corner of which he had mortgaged to equip himself for this expedition on his son's behalf, and more than a little anxious to return to it, being in much the same predicament as Apu in having no sons. The two men found, in their common affliction, much to unite them: a unity which alone enabled them to override Jayamma, who in this matter of the marriage of her last remaining daughter yearned for the slower cadences and ceremonious rhythms to which she was accustomed.

She said so in carrying tones to Thangam which Apu pretended not to hear. Thangam, naturally enough, allied herself with her mother; while Nalini, a bashful neutral, affected not to know anything of what was going on. Ravi, in the brief moments when the mists that enveloped him lifted, trembled: the last thing he wanted was to incur the displeasure of his masterful mother-in-law to be.

53

What she most wanted, he well knew, was for him to remove himself: to go away, anywhere away from this hub and centre of things, where it was unseemly for the prospective bridegroom to be. Ravi would gladly have fallen in with her wishes, but what could he do? Here he was and here he worked from morning until evening, and Apu saw no reason to release him from his labours.

Undisturbed by these cross-currents, the two old men provided an island of peace. They talked of land and what it cost, of the high price of rice and grain, of the unpredictability of demand and the uncertain return for one's labour. Apu, town-born and bred, knew little of rural living: yet he was only a first-generation townsman. His father, like Ravi, had joined an earlier exodus from his village following the recurrent famines at the turn of the century; and if Apu knew nothing at first-hand, yet his earliest memories took in the bitter experiences of both his parents, accounting in part at least for the assiduity with which he, as a boy, had applied himself to apprenticeship in a totally new craft. He had prospered. It did not make him look down on those who had not.

Ravi's father, on his side, did not envy Apu. He admired him. This was due less to the innate sweetness of his character than to the thorough grounding in acceptance he had undergone. He knew that his lot could not, would not, be any better. Now he preferred to husband his strength rather than to expend it in the meaningless, eroding anguish of grudging another man what he could not have.

In between these conversations, and before the working day began or after it ended, the details of the marriage were quietly settled. Nalini would bring her husband no dowry: on the other hand Ravi was being paid during apprenticeship and, said Apu spreading empty hands to illustrate his lack, he had no sons and was he to leave his business to worthless idlers? Ram concurred. It was a problem that often exercised him, during those daydreams when he imagined having something to leave.

Both men were well pleased with the bargain they were striking. Apu liked Ravi: he was a good worker, a sound and willing one, and he badly wanted someone to whom he could hand over the reins when the time came, allowing himself some relaxation

54

in the meanwhile. To Ram, Nalini was everything a man could expect of his son's wife, and his son's prospects seemed to him to be eminently promising. Indeed Ram was frequently dazzled when he thought of how well the boy had already done for himself, setting up here in town and prospering, all by his own endeavour.

He did not know—and Ravi scrupulously kept it from him by ingenious and exhausting effort—that his son was not really 'set up' anywhere, except perhaps on his pavement pitch that until lately had been outside the coffee-house they both now slept in. And Apu did not tell him of the reprehensible and violent events of their first meeting. This, as Apu often said to himself, was all in the past: a sowing of wild oats by a young man, meant to be forgotten. But this he kept from Ravi, believing that he should suffer for his sins—which Ravi did over many nights, for the old authority had to his annoyance reasserted itself, so that he found completely ineffectual his own repeated assurances that he really didn't care what his father thought.

Jayamma, excluded from their weightier counsels of dowry and endowment, turned her attention to other important matters. She outlined to Ravi a husband's responsibilities, the duties he owed to mother-in-law and wife; she drove him into corners and lectured him; she even dredged up the past in order to exhort him in fierce whispers as to his future conduct. This last she did with marked reluctance, for she would have preferred to be done with this particular episode over which she suffered strangely ambivalent feelings. It was not what was done: not much had been, and anyhow if there were thieves in the house one had every right, even a duty, to thrash them. What troubled her, she liked to believe, was that *she* had done it: she, who had been brought up to respect every living being as the fragmentation of an eternal God. But going deeper, which she could hardly bring herself to do, she knew that what really troubled her was the lust that had risen in her like a tide, the surging exultation that glutted her as she felt her blows falling on his flesh.

She had not spoken of that night to either of her daughters, or to any other member of the household. Indeed, she often felt thankful for the marriage party that had claimed them all, so that none had seen her with her hair loose, in an abandoned frenzy. Except of course her husband: and he had been too appalled by blood and violence to notice. Sometimes she wondered at the reasons that kept *his* mouth tightly shut; but she never gave herself an answer, instantly smothering whispered disloyalties that suggested it might be his spiritless performance he did not care to remember.

Ravi, beset by fears and longings that made him botch his uncongenial work, the cocoon he had wrapped himself in rent by the hectoring Jayamma—even he dimly realized that negotiations were working out in his favour. Nalini was withdrawn from him still further, as a betrothed girl should be. There were no more cinema or any other outings, and Jayamma watched like an eagle to see that there were no lone occasions when desire might be fired beyond control. Thangam's smiles grew more and more arch. She had acquired a small repertoire of lewd jokes, and as a married woman she now felt free to corner Ravi and air them. More subtly, and agreeably, his status in the household changed. Varma's insolent lip kept pleasanter proportions, and he slapped Ravi's back now, where he had previously toed him out of his path with one fastidious, un-shod foot.

Then it was done: the day fixed, the hour chosen, the bride-to-be informed. Stones rolled off Ravi's shoulders, he felt light-hearted, almost light-headed with relief. For the first time since, as in bleak moments he put it to himself, he had set this fearful juggernaut in motion, he really began to believe he would benefit by the end of the run. Covertly, now, he imagined himself beginning life with Nalini—settling down, that despised state to which elders were forever propelling youngsters, which had suddenly shed its drab garb and acquired a cosy magic. Even more covertly, nibbling only, he imagined himself lying beside her, drawing her close to him, covering her body with his own, and feeling her warm and ripe beneath him.

'Ai, Ravi! Whatever's the matter with the lad?'

Ravi pricked himself and cursed, silently. As if they did not know what the matter was with him! There had been ribaldry enough about it.

'The best person, since your mother is no longer alive,' Jayamma was saying, 'as I said before, only you didn't hear, would be your aunt.'

'Which aunt?' Ravi started violently.

56

'The one you had staying with you. Now she would know how many people to invite and—'

'She's dead.'

'What?'

'She died. I told you she was ill.'

'But you never told me she had died.'

'Well she did. Soon after she returned to our village.'

'Then I suppose I must depend on your father.' Jayamma sighed—the sigh of a woman forced to struggle along with the known ineptitude of a man. 'Perhaps he can tell me how many to expect from your side, otherwise how can the arrangements proceed smoothly?'

She bustled off, leaving Ravi to the sombre realization that the return from his side would be nil. His mother was dead. His brothers and sisters, who with their progeny would have provided the cohorts, were gone, forced out by the relentless pressures of their existence, in the upsurge of revolt that had begun to dismantle the old pattern of family life first in one village, then in another. There were many villages: it was a slow process: but it had begun, and it had taken them. So they had gone and not returned, not kept in touch, accepted the rift as he had come so close to doing. He was glad now that he had not. Where would he have been without his father to give him identity and status, to gesture over his shoulder to a background and roots that were solid and stable and reassuring in his in-laws' eyes? Yet he knew the gestures were empty, the final rupture only postponed, for he felt there was nothing for him in his village, and its people and their living had become so remote as to be utterly meaningless to him.

But whom to ask?

'There is hardly anyone left,' said his father sadly. He had emerged, looking a little ruffled, from the room they turned him out of early each morning to make way for customers. 'Nothing is what it used to be. Now I remember when your mother and I were married—'

Ravi registered fleetingly the irritation he always felt when his father began drooling over a hideous past, and then he ceased to listen.

57

Chapter 10

NOWADAYS the door between the working room and the open courtyard was never closed, for in this way it saved Jayamma precious time while she hurried about her various missions, or ran in and out raising points of order with Apu and Ram or settling problems with them. Ravi, the centre, all three ignored: but it was a pointed ignorance which made him aware that really they regarded him as a stumbling block placed right in the middle, so that he hunched himself painfully in a vain attempt at effacement, and went on with his work as best he could.

It was not a very good best: there were far too many distractions. Even now, as he tried to concentrate on the rolled hems of which Apu made such a fetish, he could hear the loud drone of Jayamma's voice, reciting those endless lists of which she seemed so fond.

'Jaggery, gingelly oil, jeeragam, lavangam, turmeric, venthiam,' he heard her intoning. 'Cardamom, coriander, cummin seed, tamarind, chillies, two bundles plantain leaves, twenty limes, coconuts another twenty, flower garlands say ten—'

Ravi frowned. Ten garlands? What did she want with so many? Too late he realized he had stopped working and was staring at her: and now she glared back at him.

'Shameless, it is nothing to do with you,' she shouted. 'You see to your work and leave me to mine, this is none of your business.'

But a few days later, almost exactly a month from his father's first jarring threshold appearance, it turned out to be very much his business, though he was in no state to realize it.

He sat stiffly in the valanced hammock rigged up in the courtyard under the hired *shamiana*, his shoulders aching from the weight of the flower garlands heaped upon them. Four on him, three on his bride who sat as stiffly beside him with her eyes downcast; but hers were lighter, jasmine interlaced with rose

58

petals and bright silver tinsel while his were thickly coiled chrysanthemum with heavy loops of gold.

His bride, his Nalini. He said it to himself, but realization would not come. Now and then he glanced at her, furtively, half-fearful, half-hopeful of meeting her eyes: but she did not look up, did not move, sat rigidly in her corner maintaining a decorous distance as if, he thought with a sudden flicker of his old savage spirit, the whole of this pageant, the slow ceremony, the assembling of witnesses, was not precisely concerned with bringing them together, their physical union. Then as suddenly he melted. She looked so young, so appealing, sitting beside him in her finery, and it must be even more of an ordeal for her than for him, this submitting of oneself to the public gaze while the men stripped and sized up the bride and the women veiled their eyes as they thought of the groom.

His ruminations terminated abruptly, the clarity of his thoughts blurred, as yet again something was required of him. He obeyed, in a trance, with an awkward clumsiness which they indulgently excused as marriage nerves. He got up, he sat down, walked around the sacred flame, and fell at the feet of his father for his blessing. Somewhere beside him in all this was Nalini, but he was not now clearly conscious of her. The fire filled his vision, that and the flowers, flowers everywhere: in women's hair and garlands, and twisted among the plantain fronds that waved above the swaying hammock. From somewhere came the smell of burning camphor, the acrid fumes leavening the heavy cloying sweetness that hung in the constricted air of the small enclosure; and there was the smell of incense too, wafting up in their blue trails of smoke from incense-sticks inserted in clusters in crannies and crevices, tiny glowing pin-points of light like eye-pupils.

Presently it was over, they were married. Married! He felt his heart make a strange side-slipping movement, and imagined this was what it would feel like if he were suffering a stroke. Then water spattered on him: they were being sprinkled with rose-water prior to the nuptial drive, he realized, and he revived. He moved to the door, urged there by the whole bevy of relatives and friends, with Nalini at his side.

A motor-car was waiting for them: an old Dodge hired for the occasion, with its canvas top crumpled right back. Ravi had never been in a car before—which did not mean he had not wanted to, for he and Damodar had often pictured themselves driving away in one of those shiny automobiles parked so nonchalantly in long lines every evening along the Marina. But the doors were always locked, and there were always people about. Now pleasure and excitement filled Ravi's breast. Certainly, he thought, Apu and Jayamma were doing them proud, he had done very well by them. And they, he vowed on the instant, should do well by him, they would not find him wanting.

The crowd were pushing him forward, someone had opened the car door. He gripped Nalini's arm tightly and then stumbled in and sank down in the relative privacy of the car, she in her corner, he in his. A sense of awe now coupled itself to the general embarrassment he felt. He could hardly raise his eyes from the seats, which were covered in blue rexine that smelled of linseed-oil and looked, he thought, very stylish. But he could not keep his eyes on them for ever: the strain of his fixed gaze was already beginning to tell, although for the life of him he could not shift it. Then in her corner Nalini giggled—no more than a squeak smothered to respect the solemnity of the moment; but it was enough to snap the tension that, he had begun to believe, would keep his eyes permanently glued to the blue rexine. He looked up, he looked round. He was even able to focus and recognize faces in the throng. Foremost among the men were Apu and Varma, as befitted members of the more prominent family. His father stood several paces behind because, thought Ravi, he had contributed little to this affair: a poor man, relegated to the fringes not from any exercised intentional unkindness, but from a sort of natural fall into the appropriate slot. If Ram was aware of this, he showed no resentment. He beamed and was joyous, his face filled with pride that all this should be in honour of his son, this grand lavish affair.

There was even a band, a jolly three-man contingent that marched behind the car as it crawled along the street. Ravi, released from his paralytic embarrassment, found a little to his surprise that he was enjoying it all—this slow ride with his bride by his side, the cheerful cavalcade following, the band playing a lively tune that he knew, a modern number with a beat and a lilt in it, much preferable to the solemn, traditional nuptial music, punctuated as it was by triumphal, ear-splitting blasts, that he had so far had to endure.

Yes, this was distinctly more to his taste. He leant back against the rexine, and stole a look at Nalini; glanced away quickly, then a vague sense that really he ought to look properly at her now if he was to form and keep a lasting impression of this important moment in their lives, made him turn to her again. She was dressed in pink—he realized, surprised, that he had not even clearly registered this before: a rosy pink sari shading to dark pink and red, with a four-inch gold border. He was used to fabrics now, he could tell the gold was not real, only the shiny silk stuff the merchants had produced after much research to satisfy the hunger that poor people had for rich clothes. Of course it did for the occasion; but if you rendered it down by fire, as women in fine houses did with their old saris, you were left with a heap of ashes instead of a big lump of silver that could be drawn into shining threads again. A sudden disquiet assailed him. Was Apu after all a poor man, who had had to call upon his entire resources to put on this show? On reflection he dismissed the thought. His father-in-law was a shrewd man, who had simply not seen any point in spending too much on a sari worn perhaps once or twice. His own daughter, the old miserly so-and-so, Ravi said angrily to himself. Then he got rid of that thought too. Apu was right. It was he, Ravi, who was wrong, who had got too many big ideas from going into all those fine big houses where four-inch gold borders were worn. In a marriage from his father's house not even sham gold would have been possible, let alone what Apu had seen fit to provide.

His father's house, with a thatched roof that always needed mending and a half-empty cooking-pot that had never been able to feed or contain its children. What would be *his* lot, as husband, householder and father? His father's, Apu's, better than Apu? Better, he thought passionately. But how? His mind swung wildly from dark to bright like a mad pendulum, and finally settled for fair. By working of course, by being astute, by putting away so much each month . . . despite the band, the crowd, the coarse jokes of street louts, he fell into a hazy, not unpleasing reverie.

It lasted until the car braked, jerking him out of it. They were back, it was over. All over, thought Ravi with a pang. He stared gloomily at the familiar doorway, from which they had departed in glory a bare hour ago. Now the awning was down, and hardly anyone lingered. The plantain stems drooped, and even the mango leaves and marigolds had begun to wilt. If only, Ravi thought passionately, it could have been different! If only the car had not stopped but sped on, whisked them away and set them down at a strange front door that spelled out the beginning of a new life and opened into who knew what exciting future! Instead here they were, back where they had been, nothing changed except perhaps for the worse, nothing to do but put as good a face as possible upon the anti-climax. Enveloped in a sense of incongruity, feeling awkward and slightly foolish, Ravi stepped over the threshold as he had done hundreds of times before.

Chapter 11

FOR the evening meal Jayamma had prepared buttermilk and rice. There were also the left-overs from the marriage feast, carefully salvaged and assembled on a platter, which no one seemed disposed to eat. They sat about, gorged, crowded together in the small kitchen, and looked at Ravi and Nalini, while Ravi wondered how long it would be before they were alone.

'Come on, eat up,' Jayamma urged. 'All these things I have made with my own hands, you must try a little to please me.' She watched them peck, hovering over them with a kind of determined benevolence until Apu said, abruptly, 'Enough. It is time for them to bed,' and then her eyes grew large and lambent, she placed a plump, moist hand on Ravi's shoulder and said, softly, 'You know where to go?'

For a confused moment, brought on by a stifled snigger from Varma, he misunderstood her meaning. Then he realized she was referring to the general reshuffling of sleeping quarters, and he nodded. Apu had apprised him of the new arrangement—authoritatively, and in the presence of Varma and Thangam, who were the potential trouble-makers, so that there should be no squabble. Thangam, her husband, and the baby, who all slept in the front workroom, were to move in with Apu and Jayamma. The cripple Kumaran, who lay at Apu's feet massaging his scraggy legs with his one sound hand until he slept, was shifted to the workroom; and Varma, lording it on his own in the box-sized room next to the kitchen, was to share the workroom with the cripple, giving up his room to Ravi and Nalini.

Their own room, however box-like. His and his wife's. All Ravi wanted to do now was to escape to it, taking Nalini with him, but despite Apu the others lingered, yawning and ready for bed, but too lethargic to rise and go, and until they did he could not budge for, quite apart from the courtesy due to his elders (which Ravi in his desperate state was ready to dispense with), the only way out of the kitchen led through the box-room. Presently Apu rose, then Jayamma, then Thangam . . . last of all Varma, with a hefty thump on the back for Ravi, and the sly hope that he would not find himself flagging.

The tap in the courtyard gurgled and splashed again, as it had done interminably as one by one they completed their nightly ablutions, and at last was still. Ravi stood up and grasped Nalini's hand. He was almost swooning with desire for her, but at the same time he trembled and felt her hand trembling in his. 'Come,' he said thickly, felt her resist and, inflamed, half dragged her into the room and closed the door. There was a double latch. He fastened both and then he turned to her.

She was sitting on the bed, simply sitting and waiting, her hands tightly locked in her lap with the knuckles sticking up through the skin. Her nervousness communicated itself to him. He suddenly felt he did not know how to approach her, what to do, recalled Varma's jeer with fright, and felt himself go limp. It was not inexperience. He had had women before—a dozen, a score, procured for him at first by Damodar, later on his own initiative. But they were easy, they made things easy, came half-way to meet a man. He would have known exactly how to proceed with such a woman—would have joked with her coarsely, asked whether she liked them big or small, questioned her without embarrassment about her own size and preferences, and disposed her limbs to suit himself.

Nalini was different. She was young, untried, a virgin. If she had been otherwise he would not have wanted to marry her. He

63

sat down beside her, noting that she looked very pale—perhaps through tiredness, or perhaps, he thought, it was the effect of the harsh light thrown by the naked bulb—then he remembered that the light might make her shy, with a girl like her it would be so, and he got up and switched it off.

The sudden darkness was blinding. He groped his way back, and felt his outstretched hand touch warm smooth skin, her soft bare nape beneath the upswept voluptuous coils of hair. Instantly his senses leapt into life, he could hardly contain himself. He pressed her back on the bed and began caressing her, thrusting aside the filmy hampering folds of the muslin sari into which she had changed until he could feel her body and it was everything he wanted, warm, soft, long, fine, supple legs, a belly that arched under his hand, and a skin like satin—he heard himself cry out as he covered her, spreading her thighs to receive him. He did not know if he was hurting her—he could not have stopped if he was. He heard her sharp indrawn breath, but otherwise she lay passively under him.

In the morning—he looked for it—there was blood on the bed. The spots hardly showed on the bridal red-flowered draw-sheet Jayamma had laid. It induced in him a deep, protective flood of tenderness for Nalini.

Chapter 12

ALL over, it was all over. Ravi had predicted more wisely than he knew. His father had gone back to his village, having waited until the marriage was consummated, as was usual, in case of recriminations or failure on either side. He had gone thankfully after blessing his son—as if, thought Ravi, twisting his lips, some great new shining future were awaiting the old man in his village. Friends and relatives who had camped in the house, but whose claims to its hospitality were tenuous, had either dispersed or been judiciously dislodged by the combined, formidable strength of Apu and Jayamma. Ravi, from the elevated status accorded to him as suitor and bridegroom, had been returned to his former role as

64

employee—at least as far as the two with power were concerned. Varma and Thangam's husband Puttanna, it is true, now treated him as an equal, where before they had given orders: but who after all were Varma, or penniless jobless Puttanna? In Apu's eyes worse than nothing, hangers-on in his house, and it was Apu who had the power, who held the household together and kept it functioning by his industry and narrow, inflexible discipline as they all well knew.

Even the bed was gone. This loss he felt most, more than the other symbols that had vanished with his relegation. It had been taken back ten days after his marriage, by Apu, to whom it rightly belonged. The rest of the household slept on mats spread on the floor, and now perforce Ravi had to follow suit. It irked him vastly. Although he had slept on baked earth floors for part of his life and on the ground or pavement for the remainder, yet in ten days he had grown accustomed to comfort, he could no longer accept the hard floor without rebellion. Soft living had become a norm.

Nalini giggled when she saw his long face. Life was light and gay to her, laughter came easily, but the responsibility he had taken on with marriage weighed on Ravi. His heart was heavy when he saw his young wife lying down on the floor to sleep while other women, neither younger nor more beautiful than she, in those fine houses whose bedrooms he was invited so casually to enter, reclined on sumptuous beds with mattresses as plump and puffed-up as peacocks' breasts. One day, he vowed, she should sleep soft too: one day they would own a bed of their own . . . he said as much to her and she scoffed at him, though gently enough.

'Such ideas! Do you think we are grand people? Isn't this good enough for us?'

'Not good enough for you,' he said, pushing back the tendrils of hair that clung to her damp brow—their small room could be stifling, right next to the kitchen where Jayamma seemed to be for ever cooking.

'I'm the best judge of that.' She turned on her side to murmur into his ear. 'And I'm happy.'

'Are you? Really?'

'Really and truly happier than I thought possible.'

'I would like to give you much, much more than I do.'

'I know.'

'Don't you mind?'

'No, of course not.'

'I will, one day . . . I'd do anything for you.'

'You do enough already.'

He crushed her hand between his. Sometimes he thought he would burst, so great was his love for her. And he was happy too, except for this itch to better their lot: happier even than he had expected to be. He had asked, it seemed to him, so much from marriage, and had been given so much more. Nalini had always been gay and pleasant, in this she did not change: but now she was beginning to respond to him, making love as he, encouraged by her willingness, taught her to, learning to abandon herself, to give her body without shame to him to do with as he willed, so that now instead of a passive submission they came together joyously.

In his more honest communings with himself Ravi acknowledged that he in turn had learnt a lot from Damodar, from the women his friend had engaged for him. Before his flight to the city he had believed he had little to learn about sex: in his circumscribed village it was the main and often only recreation, the most frequent activity, too common, too easily observed for them to organize even the sniggering spy-sessions that young men did in cities. Yet there were extensions and refinements of which he was ignorant; and in his pre-flight fantasies, the sexual yearnings and imaginings, he had never once contemplated in a wife of his the abandonment he was now busy coaxing from Nalini—an abandonment he had once believed proper to coarse women, the sort one went to, if one had the money, to satisfy one's lust.

On the whole, however, he preferred not to think about Damodar. That life had been heady while it lasted (he thought, overlooking the abject interludes), but from his present stance of regained respectability he could clearly see its sleazy undertones, totally unfit for someone like Nalini, which made a return to it unthinkable. Jayamma thought so too.

'I knew you were a decent boy,' she said meaningly, 'right from the beginning, you know.'

This tribute, which not so long ago would have drawn from him a sarcastic bray, he now accepted. He was a decent boy—a decent part-householder, living decently. What he forgot to take into account was that there was no reason why he should not do so with much of his disaffection stifled by happy marriage, steady work and a steady wage.

Ravi would have liked this steady wage to be higher. He wanted to buy a bed, a nice new sari for Nalini, material for some smart new shirts for himself, a safety razor, a mouth-organ (all the old gang had had either mouth-organs or flutes), and sundry other essentials and luxuries the list of which grew daily longer. The longing for them grew too: and from constant denial affected him like a deficiency disease. Apu, however, saw no reason to increase his wage (nor indeed could he have afforded to do so) since Ravi was fed and lodged at a reduced rate, and Ravi therefore tried to count his blessings while he held his peace.

The business meanwhile was thriving. Apu, with his steady worker to rely on—bound to his side by ties stronger even than a steady wage—was gradually taking on more work, even nibbling at smaller contracts that hitherto he had had to turn down. They had two in hand now: one was stitching nurses' aprons for a private nursing home, and the other was making quilted silk jackets for ladies for a small shop that had recently opened in Mount Road.

The aprons were easy but dull. The shop supplied the material and the pattern, all that had to be done was cut out and sew, cut out and endlessly sew. Ravi grew heartily tired of this, the bolts of tough white material that thudded monotonously onto his lap, the straightforward, uninspired stitching he had to do. The jackets were another matter. He loved the feel of the silk, the quilted diamonds that came up in little puffs, the tiny standaway embroidered collars. But he had to work slowly on these: if he did not his diamonds became squares, or the needle jammed in the wadding, so that out of a batch Apu allowed him only one or two to keep his hand in.

'You like it better than you thought you would,' Apu remarked drily one day. 'Didn't think much of being a tailor did you—oh yes, I could tell from the uppity airs you gave yourself.'

Ravi hung his head. The truth was he still didn't think much of it, this womanish trade that made no call whatsoever upon a man's strength, or valour or spirit—a call that he would have been glad to answer . . . still, there were times like now, when it wasn't so bad, and he knew he would put up with worse for the sake of a regular pay packet.

'I like making these,' he said shyly. 'The jackets are beautiful.'

'They sell like hot cakes,' said Apu, 'especially the beaded ones,' and his old man's hands that trembled to light a match firmly placed in position and secured with neat invisible stitches bugle-beads and seed pearls along the elaborate curlicues of arabesques traced on cuffs and neckline.

'I wonder who buys,' said Ravi, 'I mean it's not cold here, is it?'

'Ah, it's the memsahibs,' said Apu. 'It's cold where they come from. They buy. Bless them,' he added, 'who else could pay such good money?'

'How much?'

'Eighty rupees a dozen.' Apu smacked his lips. 'You work up to my skill, lad, and we'll be on easy street!'

Drawn by curiosity, and getting the address from the old man who had no great interest in such things and had to search for it, Ravi went one day to the shop that sold their handiwork. It was right on Mount Road, among the big buildings, painted white and gold, with a huge floor-to-ceiling show window and the name EVE in large gold letters above. The name struck him as eminently apt, for Damodar had once told him that Christians believed Eve was the first woman ever, from whom all were descended, and this shop was full of woman's things. Damodar had added, sniggering, that incest must have been rife and had then, having whetted Ravi's curiosity, broken off abruptly, leaving him to interesting conjectures of his own.

EVE . . . how clever of them to have thought of it, Ravi ruminated, gazing in fascination at the goods displayed. All colours, all kinds. Bead bags, brocade sandals, jewelled belts, swathes of chiffon, handfuls of sequins carelessly scattered, and in the midst of this golden litter on a figure made, he saw with astonishment, of plaited straw, was one of their coats. It did not look the same here: it had become vastly richer, more sumptuous, since leaving his hands—he had to look twice to make sure it was the same. But there was no doubt about it, he could even see one little diamond where the quilting line wavered. Pleasure filled him. He felt like grabbing the nearest passer-by and pointing it out with pride, until his eyes travelled down to the straw hand-span waist where the price tab was. Rs.125/- it said, quite plainly. Ravi was stunned. He and Apu between them got Rs.80 per dozen, while they, doing no work that he could see, got Rs.125 for one. It shook him.

Apu took it calmly. 'Of course they get twenty times what people like us get. That's because they're not people like us.'

'What sort are they then, devils? Gods?'

'Different, that's all.'

'Then the sooner we become like them the better.'

'Just you try, my lad. Just try and see how far you get!'

But twenty times as much! Ravi felt like shrieking. The fact stuck in his gullet like an outsize stone, yet here was this old fool apparently able to swallow it whole.

'It's wrong,' he cried.

'Maybe, but that's the way it is.'

'Then the sooner it's changed the better.'

'You aren't going to change it by shouting.'

Ravi seethed. 'I know, but you could if you refused to sell.'

'What?'

'Refuse to sell cheap!'

'Are you mad?'

'What about you? Haven't you any pride? Doesn't it mean anything to you to get a decent price for decent work?'

They were both shouting. Jayamma ran in, clasping her hands together theatrically. Nalini and Thangam were peeping from the window, nervously, with pale faces. There was a pause.

'You go on like this, my lad,' said Apu at last, controlling his shaking voice, 'and see where it gets you. Just wait and see, that's all.'

Ravi was almost too angry to reply. 'I'll wait,' he said in a thick choked voice, and slammed his way out.

He walked blindly, rapidly, wanting only to get as far away from the house as possible before his brain too, his thinking, became contaminated. Of all his emotions, disgust was uppermost. To be ground down like that. To lie down and take whatever they cared to give. To believe such a state was unalterable. My God, he thought, what is wrong with them? What can have addled their brains? Apu, his father—all that generation, clinging trembling to what was for fear of what might be. But these were words to conjure with, not quail before. Ah, what might *not* be, if . . .

Damodar had taught him that. At least, he had given form to formless suspicions that were at the roots of the restlessness that had driven them one by one out of their villages. The trouble—to him, Ravi, first as city innocent, now as husband and householder —lay in the working out of that 'if'. Damodar would have had no doubt at all, had never had any. What might be would be if you were prepared to do this, and this, and this.

But what could *he* do, within the narrow frame of respectability he had slung round his neck like a penance? Rebel, and a contract might be lost, the steady wage would come to an end, and then what of Nalini? He had to think of her, he had to think of himself for that matter. There seemed to be no answer.

He kicked angrily at the stones in his path as he went along. A dog prowled past, sniffing at the gutter. He took a little run at it, aiming for its flea-bitten hindquarters, but the animal dodged his kick and vanished. He cursed. There was a kind of pressure inside him that made him want to break and tear, to do violence although violence was foreign to his nature, simply because of what was pent up in him. Then he saw it: a jagged stone, waiting to be thrown. He bent to pick it up, and a heavy hand descended on his shoulder. He very nearly yelped, but traces of his training lingered: he smothered the sound, and at the same time the fingers that should have closed round the stone began searching out gravel between his bare toes and the soles of his chaplis.

It was wasted by-play. There were no boots here, no sergeant, only another pair of ordinary feet in ordinary chaplis and—his glance travelled cautiously upwards—the familiar face of Damodar.

'Why Ravi, you old renegade!' Damodar had evidently noticed nothing.

Ravi straightened up. He was a little short of breath, but he managed the civil riposte. 'Well, speak of the devil!' he said in unbelieving tones. 'Do you know not five minutes ago I was thinking of none other than you?'

'Good for you,' Damodar spoke with transparent pleasure. 'I was beginning to wonder if you had forgotten us altogether.'

'No, no, of course not. Whatever gave you that idea?'

'Well, you haven't exactly been to see us, have you?'

He stopped and peered at Ravi closely. 'Were you about to come round today perhaps?'

'I—I hadn't thought of it,' Ravi found himself stammering. 'Why—why do you ask?'

'Well, naturally,' said Damodar, 'seeing you're practically outside my front door.'

Ravi stared at him mutely. He did not want to take up with Damodar again, he did not mean to, for all that he had spent half the day mentally endorsing the other's creed; and yet, quite unconsciously his steps had led him to their old headquarters.

'I was just mooching along,' he said lamely, 'not really going anywhere . . . you know how it is sometimes.'

'Troubles?'

'Sort of.'

'Soon cure that.' Damodar winked. 'Spot of the old medicine.'

'Don't go in for that now,' said Ravi, nervously. He tried to be facetious. 'Old married man and all that, you know.'

'Oh, come on!' Damodar coaxed. 'What's the matter with you?'

And Ravi thought, why not? He had been too good too long in a rotten world. Damodar linked his arm through his, and it was like old times again as they set off down the road.

Damodar insisted on paying for their drinks. He was flush. His wallet was fat with ten-rupee notes, he must have had two or three hundred rupees on him. Ravi tried not to be envious, it was wrong to be envious of friends: yet he could not help calculating how long it would take him to earn as much.

'Haven't done too badly this month.' Damodar correctly interpreted Ravi's silence. He leaned forward confidentially, 'That was a bad patch you know, just before you pulled out . . . never known it quite so bad. Went on so long too, never known such a foul run, not in all my experience and I've been at it how long now, ten years? No wonder you quit.'

'I got married,' said Ravi.

'I know, I know, I heard. I would have bought you a present if

I hadn't been so short. And worried, man! What with you gone and the others talking of going—'

'Going? Why?'

'No brains,' said Damodar sombrely. 'They thought the bottom had fallen out of the booze market the moment there was talk of Prohibition lifting. I told them different, but half of them flitted. Fools! As if anything could really change—a little shift of emphasis, that's all!'

'You mean,' Ravi hazarded, 'Imports—contraband?'

'Of course!' Damodar kissed his fingers. 'And prices are sweeter than they were. Up and up they go, the more they slap on the duty. That's why they come to us, we're dirt cheap, compared. Our trouble is we can't get enough in fast enough.'

'Police bastards?' Despite himself Ravi felt his interest stirring. He had almost forgotten his earlier rage.

'Specials on the job,' said Damodar. 'Wharf rats. Never mind. Drink up and damn them.'

Ravi was not much of a drinker, he got drunk too easily, but the interregnum of companionable tippling before he arrived at this blind state was agreeable, and blunted the thoughts that had griped him all day. Relaxed and mellow, he gazed at Damodar with a distant affection, and wondered why he had ever considered him sub-standard, unfit for the strait-laced, dull, foolish, craven and killjoy company in which he had landed himself.

Damodar's drinking was of a different order. He drank with a kind of dedication, in a cold, systematic rebuttal of the tenets of a religion which had been thrust upon him with relentless fervour, his grey eyes grown harder in his pale face as he watched his weaker companions reel from a consumption that left his own faculties as sharp and chiselled as ever. Sometimes—now—Ravi speculated whether Damodar could possibly enjoy this kind of drinking, only to have his doubts dispelled by sudden outrageous clowning, or a general hilarious bonhomie that only in his more sober moments did he question whether put on.

But there was no disputing Damodar's head for liquor. He could see the evening out, and rise as steadily as when he had sat down. Because of that one felt safe with him, could always depend on him to see one through; and because of that one drank the more.

As they rose to go Damodar said, with a slow, cold cruelty, not caring to hide the contempt he felt: 'If you like decent money, you know where to come. Of course, you'll have to get rid of your beggar mentality first, otherwise you will never want decent money, will you?'

Chapter 13

IT was after midnight when Ravi arrived home.

The door was locked. He leant against the wall, a little breathless from the long walk, more than a little unsteady, looking up at the small window with the grating set high above him. He seemed to have done this before, a very long time ago ... ah, yes, he thought, that very first time. How long ago would it be, five months, six? Since then he had lost his freedom, tangled himself up with respectability, acquired a wife to support—he scowled in the darkness. Now where exactly was this wife of his, who ought in turn to be supporting her husband? In bed no doubt, sleeping comfortably while he hung about outside, shut out like a stray dog. He went back to the door, jiggled at it impatiently, and to his alarm it gave way in front of him.

Jayamma had opened the door. (Couldn't Nalini have come? he thought sourly as he picked himself up, did it always have to be Jayamma?)

'It's you,' she whispered stridently. 'Nice time to come home, this is.'

'I'm not going to be—' he began loudly.

'S-sshh!' she hissed at him with a fury that silenced him instantly. 'Do you want the whole street to find out what a worthless vagabond we have taken into our house?'

It pierced his fuddled mind. He saw, more starkly than ever he would when sober, how grievously he suffered from having no roots here, no family to give him a background, to arrange itself if need be in line of battle with him. It solved a riddle he had shoved well to the back of his mind—why, despite his marked and satisfactory rise in status in this household, Jayamma could still speak to him in a way such as he had never known mothers-in-law to

73

speak to their sons-in-law. It was because he was a vagabond. He had been accepted as a steady working addition to the household, welcomed as a daughter's husband, and yet at the crucial moment she always remembered he had come in off the streets. Well, he thought resentfully, let her! One day he'd show her it didn't matter, if it came to that.

'Can you at least walk? Well, come on then!'

He followed, hangdog but rebellious, in the wake of the lantern she carried.

'And be quiet.'

He did not answer. He tiptoed past the workroom, where Varma and the cripple were stirring and muttering in their sleep, into his room. It was pitch black when he closed the door behind him. He stood stock still for a moment, then he lowered himself, his head swimming, into the dark vortex that surrounded him and began groping and crawling on all fours towards their sleeping-mat. He thought he was being soundless, even congratulated himself upon it, but Nalini woke. He did not know how he knew but he did, and he stopped. She said nothing; he couldn't even hear her breathing.

'It's me,' he ventured.

Silence. 'I met an old friend,' he said. 'We got talking. Time ran away.'

'You've been drinking,' she said in a flat, low whisper. 'You're *drunk*.'

He might have spared himself, Ravi thought. Despite his head, the hour, on his way back he had found a tap and gargled vigorously, had raided a stall for betel-leaf and chewed it until his tongue was furred with the juice. So how could she know? She was just guessing, he thought angrily, saying the first thing every woman said when her husband came home late.

'I'm not drunk,' he said firmly.

'You are.'

'I'm not.'

'You are. I can smell it. The whole room reeks.'

No smell came to his nose. Still, if she said she could smell it he supposed she must be able to.

'Only one small drink,' he said. 'That's all I had. For old times' sake.'

'No. A lot more than one. Don't lie to me.'

He thought it best to say no more. He resumed his crawl in the blackness and a pleasure as warm and diffuse as any produced by alcohol permeated him as his hand encountered mat and pillow. Sleep: it was his supreme desire. His senses gave the lurch preliminary to sweet unconsciousness as he imagined head sinking into pillow. But there was something that would not wait, of even greater import: the appeasement of his wife. He touched her tentatively, hoping she was somehow asleep but she was not, and he said, hoarsely, 'I'm sorry.'

'Yes, but why did you do it?' She had raised herself on an elbow. His eyes had grown accustomed to the murk, he could see the sharp triangle formed by arm, head and supporting palm. 'It's not as if you lacked anything, or were unhappy or something.'

'I told you.' He was intemperate, thinking of the last few hours of rest vanishing. 'I got carried away: it could happen to anyone who wasn't a saint!'

'Just because Apu told you not to be silly,' she said. 'If he didn't who would? He was right too. You are getting high and mighty, putting yourself on a level with high-class folk. How can we ever be like them? Why can't you be content with what we have?'

'Because I want more,' he cried, his temper rising. 'I want a bed for one thing! I'm fed up sleeping on the floor. They all have beds, the people we slave for, do you know that? Day-beds, night-beds, double-beds, divans—'

'You've been corrupted,' she said. 'You go into all these big houses, see all these things, it gives you impossible ideas.'

'They're not impossible ideas.'

'They are. How can people like us ever be like them?'

'They're not made of different clay are they? There's nothing lays down they should always have the best and trample over us and do us down, and we should always come off worst?'

'They're a different class, that's all,' she said with a catch in her voice that should have warned him. 'Ordinary folk like us can never be like them.'

'Oh yes we can.'

'We can't.'

'We can, if we stop thinking like stupid water-buffaloes.'

He could not see much of her face in the dark, but he heard the loud, shocked gasp she gave. At the same moment there was an exasperated snort from Varma next door, followed by three or four thuds on their door.

They lay side by side on their mat, quaking. They were not particularly afraid of Varma, but sometimes if they were too noisy the thudding would increase until it wakened Apu—normally insulated from any sound by the intervening courtyard—who could be terrible when roused. His wrath was invariably directed against them too, for he took the view that a man and a cripple were hardly likely to be as jovial at night as a young married couple.

The breathless silence went on. Even straining his ears Ravi could hear nothing, all was quiet. This time at least they had escaped. But he knew he had to do it—break this crackling envelope of silence, disturb the peace despite whatever the consequences.

'Nalini,' he whispered, nudging her, 'I did wrong. Please forgive me.'

She did not answer. The flank he had prodded began to heave, and presently he heard a soft muffled sobbing.

'Please don't cry,' he said. Her crying tore at his heart. He wanted to draw her close to him and comfort her, but he knew he would have to choose his moment, otherwise she would only withdraw still further, raise a hard hostile wall between them that would mean misery for both for hours if not days to come. He waited, and presently touched her arm.

'I'm a thoughtless monster,' he said. 'The last thing I ever want to do in this world is to bring you pain. I'll never do it again, never.'

He meant it. He loved his laughing, dimpled, gay young wife, he wanted passionately to keep her so, never to oppress her with his own dark broodings, to bear her down by his own misdoings to a sullen stoicism with which his village life had made him so dismally familiar.

'I know.' Her sobbing increased momentarily, then died away into small choking gasps. 'It's just that sometimes I—I don't know what's eating into you, there must be something but I don't know what and it worries me ... and tonight I—I just don't want to hear them calling you vagabond again, that's all.'

She had been made to suffer because of him, because she cared for him. His heart constricted within him, and at the same time he almost felt like swooning with the joy of it. Pain and happiness, bitter sweetness.

'Dearest, my dearest,' he said gently. 'You should not have minded for me. I have a broad back, haven't you noticed? I'm not worth it.'

'You are.'

She snuggled up to him, warm and loving, and instantly his senses quickened. He was wide awake now. All desire for sleep had vanished and instead came this other desire, full-blooded and passionate. He turned on his side and began caressing her, slowly and very delicately, content to wait until she was ready for him. His wife, he thought with a surge of possession, his to have, his to hold ... his excitement grew, externals fell away, there was nothing at all in the world beyond this feeling between him and this woman—and then the door shuddered again, the thudding that meant they had woken the finicky Varma was resumed with an increased violence.

They lay still, defeated. The glow so quickly kindled as rapidly died, leaving the unquiet residue of incompletion. There was no peace for them, Ravi thought bleakly, not even in this one room that was nominally their own. All day—afternoon—evening, people passed through it: they had to, to get to the kitchen. And at night there was Apu, and Varma, and the needs of the two other households, milk for the fretful baby, or kasayam for Jayamma, or a rice-poultice for the old man's ills. Interruptions, curbed in their first married days, were now legion. If only, Ravi thought irritably, with longing, then savagely, if only they had their own small house—however small, a doll's house—just somewhere to call their own! One day, ah yes, one day, he said wordlessly to his wife, and heard her sigh as if in sympathy. She had turned on her side, with her back to him. He turned too, encircling her waist with an arm and fitting his body consolingly to hers in the position they called stacking spoons; and so at last, achieving some kind of comfort, they slept.

77

Chapter 14

ONE result of this drinking caper—as it came to be called when
Ravi was within earshot but ostensibly not meant to hear—was to
alter Apu's treatment of him for the better. It was not that he
barked at him less, or lowered his craftsman's criteria by an inch,
or spoke with other than his usual high authority; yet somehow
he seemed to tread more warily, almost as if he were sounding
the ground before advancing into critical territory in case of an
explosion. Varma and Puttanna too looked at him with respectful
eyes. Vagabond they might have combined in calling him, in his
absence, in unctuous echo of the angry old man: yet neither—the
one with the capacity for it, the other with the liking—had ever
had the nerve to return drunk at midnight. The street loafer, the
unwanted leech, the bridegroom and husband in astonishing meta-
morphosis, had now attained, as it were in his own right, higher
levels than ever in their estimation.

Ravi was well aware of the change. His sensitivities had been
honed to too fine an edge by the flick-knives of city living for him
not to notice: but he did not see that his new status arose from
his strength in measuring up however unconsciously to the old
man, and after searching around he assumed that in some obscure
way Damodar's gloss had rubbed off onto him—the high gloss of
success, of sophistication, of a city suavity that came from knowing all the answers to the vexed problems of easy living calculated
to make the most appeal to Varma and Puttanna, who by any
reckoning were failures.

Primed by this erroneous conclusion, Ravi took to swaggering a
little. Here he was, a villager for all but a few years, the simple
village ignoramus whom all city men looked down upon from an
inbred superiority which no amount of informed exhortation
could eradicate, outstripping two people whom he knew to be city
born and bred. He even began to believe that, in general terms of
success, he bore the same relation to them that Damodar bore to
him: and pursuing this theme he spoke easily and glibly of riding

the market, of clinching deals, and streamlining the business. Luckily for him, and partly because his sense of prudence had not altogether abdicated, he gave his lectures in Apu's absence, which was less difficult to do than it had once been.

Keeping to his own careful plans, the old man was gradually handing over more and more of the work to Ravi. He rested more frequently now, rising from his labours over the machine which had left him with an almost permanent stoop, to retire, grumbling and stiff, to his own room from which Puttanna, dislodged, emerged grumbling and ruffled to make an unwilling audience for Ravi. For the old arrangement still held; Puttanna and his wife Thangam still shared the older couple's room, although with Apu's increasing demands the only use they had of it was a few hours for sleeping at night.

This was particularly irksome for jobless Puttanna, who found himself rather less welcome at his former haunts now that even his small change was exhausted, and, as he querulously said, he had to be *somewhere* during the day. By now he had given up all pretence of running a shop, and the current face-saving legend, strenuously put about especially by his wife, was of a defaulting partner, a scoundrel who had decamped with all Puttanna's hard-won wealth.

Nobody believed the legend: yet no one nailed it down for the myth that it was. Even Apu said nothing. His lips tightened in contempt when he came upon his son-in-law eating in idleness, eroded by it, but he knew better than to press him into service, after the disasters that had attended previous efforts. For Puttanna was no good at tailoring, and had no mind to be. He looked down on the trade, regarded it as a come-down to have married into such a family, for he had once been a shop-owner—that is to say he had inherited a stall from his father, which after three years' trading he had had to hand over lock, stock and barrel to his creditors. Puttanna never referred to it except as a shop: and the stock it carried was a miscellany, for Puttanna had branched out from the narrow specialization that had returned his father a fair living. There were cheap plastic dolls, flowers and toilet sets, tin trumpets, mirrors and fake jewellery, and, as a side-line, the little boys' shorts and white frilly shirts that went down so well with Indian Christians for church wear, as well as the little girls' print

79

frocks and *cheety* pavadais that even quite poor people could afford, which had once been the stall's mainstay.

At one time the stall had drawn its supplies from small backyard factories, often no more than family group co-operatives, which turned out these garments in hundreds and sold them mostly to places like the Market; but there were odd surplus dozens, or rejects, which were made available for stalls. Then his credit grew shaky, and Puttanna had to turn to such tailors as were willing to oblige him—a dwindling number. He had lorded it over them, Puttanna implied when he recounted this business saga, these humble men who came soliciting his orders and whom he had often, he said, had to turf off his porch. Of course, he would add hastily, seeing the wrath of his listeners rise, these were only small men, not at all like Apu who sold to grand shops in Mount Road, not at all, his father-in-law was quite different.

Mostly, however, it was not Puttanna but Ravi who held forth. He had reached that degree of skill where he could work without thinking, let his fingers get on with the stitching while his brain and tongue unleashed lectures and schemes upon his imprisoned audience. Apu heard. His mental alertness was undiminished, sharpened even, by his encroaching physical infirmities; and even when the drone from the workroom became indistinguishable, he was well aware of its tenor. He saw, however, no reason to intervene. Ravi never neglected his work, however much he talked, and that was the important thing. Industrious worker, good husband: Apu felt he had not been far wrong in his estimate of Ravi. Yet he wondered about that last peccadillo, unable to dismiss it altogether as of little account. What was it—a young man's folly, bad influence, a sign of the times? The precipitating cause he knew: their difference of opinion over the pricing of a jacket. But was that all, was there more?

One day, abruptly, he summoned Ravi to his room. It was the only place with any sort of privacy, and that only by day, before the sleepers trooped in with their bedding rolls. Ravi was fashioning, with some pride, silk loops for the frog-fastenings of a woman's pyjama jacket; but he dropped everything, as everyone did, to obey the summons.

'What,' said Apu forbiddingly, 'made you get drunk again?'

Ravi's heart sank. He disliked these frontal attacks, which the old man seemed to specialize in. Moreover weeks had gone by, he had thought himself safe, it seemed grossly unfair to drag it up now. Morosely he began sounding out possible answers. Why *had* he got drunk? Well, why not? Drinking agreed with him, he found it warming and pleasant. And he had met Damodar, and what more natural than that two friends should linger over a drink apiece?

'I met a friend,' he said, nobbled a little by those searching eyes, 'and we—you know how it is.'

'Is that all? Think.'

Ravi thought again. Of course it wasn't by any means all. There had been, there was, his sense of outrage that *they* shoul ' grow rich at *his* expense: he and his ilk perennially scratching round for a living, while *they* sat still and waxed fat on huge peremptory margins. He said, resentfully, 'I was upset. Anyone would be.'

'Over the jacket?'

'The pricing. We do all the work, they make all the profit.'

'We make a profit too.'

'Oh yes,' he said sarcastically, indignation overcoming his awe of Apu. 'I daresay we do, by permission. It's so small it's not worth having.'

'Really?'

'Yes, really,' he said robustly, upheld by heady currents. 'What's more, we *never* charge enough. Five rupees for a dress! Do you know it takes me half the day just to do the buttonholes and buttons?'

'You must endeavour to be quicker.'

The dry voice punctured him. He said, miserably, 'I do try.'

'I know. I find you quite satisfactory. I'm not complaining.'

Ravi rose to go, but the old man had not finished.

'You want to charge more,' he said. 'What would you do if our customers went elsewhere?'

'Where would they go if everyone put up their prices?'

'Would everyone?'

Ravi stared wordlessly at the old man. He knew the answer: they wouldn't, they were all like Apu, the older men, too scared to make a stand for fear of falling, too disorganized to get together to fix prices; and the younger men who were bold had neither the skill nor the resources. What a losing battle! Depression settled on Ravi like a sodden grey blanket, and there was no Damodar to lift it, or resuscitate the rebellion that had flared so brightly and flickered out.

Chapter 15

FOLLOWING this conversation, Ravi was given a rise which he instantly chalked up as yet another score on the credit side of his drinking caper. Here he was, he thought with a certain smugness, prospering as a direct result of his misdeeds, what with more money in his pocket, deferential treatment by members of the household, and going further back his very entry into this house. Certainly no one could say it hadn't paid dividends! So compulsively appealing was this line of thought that he even considered deliberately indulging in a little discreditable activity, but the thought of Nalini restrained him. Instead he fell to spending the money he had yet to receive, setting his sights higher than the mouth-organ and the bed he had previously focused on.

A bicycle: that was what he needed now. The long walks to the big houses wearied him, and more and more loomed ahead as Apu extended his circle of work, careless of his weakening legs. Then there was the time it would save, which would give effect to the policy of streamlining the business he had been advocating. Talking was fine, he felt, doing would be more impressive. He could see himself on a bicycle, a shiny black Raleigh with glittering spokes, the piles of tacked and finished garments neatly strapped to the carrier behind. What happened now was that Apu made him carry everything, either in stiff folds over his arm, or done up in a huge bundle as if he were a *dhobi* carrying the washing. And they walked, everywhere. The old man was too mean to pay bus or any fares, he wouldn't even take a jutka now that, Ravi told himself acidly, there was a human donkey to hand. To be fair—and Ravi was scrupulously trying to be—Apu did not spare himself either. Sun or rain, his thin spindly legs kept going like pistons, at a pace Ravi found it an effort to emulate.

'You are too soft, you and your generation,' Apu liked to cackle at him. 'Brought up soft, can't take anything.'

'We don't *want* to take anything and everything,' Ravi would retort, angrily, but only sometimes. Mostly he let it pass. The old man was right. He could not see himself, at Apu's age, tramping these absurd distances.

Actually Apu could not see himself keeping it up much longer either. It was only his strong spirit, and the long rests he allowed himself which acted like a rejuvenator, and the lesser fact that he enjoyed riling his swaggering son-in-law, that enabled him to manage at all. Apu recognized this, and in recognition of it, methodically preparing for the future as he always had (although he never tempted providence by admitting this even to himself) he began taking Ravi as often as he could, and even more frequently than hitherto, into the big houses where his patrons lived, the large bungalows behind high-walled gardens to which his craftsmanship gained him admission.

In the beginning Ravi had been made to wait on the veranda, in the company of cobblers and fruit-sellers, while Apu went upstairs for measurings and fittings and ladylike preenings in mirrors. Sometimes he had accompanied Apu, walking behind the old man up wide polished flights of stairs into bedrooms and dressing-rooms where his rôle was that of dumbwaiter instead of assistant tailor that he felt he really was. Now Apu deliberately made a practice of it.

'My son-in-law,' he would say deferentially, 'he is learning the business.' And if the lady of the house was not too preoccupied to be gracious, he would add, 'He is doing very well too . . . one day he will step into my shoes,' and he would thrust Ravi forward, so that she could take a good look at him and not be fobbed off with some other tailor in the future. Then they would sail upstairs, the lady, Apu, Ravi and bundle—always in that order—and on the way Ravi would peep into other rooms, catching glimpses of silk hangings and tall windows, gleaming floors and fine furniture, and feel an awe of so much wealth. What did it feel like, he frequently wondered, running his fingertips over satinwood surfaces, sinking an inquiring toe into inch-thick carpets, to live like this, without worry, without wanting, every need and craving satisfied? He tried very hard, but his imagination never quite stretched to cover it.

'Don't dream!'

Apu's husky voice, his elbow in his ribs, often recalled him to his duties and he would sit down hurriedly, un-knot the bundle, and, shaking out the folds with a professional panache, hand whatever it contained to the old man. Sometimes the dress was near complete, perhaps only a hem to be pinned up or let down. Sometimes it was merely cut and tacked and the fitting would drag while Apu pinned here and there, signalling to Ravi to watch, his hands full of pins, the lapels of his drill coat bristling with silver pinheads and pinpoints.

At other times they began from the beginning, with a pile of new material, and shiny magazines open at pattern pages sprawled all over the tables. *Woman, Vogue, Femina, Vanity Fair, Eve, Elle*—his eye wandered over the alluring foreign names, half-stupefied, half marvelling that virtually a whole industry should be devoted to women.

Apu, unable to read, concentrated on the pictures, cautiously recommending suitable patterns but quick to withdraw if the response was lukewarm. Yet if his advice were honestly sought it was shrewdly given, for Apu had developed a good eye for what figure looked well in which creation. This was something that completely baffled Ravi. With Indian women he was on firm ground, he knew what would suit such and such a colour, or figure, and anyhow saris needed no tailoring, which left only blouses or petticoats or jackets. But Europeans? He had no idea of how they wanted to look—whether they wanted to disguise or display the qualities that seemed unattractive to him, the big raw bones, the square, long-waisted bodies, the long, shaved legs jutting below their hemlines that to him looked distastefully unclothed.

The cause, he realized, was that he had never really looked at European women before, certainly never as he looked at other women, for they had always been a breed apart, living in another world. One noted their skins of course: some red and awful, but a few so dazzling, so unutterably white and beautiful that it had stopped him in his tracks, literally, many a time, especially when he was fresh out of his village where there were no white women. And there one had sniggered, if one were accompanied and courageous, in those far-off bachelor days, over pale eyelashes and orange hair. But not having looked at them as *women*, until lately, made it extremely difficult for him to advise on what they should wear.

'It will come,' said the old man serenely. 'After a while you will be able to tell what will look best on them—even when they can't.'

Ravi doubted it. He also doubted whether he would ever match Apu's skill in cutting out and in copying patterns. Nothing seemed too difficult for the old man. He would carry away a fashion plate cut from one of those sumptuous magazines, and his gnarled shaking old man's hands would grow steady as he chalked and cut out the pattern, adroitly adapting it to measurements often far from ideal.

'It will come,' Apu told him. 'But you must try.'

This Ravi was loth to do, for if he made a hash of it, the material hacked beyond salvage, half the cost of replacement was deducted from his wages. This arrangement had been foisted upon Ravi, rather than mutually agreed, and every time it was put into operation he rebelled silently, almost hating the old man for the inroads made into his cash-pile.

The pile grew steadily, his savings from what he considered a meagre and hard-won wage. This same wage had seemed adequate, even ample, to him in the early days when he had just started, and again, briefly, when he had been given a five-rupee rise. But that was a long time ago, he could not warm himself by that glow for ever. Still, he thought smugly, at the rate at which he was going in a year he would be able to put down a sizeable deposit on a bicycle, or in two even be able to buy it outright. He said so to his wife, and she placidly reminded him he had wanted a bed.

'That will come, first things first, just be patient,' he urged her. 'Once we have a bicycle we can do so much more work, I mean think of the time we waste walking here, walking there!'

Nalini agreed. She was perfectly happy sleeping on a mat on the floor, she had only wanted a bed to please him, to show wifely appreciation of the bursting fervour with which he looted the future to lay promises at her feet. And secretly she was more than glad to see him absorbed in his bicycle, concentrating his energies on an understandable, attainable object, instead of consumed by vague dissatisfactions and frightening ambitions. Abstract ideas, such as Ravi had been so fond of airing, only made her confused and nervous. She felt much safer with him as he was now.

They often discussed the future, in the little retreat they had made for themselves. Actually it was Ravi's doing. He was staring up at the ceiling one night, in a sweat of irritation brought on by the usual frustrations, when it came to him that the section of roof over their room was flat. The rest of the house sported gables —useless pointed structures off which tiles were for ever falling: but between the twin gables over the kitchen and their room was this small flat forgotten area. He had seen it months ago, while re-fixing some loose tiles, but had not then realized its potentialities. He was so excited that he woke Nalini and told her, and thereafter he could not sleep but lay in the dark working out in his mind how best he could construct what he envisaged as a refuge, a place they could call their own, where he and his wife could talk, plan, dream, make love, undisturbed, for all these things were very important to him.

He did not get up early enough the next morning, then he had to work; in the afternoon there was a fitting, and it grew dark at seven. But there was a brief twilight before that, not enough to work by, when Apu would look up at the windows and sigh for the failing light, and stitch some more, and finally give the order to pack up; and he waited, chafing, for the moment to arrive.

At last. He flung on the covers—oil-cloth for the precious machine, mull drapes over all unfinished garments, which Apu insisted on—then he was out of the house, sprinting up the street to borrow a ladder from his friend the blacksmith.

Kannan kept the ladder because the stairway leading from his forge to his living quarters above had collapsed, and he could not afford to put it up again. In his good-natured way he never minded anyone borrowing it, provided they returned it in time for him to go to bed, and provided they did not implicate him in subsequent proceedings should it be used for nefarious purposes. Ravi, however, he seldom bothered to caution: he knew the rules and, besides, he was now a respectable young householder.

'What's happened,' he asked mildly, as Ravi came in with a rush. 'Roof fallen in?'

'Had an idea,' Ravi panted. 'Tell you later, can't stop now.'

Kannan shrugged. Some impossible scheme no doubt, he thought. He knew Ravi and his enthusiasms.

The ladder was long, heavy, hazardous round corners. Ravi would have liked to sprint back, but he had to go slowly, and even so he earned the dark looks of passers by. It was with relief that he reached his own door, manhandled the ladder through the narrow entrance, and gained the courtyard.

By now the whole household, alerted, had assembled to watch.

'Has another tile gone?'

'I didn't know the roof was leaking again.'

'What are you doing?'

Ravi gritted his teeth. 'I saw a black scorpion,' he said. 'I am going up to deal with it. Anyone care to come?'

They cowered, as he had meant them to—chattering, inquisitive crows, for ever denying him his peace and privacy! And, he thought with fright, supposing there was a little pure space and Varma or Puttanna nabbed it?

He began to climb. There was not far to go, it was a small house, but the ladder projected beyond the gables, which meant an awkward sideways leap on to the coping between them. He stretched himself and made the leap, successfully, landing lightly on the stone coping. Below him, as he had calculated, lay an enticingly flat and empty area, adequate for his purpose. Pure peace flooded into him. Here he would build a little shelter, a sanctuary for himself and his wife.

Despite his urgent efforts, the venture took time. Apu's consent had to be obtained, and he had first to be convinced that Ravi's shelter would not bring down his roof. Varma, Puttanna and Thangam—all had to be kept at bay, for quite early on they had ceased to believe in the black scorpion. Verbally he had staked his claim, would have first rights over the space he had discovered, whatever subsidiary rights Apu might grant (he hoped none) to other family members out of a sense of fair play. Nevertheless he remained a little apprehensive. What if the others simply took possession? Apu was getting old, finding it not so much difficult to assert himself as less willing to exert himself to do so. And didn't they say that possession was half the battle?

Feverish and haunted, Ravi redoubled his efforts. The area had to be cleared. There was several years' accumulation of dust and dirt, soot, grime, cobwebs, dead leaves and insects, and inexplicable lumps and bumps of cement left by the builders which he had to chip off with a chisel. On this base, after much thought and experimentation, he rigged up a structure of plaited-reed panels and matting. The panels were costly. So was a ladder of the right length. Having bought it, he wondered if it was a good buy, for soon after Varma, who had never attempted the sideways leap necessitated by Kannan's ladder, joined him on the roof.

'Building yourself a love-nest, I see,' he said.

Ravi, vastly annoyed, looked up from his labours. 'Just somewhere I can think in peace,' he answered loftily, 'without having you hammering at the door.'

Varma withdrew; but thereafter, to Ravi's disgust, he reappeared sporadically. In an attempt to dissuade him Ravi sold the ladder, recklessly, at a price far below what he had paid for it, and bought himself another—a rope ladder that he pulled up after him.

It put an end to unwelcome visits; but that month there was nothing left out of his wage to give Jayamma for their keep.

'Pleasure should always come second,' she lectured him. 'Otherwise what will come of it but ruin? Pay your way first, other things afterwards, that should be your motto.'

He granted that her stricture was justified, but he took it badly. Neither Puttanna nor Varma nor the crippled boy (though there was more excuse for him) contributed a pie to the household: yet here he was, on his first defection, being pilloried.

'You must tell the others that,' he said sourly. 'Am I the only one that eats?'

'You are the only one that earns.'

'Then it's high time the others did,' he said. 'Healthy young men like them ought to be out working, not sitting around idling and dicing—'

He listened to himself in some amazement and thought: why,

how I have changed! for the virtuous words he heard himself uttering might have come from his respectable elders. They distinctly displeased Jayamma. She could have listened all day to criticism of Puttanna, whom she referred to as her worthless son-in-law, but Varma, who flattered and teased her as if she were a young girl, for all his lazy habits was something of a favourite.

'Not everyone can fall into jobs as you did,' she said pointedly, and as she turned away he heard her mutter aside, that he was getting above himself. Ravi in his turn fumed. This was roughly what young men were always being advised to do, yet when they did they were instantly slammed down. Well, he thought, he was not going to stop in a rut just to please her, the old bitch!

As a result of this quarrel, or perhaps to rub in the fact that he was living on charity, she kept him on short commons. It was not that he actually went hungry: but there was never a second helping, and the choice morsels went elsewhere—the crispest pancakes, the whitest *idlies*, most of the vegetables in a stew, while he had to make do with watery coffee and the thin gruel that was left after most of the dhal had gone.

Ravi was not new to this. Much of his early life he had been fed largely on water in which things had been boiled, while the things themselves went to his father, who was the breadwinner, or to his older brothers as they became breadwinners. It was simply that he had grown unused to it: and he watched with a sense of outrage delicacies going to Varma and Puttanna that had previously come to him. But if he fared badly, he noticed that the crippled boy fared worse, and some faint feeling of kinship awoke in him, making him realize that he always had fared ill, and always would, the crippled by birth crippled further by life.

He was a silent creature, this boy Kumaran. Actually he was not a boy, he was a fully grown man. They called him boy because sub-consciously they felt he was inferior, rather like sahibs who shouted 'Boy!' at their quite elderly servants. His right arm was withered, the hand and fingers hanging helpless and wizened at the end, the upper arm so attenuated a child's hand could easily have circled it. There was not much he could do: but a tart and reluctant charity over the years had induced him to do as much as, and then a little more than, he could. His left arm was fore-shortened, but less severely malformed, and with these two imperfect limbs he somehow managed to press finished garments, or to pin paper patterns on to the material ready for cutting out.

'Time you spoke up.' Ravi nudged him one evening after the usual meagre ration had been dolloped on to his leaf. 'Tell the old cow you want something better.'

Kumaran started violently. It was seldom that anyone spoke to him.

'Oh no,' he answered, shocked. 'It's good of her to feed me at all. I've been on the streets, I know when I'm lucky.'

Mouldy old fool, thought Ravi, too cowed to realize that the less one asked, the less one was given! As for himself, he wasn't going to ask for anything—no, not for anything was he going to eat that particular humble pie. And as for her, he'd show them all, just wait and see.

Exactly what he would show them he did not know, except that it would be something splendid and respect-worthy. But quite clearly defined was his intention to dock his contribution to the household which Jayamma always maintained was nominal, although he felt it to be exorbitant. Well, in future let her ask for it: come to him and ask, and he would hand over what he thought was right, not what she expected as her due. After all, this had been Apu's intention, when he had arranged to give Ravi his full wage, without any deductions, so that he in turn could hand Jayamma what he considered a fair share towards running the joint establishment.

Chapter 16

WHEN at last, however, the shelter was completed, Ravi's rancours and resentments melted away. He no longer felt like wrangling with Jayamma, and handed over his usual outrageous contribution without dispute, while she in her turn desisted from the petty deprivations which had so maddened him. Indeed she was quite glad of this, for she liked her hardworking, handsome son-in-law—handsome, that is, when he didn't have that sulky, unsatisfied scowl all the young men seemed to have stamped on their faces these days.

'It is so awful for everyone,' said Nalini soberly, 'when you and mother quarrel.'

'It would be worse if I quarrelled with you,' Ravi answered, reasonably.

'Would you?'

'I wouldn't want to . . . but I'd have to, if there was no one else.'

'Why would you *have* to?'

'Well,' he said honestly, forcing himself to hard straight thinking for her sake. 'When I feel that way, I have to take it out on someone.'

'You don't have to,' she said. 'You just do.'

'No,' he said helplessly. 'I have to. I can't help myself.'

He could see she didn't agree with him, but she didn't pursue the subject. She was unlike other women in that, he thought, and so much the better for it: what man liked being hounded into corners? He squeezed her arm, affectionately but carefully, for she was busy knitting.

They were sitting companionably together in their roof-top shelter, making the most of the brief twilight. He liked to be idle, to relax alone with his wife after the day's labour; but Nalini always brought something with her, a piece of sewing or mending, or a lapful of flowers to be strung into garlands that she and Jayamma took to the temple, or occasionally wound in their hair. Now she was making a pink bonnet for the baby her sister was expecting. He watched her monotonous movements, finding them oddly restful—although he would have preferred her to be knitting for his child instead of Puttanna's. But there was no sign of one: while Puttanna, who could scarcely support the child he already had, who seldom had any privacy in the quarters he shared awake and asleep with Apu and Jayamma, had somehow succeeded under cover of shawls and coverlets in impregnating his wife, who had not imagined she would conceive with a baby still at the breast.

They were all glad about it though. They all liked babies. He did too, dandling the infant Puttanna and never holding it against her that she had a superior, insufferable father. He wished he had a child too, preferably a son rather than a daughter, a little boy who would run after him and call him father, who would look up to him and to whom in time he would pass on his skills, so that he would never have to worry about whom to hand over to like poor old Apu . . . Quite suddenly, weaving his conventional fantasies in the falling light, he became aware that Nalini's thoughts were racing after his. Her eyes were downcast, but he knew. Babies lay between them, the babies they had not yet created. He could not speak of it, and neither could she, from the same shy reserve that starting from her now bound them both, so that sex had become an unmentionable subject by day, despite the frenzies of their nights.

He had sometimes tried, in the tension that mounted before their love-making began, to make her talk of it as unashamedly as she acted: but she never would and he had let it go, in much the same way that he accepted that his knowledge of her would always come in the darkness, so that if he had seen her naked by daylight he would not have recognized his wife. Occasionally he pondered on these things as deprivations, deeming them so from his experience of women in what he now believed were his disreputable years: but mostly he advised himself to forget these and latch on to his benefits. What did a little verbal prudery matter, so long as her abandoned action gave him so much exquisite pleasure?

'What are you thinking about?'

'I was thinking about that bonnet,' he said.

His thoughts, disturbed, rose from the depths and wandered at surface levels. Why, he wondered, did they put bonnets on babies? It must be vastly uncomfortable for them in this hot climate, no wonder they cried. Especially Puttanna's baby . . . and she invariably chose the night, so that Puttanna had to bolt from the room for fear of Apu, and tramp up and down the courtyard with his child on his shoulder. He would have slept there too, poor Puttanna, out of sheer weariness, but the floor had never been cemented over, it was baked earth that was always damp and sometimes squelchy from the leaky tap and the constant washing and splashing that went on at it. Ravi chuckled. It could be extremely irritating, listening to those shuffling steps outside one's door at night, but all the same Puttanna's plight was really quite funny, when you thought about it.

'What are you laughing about?'

He told her, finding it funnier still, and she said, reprovingly, 'You mustn't laugh at him, poor man. Remember it may soon be your turn.'

He turned sharply and looked at her, but she did not raise her eyes, her hands went on steadily knitting. At last he said, in a kind of fear in case he was wrong:

'Do you mean—are you going to have a child?'

She finished the line, poked both needles into the wool, placed them in squares of clean muslin and made a neat parcel.

'Well,' she said. 'I'm not sure. I would like to have been sure before telling you. But the way you rush at things, it is not possible to do anything in the way it should be done.'

He did not care, his heart was singing. More than anything on earth he wanted a son. A bed, a bicycle—he had wanted these, but now in an extravaganza of divestiture he flung them away. They no longer mattered. They were externals. This was something real and precious: a son.

'You know I'm not sure,' said Nalini soberly.

He hardly heard her. Already he was busy making the boy a little round velvet cap that he could wear when they took him out, perhaps to see the fireworks in the Park during Deepavali, or to the Fair that usually came round after the hot weather. The prospect intrigued and absorbed him.

Insistently over the next few weeks Nalini warned him that she might be wrong, their hopes unfounded. She was cautious by nature, taking after Apu who seldom spoke of anything that wasn't already half achieved, and after Jayamma, who believed that to anticipate happy events was to blight them by provoking the wrath of Heaven, whose prerogative the future was. But Ravi did not listen. His wish for a son was so strong that he could not even imagine it would not come true. He had always been a believer in the force of wishing, wishing so hard that things came true.

By the end of the third month Nalini capitulated. A baby was definitely on the way. It was time for them to start taking in the slack a little. Ravi agreed. They gave up their snow-fruit and Kola, which were still an occasional pleasure, and Ravi flung his new shirt and mouth-organ the same way the bed and the bicycle had gone. They began buying for the baby—cotton material for little jackets, and one really good Binny's towel, more wool for a bonnet, and bottles of coconut oil to massage the baby's body.

Thangam, the expectant mother, watched with interest which she tried to stop turning sour but it would not work. For what preparations could a woman make married to a man who brought home not even one rupee? Puttanna tried, he said, it was just that there were no jobs available. Perhaps he did. Sometimes he was out all day, and came back at night worn out and tired, slumping down wordless and sullen beside Varma. Varma had no job either; but he had had the sense to remain single, there were no pressures to bear him down.

'I don't know what you have to grumble about.' Hands swollen, ankles swollen, belly big, the irritated Thangam confronted him. 'One would think you were bearing the child, whereas you can't even work like other men do.'

'I have been trying to find some work,' Puttanna answered, patiently as he had done before. 'Perhaps tomorrow I shall be more lucky.'

'Tomorrow, tomorrow!' said Thangam. 'The baby will be born before your tomorrow arrives.'

Privately Puttanna wondered what had come over his easygoing wife. He could not make it out at all. With their first child, there had not been much money either and she had not seemed to mind and did they not manage? But over this one she behaved like a tigress.

Nalini understood her sister's feelings better. In sympathy she knitted yet another bonnet and presented it to Thangam, but there was not much more she could do, she had her own little stockpile to think of and she and Ravi were by no means flush. Jayamma might have helped but was too mean to do so—a meanness which she privately explained away as a prudent care for the future, when she might be widowed and have to count every pie. The truth was that she did not like Puttanna, who had no laughter or graces like Varma to make her overlook his pauperdom, who inhabited her house like some great sloth that she could not shift, that she had to feed and keep and clothe. She said so to Apu.

'And now we are to do the same for this child,' she grumbled loudly, 'as well as the other. If he cannot support children, why does he have them?'

Apu lay on his bed and stared at his toes and felt tired. Puttanna had fathered the child because he was vigorous and because he could not control it. Apu could understand this. Not many men had the discipline that he had been able to exact from this wiry spindly frame of his. But there had been a price to pay, he remembered, for all those agonized interruptions. He had been willing to pay it, and as part of the compact had come his present peace, his freedom from financial stress. But he could forgive Puttanna for being unable to do so.

'You will feel differently when the child comes,' he said to soothe his wife. 'I am sure you will like a little baby.'

Jayamma softened. 'Of course I will. Do you think I am an unnatural monster? Never think that, not for one moment. I am very glad, very happy, that our daughter is to have another child. All I said was that its good-for-nothing father should not expect you to support it. But babies—ah! they are lovely. Who would be without them?'

Puttanna, twiddling his thumbs outside, picked up the undertones of this conversation without difficulty. His wife and his children were to be welcomed and warmed within the family circle, while he, the nominal head, was carefully penned outside. The situation was the more galling because at the outset *they* had fawned on him and *he* had conferred the favours—he, a shop-owner, trapped by Jayamma's wiles into marriage with a lowly tailor's daughter.

'She is a she-devil,' he said intensely and theatrically to Varma. 'Do you know she even grudges me a handful of rice?'

'She's not so bad,' said Varma comfortably. 'You have to jolly her along, that's all.'

Ravi agreed—not that he particularly wanted to, he had no great liking for Varma, that pet of Jayamma's; but since his reinstatement in his mother-in-law's favour he found it easier to treat her justly. And Puttanna's idleness rankled. If he had put his share in the kitty Ravi might have been able to hang on to his bicycle, that beautiful machine with the flashing silver spokes he had ridden so often in his dreams. Instead, his earnings, and of course Apu's, went to support the whole brood. He said, darkly, his resentment boiling over, 'Mother-in-law is quite right to be careful. It would be different if everyone pulled their weight.'

'You mean I don't,' said Puttanna. 'Why don't you come out in the open with it instead of behaving like a jackal?'

'All right then, I will. I do mean you don't,' said Ravi.

Puttanna turned his back on him and spoke over his shoulder. 'You speak too freely,' he said, 'for someone who used to sleep on the pavement.'

'So do you!' cried Ravi. 'So do you speak too freely for a man that owes his full belly to the efforts of others!'

'Guttersnipe.'

'Blood-sucking leech.'

Varma, this time, separated the two brawling men and calmed them. At other times Ravi was the peacemaker, or Kumaran, or even Puttanna.

The relationships of the household were fluid too, constantly changing and re-grouping to meet the exigencies of the intermittent quarrelling that went on. This was nothing new to Ravi. In his own home they had bickered steadily, the irritations of ordinary daily life grown large because there, as here, they lived so much on top of one another. In a way therefore he was used to it, but with his work, his wife and the coming child to preoccupy him Ravi found it wearisome, for all that he joined in as pugnaciously as the rest.

In these days the roof-top shelter became even more of a haven, to which both he and Nalini escaped whenever they could. Several refining touches had been added to the original structure. There was a khus-khus blind, which kept out the worst of the glare without shutting off what little air there was. Inspired but clumsy, Ravi had rigged up a kind of extra thatching of palm leaves, which kept them cool and dry. There was a small punkah too, precariously hung from the roof of the lean-to, and functioning through a cord and pulley, which he gingerly worked by a toe on days when it was stifling.

It was the hot weather, most days were stifling. The sun rose early and at full strength, and by nine or ten in the morning brick walls and cement floors were saturated with heat and sending it out in waves. In the workroom, airless, its one window letting in the strong light, Ravi could feel the heat beating in on him from all sides. It sometimes felt as if the walls had narrowed at the top, creating a blast funnel in whose burning draughts they roasted. They also worked. Apu saw to it that they did. He appeared to feel the heat less than any, and his parched, greying old man's skin stayed dry while the sweat ran down their bodies.

Round about six they laid off. Not even Apu could keep going much longer in this weather.

Usually at this time a light breeze sprang up. There was a perceptible tailing-off of sound and activity as people put aside whatever they were doing and came up for air. Alone in their shelter Ravi and Nalini found a new peace, Ravi from the pressures that built up over the long day, Nalini from the chafing discomforts of a first pregnancy. If only they had a place of their own, Ravi sometimes thought, though more and more fleetingly as the months went by, they could be peaceful like this always ... but meanwhile he was grateful for what they had.

To them it was a new world of charm and novelty, this rooftop living that was part of the city's way of life. From where they sat they could see scores, hundreds of people dotting the acres of flat roofs around them. Most of the houses in the quarter had flat roofs, at least those that were new or newish, square little cement boxes that possessed this one great advantage over older ones like Apu's; and at the first hint of dusk up came their inhabitants, thankfully emerging from the steamy ovens below.

Ravi enjoyed watching them. So did Nalini. Their activities, the antics of their children, provided an endless intriguing panorama, and a friendly fellow-feeling, a kind of sociable intimacy, established itself between them and these other roof dwellers. When they came up now people waved to them or called out greetings, and occasionally a half-packet of cigarettes or a wad of betel-leaf, wrapped and weighted with gravel, would land at their feet. Yet, when they wanted they could isolate themselves: the height of the gables, and the screens he had provided, easily ensured this.

'You know I always wished we had a terrace,' said Nalini

dreamily. 'When we were children we used to go to our grand-mother's house and it had a lovely terrace ... we used to play there—there were railings all round to stop us falling over—and sometimes we would watch the processions, there were lots of them because there was a temple near by ... we used to love going to our grandmother's.'

This must be on her mother's side, Ravi thought. Apu's origins, like his, had been in a village to which his parents, defeated by the city, had returned. The old man had once told him of this, and of his regret that he had not been able to provide grandparents for his two young daughters. Well, he, Ravi, would not be able to either, for his village was part of his dead past.

'I don't believe you're listening.' Nalini broke the chain of his thoughts. 'What are you thinking about?'

'Oh,' he said painfully, 'just that there won't be any grand-parents ... on my side, I mean.'

'Of course there will,' she said reassuringly. 'We can always go for a short visit, or your father could come here, it is a simple matter.'

He was silent. He knew better the economics of village life, knew the superhuman effort, the begging and the borrowing that went into raising the train fare, the money for the extras de-manded by pride and the standards of a city. His father had managed it once, where many men like him never managed it at all. He would never do it a second time.

The light was going, grey edged the extravagant swathes of colour in the sky. Punctually, as if set in motion by a clock, a light breeze wafted up, fanning out over the blistered city, bring-ing a hint of cool showers and the sharp scent of mango. Pale gold bruised flowers fell, swirled round in a last eddy and were still. Ravi scooped up a handful of the tiny stars and crushed them for the smell. There must be a mango-tree near by, though he could not think where. In this quarter so far as he knew no trees grew.

Darkness, soon. Inky black here between the gables until later, when the stars grew hard and brilliant.

'We must go,' he said reluctantly. There was no answer. Nalini was dozing, her chin fallen forward on to her chest. Her face was puffy and streaked with sweat, her body heavy and ungainly from

98

the child she carried. How ugly she looked, he thought, and tenderness filled him, sudden and sweet. His wife, their child. He nudged her awake. Both were too precious to risk on that dangling ladder down which descent grew perilous once the light went.

Chapter 17

IN the summer months they woke at six o'clock, all except Thangam and Puttanna, who took turns rising at five and sometimes even four to attend to their fractious child. After this they all washed, not in any set order but hanging around limp and tousled until the tap was free. Ravi hated this part of the morning. Hardly one went by without some degree of friction and acrimony, and he sometimes thought he had never known anyone wash so much and so slowly as his wife's family did.

Thangam was far and away the worst. She brought a wooden plank with her, and sat herself comfortably on it while she scrubbed hands and face and arms and legs and feet, blowing and snorting and quite careless of who was waiting unless it were Apu, and then of course she did give way.

But others? They might as well be stone statues for all the notice she took, Ravi thought, watching her with glum fury. She was being especially slow that morning, hogging the tap in her bathing sari, which was full of holes and showed almost half her body. There were two shallow tins beside her, one filled with a green mess of crushed leaves, the other full of coarse ash which she was scrubbing into her arm-pits. Rub, and rinse, and the green stuff on. And again. And more rubbing-in. All to get rid of hair. As if, Ravi thought, she were some lotus beauty removing a last blemish that flawed her skin, instead of an unprepossessing woman with a swollen belly and shapeless breasts he could see all too clearly each time those thick arms went up.

'What are you staring at?'

He started guiltily. 'I wasn't staring at anything.'

'Yes you were. You were staring at me.'

'I was doing nothing of the kind.'

'You were. I've seen you at it before. Indecent, that's what it is. I tell you—'

He slung his towel round his neck and went to his room. He could not bear her shouting and ranting, whatever was wrong with her? But when she wanted something she could be very different, sweetness itself. He had grown wise to that, recognizing the honeyed trail that she laid well in advance, standing submissively back day after day to allow him free run of the tap or bringing him her bright-eyed baby to dandle, before she came out with her request for some favour. When, therefore, later that day she tried to be conciliatory, he curtly refused both her offer of *pan* and her request to go up to the shelter.

'Keeps me hanging around for hours,' he said tartly to Nalini, 'and then expects me to put myself out for her.'

To his surprise she rounded on him.

'You're always getting at her! What's the matter with you? She's eight months gone and you grudge her even a little fresh air.'

'But it's our shelter,' he said, deeply wounded. 'The only place we have ... let her up once and she'll make it a habit, you know what she is.'

'She's my sister,' said Nalini, offended. 'All this fuss simply because she's my sister. If it were your sister would you grudge her also?'

'That's nothing to do with it!' cried Ravi. 'I just want somewhere we can be on our own, without your family or my family—doesn't that make any kind of sense to you? It's *our* shelter, built for us—'

'Well, what of it? The house doesn't belong to you, does it?'

He seethed; but already Apu's querulous voice was calling from the workroom, and presently work absorbed his anger. Perhaps, he thought, he was being selfish ... after all, there was no real harm in Thangam.

Later in the evening he made his peace with Nalini, and she, gracefully accepting his overtures soberly said: 'It won't be every day, just this evening because Thangam wants to see the procession if it comes this way. She says it might, and you know how dull it is for her, she never goes anywhere—'

100

'Do we?'

'No, but it's different. We're saving up, she has nothing.'

Ravi gave in, less grudgingly than he had thought he would. He even steadied the rope ladder for his sister-in-law, helping her up the swaying rungs. Hardly recommended for a woman in her condition, he thought, as he watched her wobbling performance, but who was he to say so? He would get nothing but odium from both sisters for his pains. He followed her silently, hoping the procession would be over and done with as soon as possible.

At the moment there was clearly nothing in the offing. Nalini, who had gone up ahead, had spread the mat and taken out her knitting; while Thangam, standing, seemed to be appraising the shelter.

'Why, brother-in-law, how nice you have made it here,' she exclaimed as his head appeared. 'I had no idea!'

'He spent a lot of time doing it up,' said Nalini with a soft placid pride. 'Even put in a punkah, like they have in burra sahibs' houses, just imagine!'

'Ah, yes, brother-in-law goes about and sees things and they give him fine ideas,' sighed Thangam. 'He is not like us, stuck all day long in this stuffy house.'

Ravi wandered away and peered down at the street. Where was this procession? There was no sign of one—not even that massing of people that began long before anything happened. It was nothing other, he thought, than a trick of Thangam's, any old excuse to ruin his retreat.

'Where is this procession?' he asked pointedly.

'Coming, brother, coming. Be patient.'

'I am being patient, but we can't stay here all night!'

'I know, I know,' said Thangam with dignity. 'Please contain yourself, brother-in-law. These things cannot be hurried.'

'They must be done in the proper manner,' Nalini agreed.

Ravi set his teeth and settled down to wait. He must have dozed, a fitful sleep during which he was half aware of matches being struck and lamps being brought and lit, but he was not conscious of passing time until Thangam's voice jerked him awake. She was calling loudly for someone, and it was quite dark, nine or possibly even ten o'clock. His legs felt very stiff. He got up

101

groggily and staggered to where Nalini was standing, gazing at the street.

'What's happened?'

'Nothing yet. Won't be long though.'

He peered down. The street was thronged with people, they packed the street completely, both sides of it to the edges of the gutter as well as a solid phalanx in the middle. From them rose a loud buzzing, the conglomerate sound he had half-heard in his dreams. A greenish light lay over everything, the pale sheen cast by the tall hissing gas lamps whose bearers, meant to line the route, were by now hopelessly entangled in the crowd. They bobbed about indiscriminately, like lost corks, only just managing to hold aloft the gas lamps that fizzed and spat, precariously balanced on cloth pads on their swaying shoulders.

Nalini, next to Ravi, was bouncing with excitement. 'He's going to fall! Look, there! the one with the yellow turban! I can hardly bear to look—ah-h, he's saved, he's managed to save himself.' She let out a little gasp of relief, which mingled with the sigh that went up from the crowd. The next instant she was agog once more, her hand clutching at his sleeve.

'It's coming, I think—the procession! Can you hear?'

He thought he heard, faintly above the noisy buzzing, the strains of a distant harmonium. While he was debating a vagrant wind carried the sound closer and a loud, long-drawn-out shout went up.

'It is, it is!' shrieked Nalini. 'Thangam, come quickly!'

Thangam was only a few feet away, but she ran, first of all bawling to her husband to come up, but when nothing had happened for a full thirty seconds she ran back and her bulky frame disappeared down the rope-ladder. Ravi could hear her shouting, loudly for her husband, civilly for her mother: and presently, to his annoyance, their heads emerged from the dark void below, Jayamma first, Puttanna next, and Thangam teetering at the end with her baby, whom she had woken to watch the procession.

Sourly, mentally, Ravi invited the rest of the household to come up. It only needed these others, he thought, to complete the rape of his stronghold. But Varma had seen too many processions to lose sleep over one more, and Kumaran the cripple knew better than to behave as if he were a member of the family, while Apu

102

heard nothing but the beating of his tired heart, lying flat on his back on his bed in the darkness with his open eyes fixed on the ceiling.

'It won't be long now,' said Thangam to her infant. 'And it will be a sight for those pretty eyes will it not?'

The baby was too dazed even to cry. It dug its fists into its sleepy eyes, and the small head drooped on its mother's shoulder. It had grown used, even in its short life, to these midnight awakenings, for Thangam never liked her baby to miss anything.

'The outriders!' she cried piercingly. This was the cue they had all been waiting for, the unmistakable sign that the long vigil was about to end. Her cry was taken up by the crowd below, a thousand shouts that coalesced in a roar: 'The outriders! the outriders!'

Craning his neck over the women's heads, Ravi could see the first outrider, a motor cyclist who puttered slowly along, creating a wake in which rode two cyclists, followed by several men carrying palms and tall wooden crosses. The musicians came behind, the drummers and flautists on foot, the harmonium-player sitting in a hand-cart and playing gallantly non-stop as they pushed and jolted him along. The tune sounded alien to Ravi's ears—not wholly so, for he recognized occasional phrases, but discordant in the main.

'What are they playing?' he asked.

'How should I know?' said Thangam. "It is a Christian festival. Did you not notice the crosses?'

He had, of course, but he had not attached much religious significance to them. Christianity meant little to him, impinging hardly at all on his life. Damodar said it was a spent religion, not only in India where people thought it a bit peculiar, but all over the world because it shied away from a contemplation of the immensities of the universe to preoccupy itself with the trivialities of behaviour in this world. It had, besides, according to Damodar, tied itself up in knots what with its leaders contradicting each other about what things really meant and having to tinker with truths which they had once treated as gospel. On the other hand, his father had held that Christians were good people, and good people were God's neighbours; but then he—Ravi's father—was going by the only one he knew, the missionary doctor who had tried so hard to help their family. Perhaps they were good people, thought Ravi judiciously, and he told himself there were good and bad in all kinds. Meanwhile he leaned forward with greater interest, his curiosity piqued, to watch the procession, alien yet oddly familiar, that wound its way below.

The waving palms had passed, the bearers of the crosses, the musicians, the torch-bearers. Now came a group of women, dressed all in white, each carrying a candle, tall, white tallow candles with great bulbous drops down their sides like the tears of some inconsolable loss where the wax had melted and run. Ravi took them for nuns at first; then he saw they were young girls dressed in white saris, with veils over their heads held by circlets of flowers. They advanced steadily, their burning candles like a cluster of stars in the darkening street. The crowd fell silent. No movement, no sound except the soft foot-falls, bare feet on the ground passing lightly without mark, and a sense of exaltation that was suddenly among them all. Ravi wanted to screen his eyes, but he could not. Instead his hands came together, palm to palm as in prayer though he uttered not a word; and he saw his gesture repeated in the ranks below. They waited, he at one with the crowd, on the edge of what they did not know but sensing climax, there must come a climax now as fitting end to the long slow prelude. Then it came.

At first Ravi was aware only of a radiance, a shimmering radiance that seemed to pour from a central point, though what it was he could not see. Out of it the vision grew, set in a shining orb, drawing every star-point of light, the magically evoked statue of the Virgin Mary. He did not know, but the murmurs floated up. The Holy Virgin. Blessed Mary, Mother of God. Our Lady of Compassion. Serenely borne above the heads of the crowd in a glass palanquin, moving in an aureole of light, a shining halo about her and about the Child she bore in her arms.

Ravi leaned closer, looking down. Beautiful mother, lovely child —ah, what a lovely child, he thought with his heart constricting, a laughing, dimpled child holding fat little arms up to his mother. And she, gentle, grave, unsmiling ... of what coming dolours was she aware, he wondered, with a sudden yearning, that could make her look upon her own child with such infinite sadness?

Thangam's voice, loud, unwelcome, broke his meditation.

'How well they are made! So life-like, who would believe they were not real! They are better made even than last year. My memory may be at fault but no, it is not, they *are* much finer this year. The colouring is so delicate, just look at those lovely rosy cheeks, and the mother is so fair ... ai, how beautiful they are!' She sighed, and her tone grew sharper. 'The robes are pure silk you know ... and all that silver lace, they say the nuns make it, it takes them the whole year, as soon as one festival is over they start preparing for the next. And those brilliants on the hem, some are real you know, every now and again they sew on a real stone. Just imagine: real diamonds and rubies!'

'They must be very rich.'

'They are, they are. Their church, brother-in-law, is far richer than any of our temples. Otherwise would they do it?'

'Do what?'

'They throw it away,' said Thangam, round eyed. 'Cast it into the sea. The palanquin, the goddess, the robes, everything. They do it just before the morning light, in the deepest part of the sea so that rogues can't dredge up anything ... and when it is done they say the waves grow tall as trees, and a strange light glows on them, for it is the Mother of God ascending into Heaven.'

They listened respectfully, awed, exalted by the majesty of the symbolism. The fall, the ascension: it was the divine cycle, familiar to Ravi from his own religion, and he visualized the figure descending into the waters, triumphantly rising again. It seemed beautiful to him, with the near-magic of nostalgia, for there was in the religious lexicon of his village a variation of this ceremony, only there they had all wound in procession to the village tank to immerse their god, who being intentionally made of mud disintegrated beyond dredging up by rogues, and the children, of whom he was one, were told he had gone to heaven.

God, Heaven ... it was all so vast it created in him a longing for what he did not know. He sighed, and felt his soul empty as he watched the procession pass. It was passing, soon it would be gone ... The glittering palanquin, the beautiful Madonna and Child, were already beyond his line of vision. All he could see now were the massed flames of the candles, closing in behind like a bright constellation, dimming as it receded. The crowd began to disperse, eddying and surging in the narrow street. Some struggled free and were swallowed by the darkness to which the street was returning. Others ran after the disappearing procession, wildly, in a frenzy of desolation, and attached themselves to the last cohorts in a kind of sobbing abandonment. Where it went, they would go. Ravi, pinned against the gables, was suddenly seized by a ravening desire to follow them. So strong was the feeling that he had physically to hold himself back, gripping the tiles fiercely enough to hurt before the feeling passed. Even so it took time, and when he ran his tongue over his dry lips there was the taste of blood where his teeth had bitten down.

'Is anything wrong?' Nalini was looking anxiously at him.

'No. I—got carried away a little, that's all.'

'Yes. It was a splendid spectacle.' She yawned. 'I'm tired. Let's go down.'

'Let's stay, just for a little.'

'All right.'

For a few moments they sat quietly, in the starlight, enveloped in peace. Then all was shattered by a heavy thud and a scream that seemed to come together, followed by more screaming and the loud, frightened yelling of the baby.

Chapter 18

RAVI went out into a fresh, pink, early morning, in obedience to Jayamma who had told them this was no time for men to be about. For Thangam was having her baby. Thangam had fallen— owing to her own crass carelessness, thought Ravi, whose room she was lying in—and premature labour had started. Jayamma had sent them all packing, except of course Apu, whom she could hardly order out, and who lay slack and still on his bed, neither ill nor well but in a kind of lethargy as if weights had been laid on his body.

With nothing in common save in-law-dom, they had taken separate routes, Varma one way, Puttanna another, Kumaran a third. Ravi stood undecided in the street, unable to think of any-where to go. His eyes were heavy with sleep, they dragged the rest of him down. The entire night had been sleepless for the whole lot of them, what with half of it gone in watching the procession, and the remainder full of Thangam's moans and the cries of her baby—the one she already had, it would be twice as bad when the new one arrived.

Ravi scuffed moodily at the withered flower-petals that littered the street. There were all sorts, he noted. Hindus would only use certain flowers for their religious ceremony: roses, jasmine, chrysanthemums, or the feathery fragrant rosemary; but Christians seemed to throw anything that came to hand, for mingled in with the others he saw scattered the petals of sunflower and zinnia, and even the papery petals of the bougainvillaea creeper.

It was a pretty creeper, the bougainvillaea, he thought, lovely bright colours although the flowers had no smell. He had not realized how pretty it was until he saw the way they used it in the big houses, slap against white-washed walls where their brilliance could show, and the flowers hung down in great heavy trusses of crimson and purple. But you had to have that wide expanse of wall first. If one planted the creeper here—not that you could, there was no earth to set a root in—it would hardly show against the drab brick and tiles, except perhaps to bring out the drabness more. That was the one thing about his village life, though he had not dwelt on it much before: there had been a small plot of ground beside their hut, which his mother had planted with chillis and brinjal and pumpkins—and how pretty that had been in season, golden swelling gourds among the vivid green vines! Ravi shook himself angrily. What was the matter with him, harking back to that putrid existence? Of course it was all right in the one good season that came their way out of five—but what about the others when the paddy fields turned brown and the pumpkins looked like wrinkled old hags? He felt his mouth working in the old way, as if to be rid of the bitter remembered flavour, and he spat into the gutter that ran along the street in front of the houses, narrowly missing the man perched on a flagstone that spanned it to form a footbridge.

'What's eating you, brother?'

'I'm fed up,' he surprised himself by saying.

'Who isn't?' The man grinned, chewing on a green neem twig. 'I'm a labourer, so to speak, but no one wants my labour. So what am I supposed to do?'

Ravi wagged his head in sympathy. The problem had been his too—before Apu, before Damodar, in his first demoralizing months in the city—and he had never been sure, either, what to do. He walked away from the man, who had begun throwing pebbles into the turbid stream of the gutter. There were, he saw, a good many men throwing stones into the gutter; he had not consciously noticed before how many there were. No wonder it got clogged and overflowed, making an unholy mess of the street. It should be stopped, he thought vaguely, though he would be the last to want any more rules and regulations, or more power in the hands of those quick-fisted police so-and-so's. He walked on, aimlessly, falling easily into old habits that had worn grooves in his system. Up one way and down another, into bazaar alleys where the stalls were opening, and along the whitesmiths' streets where *kujas*, *hundas* and *lotas* were piled in shining cylinders. Sometimes he paused, conscious of a rootless feeling with which he was quite familiar though he had not known it since—since his marriage, he thought, since he had become a responsible householder, a decent citizen with a decent job and a wife to support. A job: work: of course there was, plenty of it waiting for him in the workroom, he was one of the lucky ones with no need to ask what he was supposed to do. He jerked himself up, a little alarmed that he found it so easy to drift, and quickly made his way back.

He thought he would sneak in, gather up an armful of jackets that needed buttons and buttonholes, and sit and sew somewhere outside where there was a little shade. He also intended not to be seen, but was hardly over the threshold when Jayamma was on him.

'Is that you, shameless? Is this a time to—'

'I only—'

She raised the towel she was carrying, wrung in hot water and steaming. He cowered. It was Apu's voice, he really believed, that saved him from a thorough trouncing like the one she had administered once before. The trouble with her, blasted bitch, he thought angrily as his breath returned, was that she never bothered to control her passions, just let rip as if she were a memsahib.

'Ravi! Come in here—can't you hear me calling?'

He went in. Apu was sitting on his bed, cross-legged, his hands

loose and flaccid in his lap. He looked pale from lack of sleep, and
he had not troubled to put on his tailor's white drill coat with its
high-buttoned collar which was normally the first thing he did in
the morning. Having called Ravi he seemed to have forgotten
what he wanted, for he simply sat and gazed at the younger man.

'Did you want anything?' ventured Ravi at length, uncomfortable under the bland pointless scrutiny. 'Shall I bring you
some coffee, you look tired.'

'Tired, who wouldn't be.' The old man passed his hand over his
face with a dry sound like dead leaves scraping along a pavement.
'Up all night, no rest in the morning either. Coffee, did you say?'
He began to smile, and something of his old alert look returned to
him. 'It's more than your life's worth, lad, to go to the kitchen
now. We're not wanted, there or anywhere . . . we're to sit mum,
do you hear, you and I, until it's all over. Keep out of the way,
that's all they want of us.'

Ravi acknowledged it readily. Childbirth was the one time
when women were all-important and the men found themselves
nobodies. In his village it was quite usual for men to become
drunk when their children were born. However he did not want
to sit closeted here with Apu, in this room where he lived and
slept, full of his old man's smell. And anyhow, what had he been
summoned for, surely it couldn't be just to squat and keep an old
man company? Though he rather feared it was. He had just
screwed himself up to the point of saying, I'll be going, by your
leave, if you're sure there's nothing you want, when Apu said,
brusquely, 'What did you come back for? Weren't you told to
stay away?'

'I came back for work!' said Ravi indignantly, riled by that
accusing tone. 'There's a whole heap of it, when I'm going to
catch up I don't know, I'm behind already.'

He said 'I' deliberately, and the old man did not contradict
him: for indeed he did all the basic and between work, it was only
the cutting out and the final fitting, the highly skilled beginning
and end of a garment, that Apu nowadays undertook.

'Ai, work, there's always work,' said Apu. He brooded, his
watery eyes fixed owlishly on Ravi. 'Night and morning, to keep
our souls in our bodies. And next door there's another soul coming
into the world, if it hasn't come already . . . ai, listen lad, though

you'll hear soon enough.' For Ravi had opened the door a crack, but there was nothing to hear, no infant's cry, only a general bustle, and commanding it a new, stranger's voice.

'Nothing yet,' he said to the old man, carefully closing the door. 'Only the midwife.'

'Then it won't be long now.

'No.'

There was a long silence. Ravi began to fidget again, wanting to go, but not knowing how, wanting to say, it's time for me to go, but unable to bring it out.

'It's time for me to go!'

Ravi jumped. His father-in-law seemed to have become a thought-reader. Then he realized Apu was shouting under the stress of some emotion. Perhaps he was not even aware that he was: his eyes were unfocused, withdrawn, as if his mind were far away.

'Yes, time for me to go,' he repeated. 'When one comes, they say, one must go ... children are born, old men must die.' He fixed his strange blank gaze on Ravi. 'When one is my age the cycle is very clear, one feels it in one's bones.'

Ravi listened, and suddenly felt weak with fear. What would happen to him, his wife, his dreams, if the old man died now? They depended on working and earning, on the security achieved in partnership with Apu, on the tranquillity which followed from these.

'Don't look so frightened, lad! I'm not on the pyre yet!'

Ravi swallowed. 'I wasn't thinking of that,' he said.

'No, but I made you.' Apu chuckled. His vigour seemed to ebb and flow at a rate that Ravi found disconcerting. 'It is a good thing that you should—aren't you going?'

'Where?'

'Out to do some work.'

Ravi in fact no longer wanted to. The impetus had died. He felt little enthusiasm for braving Jayamma again, gathering up an armful of clothes, and dashing out into the blazing midday sun to work. All he wanted was to stay here, old man's smell notwithstanding, unmolested and forgotten in a corner. But Apu was edging him out, physically, prodding and nudging until he found himself at the door, while he droned on about the virtue of work

110

and the fleetness of time—though what would *he* do, thought Ravi sharply, but collapse on to his spring bed again once he had the room to himself! Still, he would have to go, he could see that. He opened the door a crack. The hubbub had if anything accelerated, but the coast was clear. He slid out, made a hasty and indiscriminate bundle of half-finished garments from the workroom, and fled.

He thought of going to the Park, but it was too far. The beach was not, but the sands would be burning, the soles of his feet would blister. He could, he supposed glumly, find a shady tree somewhere, or a doorstep shielded from the sun on which no one would mind if he parked himself; but neither alternative appealed. Then there was the blacksmith, who would always give him a welcome and sometimes even a meal: but the smithy would be like a furnace, and with all that charcoal around it was a dead certainty that some of his customers' clothes would suffer. He cast around in his mind, but he could think of no one else. He had no friends left. His former associates were nomads, flitting from quarter to quarter as official surveillance tensed or relaxed, and unless one belonged to that band there was no way of locating them. Not, Ravi told himself piously, that he would want to. He would never condemn them of course: never would such heresy fall from his lips: but the fact remained that they were vagrants, seedy failures whom the city had defeated. And even more than that, though he hardly dared admit it to his consciousness, he knew how sweetly and fatally easy it would be—no more than one false step—for him to give up his austere living for their narcotic existence.

So no old friends. No new ones. The family completed his circle, night and day. Relatives? None of those either, he thought ruefully and with some consternation. Not like his father, who, ejected from his hut at a birth, had been able to call upon aunts, brothers, cousins, to provide a temporary shelter and bolt-hole. Even at dead of night. He could remember this quite clearly. They had been awakened—all being asleep in their one-roomed hut—by the moans of their mother, and used to various kinds of disturbance he and his brothers had turned over and gone to sleep again, only to be shaken into wide wakefulness by their father who was standing over them holding a hurricane lantern, his shadow huge, like a giant's, thrown right across the hut. Muzzy with sleep and a little frightened, they had gone out with him into the pitch black night, and had followed his swinging lantern down a footpath that led to the hut where their aunt and her family lived.

They simply went in, all of them. No questions were asked, no light lit. A few bodies shifted to make room for them in the darkness, and they wrapped themselves up in their tattered shawls and lay down where they could to sleep.

There was something to be said for that way of life, he thought, even if it *was* the only thing. At least you were never stranded, left gasping like a fish out of water. Of course, independence was fine, who on earth wanted relatives ruining every moment of your privacy, strung like so many millstones round your neck? But one or two would undeniably come in handy at a time like this . . .

Then he thought of Damodar. He had deliberately fended off thinking of him so far, because he had been the cause of his first serious quarrel with Nalini. Yet why not? All he had to do was to keep his head and not drink and all would be well. Besides, he had heard various intriguing rumours about him in the market—that he had bought a big house, that there was an inner courtyard paved with marble, splashed by the waters of a central fountain. The idea entranced him. He began to feel very hot and dusty as he thought of cool marble and water, and presently he found himself on his way to those quarters where news of Damodar was normally readily available to the right people.

Chapter 19

DAMODAR had always been—and it was accepted that as leader and brains of their one-time outfit he should be—the most affluent among them. Now he was rich. One did not need more than half an eye to see that, and Ravi had far more than that, trained as he

112

had been in the art of gauging wealth to a nicety, for it was on this that they based the size of their tailoring bills. Yet outwardly there was no change. Damodar still wore the plain white trousers and loose white shirt with the tails hanging out that was the common man's uniform; and he still had the hungry student's leanness, with thin jutting wrists and incurved belly that signified only eating, not eating too well as quite clearly he could have afforded to do.

Ravi respected him for it. He himself, he knew, would have gone in for rich food, for silk shirts and enamel cuff-links: yet his upbringing had taught him to focus inward, upon the constant light within, to see the raging obscenities and miseries of their life as essentially external and ephemeral; and for all that he angrily repudiated this teaching, shreds of it obstinately clung, forcing him to admire a personal austerity he would not have practised.

'You're very silent,' Damodar said suddenly, his grey cat's eyes fixed intently on the withdrawn younger man. 'Is it that nothing ever happens, or you don't want to tell?'

'Oh well,' said Ravi humbly, 'we live very quietly, you know ... no fireworks down our way. Besides,' he said and sighed, 'it's so restful here ... not like our house, there's always someone shouting or quarrelling, you can even hear it up on the roof.'

'I thought you said you lived quietly.'

'I meant without any excitements ... nothing much happens, if you know what I mean. Work, eat, sleep—it's all pretty humdrum and ordinary, hardly worth talking about.'

'You chose it. No regrets, I hope,' said Damodar, and studied his fingernails.

'Not really,' said Ravi. 'I'm quite happy, really.'

They were both quiet again. Behind them the fountain played, tempering, slightly, the heat of high noon. That rumour had proved true: there was a fountain, set in a small square pool in the courtyard. But there was no marble, only a shallow catchment basin of black polished stone over whose rim the water spilled gently into the pool, scarcely splashing the low paving-slab surround.

It was on this that they were sitting, holding glasses of rose sherbet, a bowl of crushed ice between them. This impressed Ravi as much as anything—as much as the house, which was large for the neighbourhood, but by no means the palace he had imagined, or the furnishings, which were severe, with not even one plump satin cushion in sight. But ice! He was used to the massive white ice-boxes in the big houses they went to, out of which trays were slid and ice tumbled into silver buckets; but that a friend of his— more or less an equal—should actually own a refrigerator, opening and closing it so casually to bring out these unlimited quantities of ice—now that really was something! To savour the pleasure again he rattled the spoon around in the bowl and scooped out a cube, intending it for his sherbet, but childish temptation overcame him and with a side glance at Damodar he picked it up in his fingers and put it in his mouth. It felt cool and wet against the inside of his cheek, reminding him, with a brief sensual shiver, of his wife.

'You know,' he said, 'my wife is expecting.'

Damodar stirred. 'Are you glad?' he asked.

'Well, of course I'm glad,' said Ravi. 'Wouldn't you be?'

'Not in your position,' said Damodar. 'I'm not keen on pinching and scraping. As no doubt you'll have to.'

'I suppose so,' said Ravi, suppressing the confession that they already were; and he added, defensively, 'most people have to.'

'They don't have to,' said Damodar. 'They just do. Cattle.'

Ravi felt himself curling up within, grown smaller, even in his own sight, under the scrutiny of this man whose views were, surely, those of the world. Cattle, in the eyes of the world. And what was he doing to lift himself out of that state? He stole a glance at the bundle of sewing he had brought, lying neglected at his feet. Perhaps if he worked hard, even harder than he had yet done, he would get to the stage where he would never have to pinch and scrape, like the people in the big houses who could live serenely unconscious of the money at their elbow, and then per-haps one day he would even be able to say, look, I am no longer cattle, I am—

'What have you got there?'

'Eh? Oh that,' he said lamely, already ashamed of the bundle which was to be his stepping stone to greater things. 'That's just some work I thought I would finish while I was waiting.'

Damodar prodded the bundle with his toe. 'Well, why don't you?'

'I don't feel like it, I suppose,' said Ravi. 'It's just—just buttons and button-holes . . . it can get quite monotonous sometimes.'

Damodar kicked the bundle this time. He said, derisively, 'You call that work? What kind of work is that for a man?'

'It pays,' said Ravi.

'Oh, peanuts,' said Damodar.

Ravi sucked his ice and tried not to feel miserable. He even succeeded, by dint of suppressing his envy of Damodar's possessions and concentrating instead on Nalini. He wished she could be here now, she would have enjoyed sitting peacefully beside him, with the fountain rippling in the background, with sherbet to drink and ice in a bowl. The cubes had melted now, there was only a little ice-water, but even that was very acceptable and he spooned it into his glass.

'There's plenty more—no need to scrape the barrel.' Damodar rose and went as casually as before to the refrigerator, housed on the veranda. Ravi watched, fascinated, as the solid white door opened and closed, effortlessly, with only the gentlest of clicks. The bowl was full again with baby ice-blocks jostling and glistening in a bed of clear water. Damodar had refilled his glass—the scent of rose sherbet wafted about his senses agreeably, pleasing nose and palate. Behind them the water played, sending out waves and currents of cool air.

'It's so lovely,' Ravi sighed, feeling himself ravished, 'truly wonderful, in this kind of weather.'

'It's nothing,' Damodar spoke brusquely. 'It's what everyone should have.'

'What, fountains?' asked Ravi, surprised.

'Oh, that, that's only a toy.' Damodar jerked a contemptuous shoulder. 'I thought you meant refrigerators. Everyone should have them. Every family.'

Ravi was silent. The possession of the one seemed to him as remote as the other.

'You think that's an impossible dream.' Damodar sneered. 'You would. I tell you, what you've got is an ant's brain. You can't think big. You've scraped together what you call a reasonable living and you cling to that rather than go for something bigger in case you lose the lot. The lot did I say? It's precious little, and that you hang on to like death.'

115

Ravi listened painfully, and remembered that this was exactly the accusation he had flung at his father. But with far more justification, he thought, for his father had mouldered in a village, still mouldered there with just about nothing to call his own.

'We're fairly comfortable,' he began, deprecatingly, but with a kind of forlorn pride. 'Of course we may be a bit short when the baby comes, but it's not so bad—'

'It's pitiable.'

'It's more than lots of people have.'

'That isn't saying much.'

'But what can one do,' asked Ravi desperately. 'Of course one would like to—to have refrigerators and—and things like that, but people like us, how can we, I mean—'

'Only one way.' Damodar cut short these meanderings. 'There's enough wealth going around, you have to help yourself to it, that's all. Nobody's going to bring it to you on a platter.'

'I've tried,' said Ravi miserably. 'You know I have. But now my wife—she—she doesn't want me to do anything dishonest, she and her family I mean, they're respectable—'

'Respectable? Dishonest?' Damodar laughed softly. 'What a peasant you are! Tell me, those people up in the posh houses you and your old man go to, are they respectable?'

'Of course they are!' said Ravi.

'They've become respectable,' said Damodar. 'That's what money does for you. And honest: do you think they are honest?'

'Yes,' said Ravi.

'You never used to,' said Damodar evenly.

Ravi was silent. It was in the old days, but not all that long ago, that he had railed at them, called them miserable hypocrites for allowing their left hands to fill nefarious coffers while their right hands remained above board, silently proclaiming their innocence. What had happened to him, what had happened to these truths of his own experience that he should now be denying them? Was it that he was now so much a member of the tribe of the respectable that tribal faults had to be pretenced out of existence?

'So,' said Damodar. 'You've gone back. Everyone put back, in their proper niches. Everyone to stay put, what's more. A happy state of affairs.'

'I don't like it,' said Ravi sullenly, 'any more than you do. But what can anyone—what can I do?'

'What I do,' said Damodar simply, 'if you want what I've got. There's no other way really, as things are. Grab or go under, you've been around long enough to know that.'

'I know,' cried Ravi, 'but how can I, my wife—I can't just—'

'Of course not,' said Damodar. He yawned. 'Once a peasant, they say, always a peasant . . . never mind, drink up . . . go on man, drink, you're not going to let a few words upset you?'

Ravi drank, but the sherbet no longer tasted so good; and when he rose to go Damodar did not press him to stay.

'Well, I'll be seeing you,' he said, nervously.

'Of course, my dear chap, of course,' said Damodar, steadily edging him out, 'any time you want to work for me, my way, just come along and say so.'

Chapter 20

THANGAM'S new baby was another girl, a small, passive child, darker than either of its parents, that looked, Ravi thought, exactly like a little monkey in the yellow bonnet Nalini had painstakingly knitted for it. Secretly, he had been glad to hear it was a girl: it gave him the chance to provide the first male grand-child in the household; and shunning hypocrisy he could not but agree with his brother-in-law, who said two daughters in a row was sheer bad luck. Thangam, too, was frankly disgruntled: here was that old fool of a father about to hand over everything to the junior son-in-law, and her own effeminate husband could not even implant a male seed in her womb! Sometimes she looked enviously at her younger sister who, placidly unaware of these cross-currents, continued to swell satisfyingly.

Practically a whole yard out of the length of her sari, said Nalini, went to clothe her increased girth, so that there was hardly anything left for front-pleating. This made her look awful, she said, and she took little mincing steps to demonstrate her narrow and restricting hem line, gasping and giggling as she nearly keeled over. Ravi righted her, feeling his child kick as he did so; and he became aware, obscurely and without really fitting words round it, that this was what life was about, not fountains or even refrigerators, nor the violent demand and dazzling fulfilment of Damodar's high-tension world. But the feeling was elusive, it passed quickly: and when it had gone Ravi despised himself for finding contentment so easily, settling for low stakes precisely as if he were a prize member of that grim herd, Damodar's lowly cattle.

If thinking of Damodar roused a sour and self-critical fretfulness, Nalini invariably restored his peace. She was so affectionate, so gay, with her soft tender ways that were like a caress, that when she was near he could even feel a little sorry for Damodar, who had no wife, who could not know what it was like to have someone like Nalini by his side. Sometimes it baffled him, this curious shift in the emphasis on what was and what was not important to him, making him wonder who and what he really was under all those feelings and counter-feelings.

In this wash of uncertainty Nalini, to his relief, assumed no sudden strange shapes. She was constant, a rock to which he could cling and keep his head level when his views and values began their mad dance. Yet if she soothed him, she was in need of comfort herself. Now in the last stages of her pregnancy, the minor discomforts were magnified, and at nights she woke, two and three times, crying from severe cramps in her legs. Other nights she lay awake, unable to sleep from a persistent backache, her clenched fists dug into her back in an attempt to ease the nagging pain. Neither Jayamma nor Thangam proffered much sympathy. Jayamma's pregnancies were too remote, what came back was only the pleasure in babies; and Thangam carried and bore easily, so she couldn't understand what there was to make such a fuss about, didn't all women have babies? Ravi almost loathed her, for he knew it was not a fuss about nothing, could feel the knotted calf muscles as he massaged his wife's legs, patiently, far into the night.

In the mornings he woke with a heaviness in his limbs, his eyes bloodshot and gritty, to confront in the workroom an equally weary Apu, whose nights were made sleepless by the two squalling infan... He could have slept in the mornings, at which times Thangam's perverse babies were usually slumbering (the older child from the exhaustion of hunger, for she had not taken kindly to an abrupt weaning, the new baby sated with breast milk which, according to Thangam, ceased to flow at night). But if Apu had kept to his bed Ravi would have done so too, and the old man seemed determined that while they lived they should work. Indeed, finding himself alive when, in accordance with his life-for-a life belief he had half expected to die, seemed to have injected a new vigour into him—a vigour that Ravi found difficult to abide. Sometimes, drooping over his machine in the mornings, Ravi felt like revolting, simply dropping everything and retiring to his room to sleep, but he could not, the old man's presence was too intimidating.

By midday, usually, Apu's energies had run out, he would rise slowly, his knee-joints creaking, and go and lie on his bed while Thangam dealt with the babies, quieting the one with tobacco juice and giving the other the breast. By now, however, when he could have slipped away, Ravi had lost all desire for sleep, and his responsibilities began to press down on him unpleasantly, reminding him of the money locked up in all those bundles of work that lay, neatly wrapped in linen and awaiting attention, on the floor. Then he would begin to work in earnest, inducing panic that was only half simulated to make his fingers fly faster, even, in his zeal, usurping the old man's place to urge his fellow workers on.

His fellow workers needed urging, but they resented it. Varma voiced his resentment, but he did it warily, for he was afraid of Apu. He spoke of uppity upstarts, of easy-bed-hunting sons-in-law who gained influence over doddering old fools; and he did so in barbed asides which, he implied, Ravi could listen to or not as he pleased.

'If you mean me,' Ravi stopped the clacking Singer, 'why don't you say so and be done?'

'You, brother?' Varma spread his hands in general disclaimer. 'Are you not our worthy bread-winner, as Apu often dins into us? No, no, I was speaking only in general terms.'

Or, what was even more infuriating, he would loll against the wall, watching the flashing needle and commenting on Ravi's

119

fine straight stitching until Ravi, goaded beyond endurance, would stop, and invite him to put in a little practice himself. But Varma would not. He was not, he frankly admitted, a good workman, he never would be. What was the point of trying, when it would only mean unpicking, the worst kind of labour? And he would look down at his smooth plump hands, lying idle in his lap, with a kind of fond disparagement. At other times, however, he was genuinely friendly, passing Ravi a wad of chewing tobacco, or some sweetmeat Jayamma had made for him, or else he would tell funny bawdy stories, which Ravi missed from his old days, which made him laugh and restored his good humour.

Apart from occasional outbursts Puttanna bottled his resentments, for unlike Varma he could not afford to be vocal. Varma stood in Jayamma's good graces, he could look to her for protection even if he fell out with Apu. But Apu and Jayamma were united in calling Puttanna, quite often in his own hearing, a worthless good-for-nothing, and he dared not risk their joint wrath. So he looked on sourly, his thin mouth pinched with disappointment, failure, the frustrations of his life, the grumbling strictures of his wife—from which his only retreat was into superiority. His father, he told them over and over again, had been the owner of a shop, he too had been a shop owner and still would be but for government policies which had more or less put the old money-lenders out of business so that men like himself found it impossible to raise credit. Once in the owner class, he implied, it was simply not feasible to settle for less, for in the one there was power and authority, the managing and the ordering of other men, and how could these inherited skills be turned to working at a craft? Then there was business acumen, wasted in this family trade. How often, for instance, had he not told Apu to buy an attachment for the machine that would make button-holes, which would by now have paid for itself twenty times over?

'Yes, and who would pay for it in the first place,' Ravi snarled at him. 'You?'

'The business,' said Puttanna.

'The business is Apu,' cried Ravi, 'Apu and me!'

'Such airs,' Puttanna looked him up and down, coldly. 'The business is you! Well, the pity is you can't see when fifty rupees would be well spent.'

'Fifty isn't enough!'

'Whatever is enough then,'

'It costs nearly a hundred,' said Ravi. 'There isn't that much money to spare.' He didn't really know: Apu kept these matters to himself, largely in his head: but he calculated that Puttanna wouldn't know that he didn't know—he, the favoured son-in-law. 'There wouldn't be any need for such gadgets,' he went on, pointedly, 'if everyone did their share of the work,'—a remark Puttanna had heard so frequently he did not even consider it worthy of an answer.

Kumaran was different: he worked hard, as hard as he could, and the end result was pitiable. It did not rouse Ravi to pity. Overworked and under stress as he was, he began to hate the sight of Kumaran's shrunken, malformed limbs, and their slow clumsy fumbling motions were a daily irritation. Why, he asked himself querulously, should they labour to support a useless cripple? The answer, as he very well knew, was simply that there was nowhere else for the cripple to go.

These were daily annoyances enough and to spare; but worse was to come. When it came Ravi fell to wondering why he had not counted his blessings while they lasted, and in a fit of alarmist superstition directly ascribed the new imposition to this omission.

Imposition it was; at least it seemed so to him, for he had come to regard as his own the small room in which he and Nalini slept. Apu on the other hand—in his view reasonably—could not see that any room was anyone's exclusively, since after all the whole house belonged to him. Finding his nights increasingly disturbed, he turned his daughter and her family out of his room. Thangam, Thangam's husband, their two children—all of them now had to share with Ravi and Nalini.

Nalini took it stoically. She was used to obedience, and saw no point in banging her head against a stone wall. Besides in her heart she agreed with her father's decision, that it was more fitting for married couples to share than for a family to sleep in with an old man and his wife. She and Ravi had had their fair quota of privacy, which most people tried to arrange for newly-married couples; they could not expect it to last for ever.

Ravi took it hard. He had never before had a room of his own. Long witness of his father's land-hunger, the stony deprivation of

121

his years in the city, had wreaked their own peculiar havoc; and desire for possesion, whether of land or bricks and mortar, was like a fever, a lust in his blood.

'We can always go up,' Nalini said to placate him.

'Up? Where?' He glared at her.

'To our—our sanctuary that you built, on—on the roof,' She stammered, never having seen him quite like this.

'What, with you like a pregnant cow?'

He hated himself for saying the words, but he could not stop them, his frustrations had built up too high. The odd thing, to his mind, was that he did not really think of her as a pregnant cow, except fleetingly, and then it only moved him to tenderness. Why then should he have said it?

The net result of his misery and regrets was that he grew even more adamant that Nalini should not risk herself on the swaying rope-ladder, thus closing off their escape route while violently resenting the irruption of Thangam and her family into what he still called, and thought of, as his room.

It was a tight squeeze. He and Nalini, their sleeping mats, their trunk, the personal possessions they ranged along the windowsill, had fitted in neatly. Now everything was halved. To maintain some semblance of privacy they strung an old sari on a cord and hung it as a room divider. The divisions would have been equal but for the electric light, fixed uncompromisingly in the middle; and when they had shifted the divider the necessary six inches Ravi, having the smaller family, found himself the glum possessor of the smaller division. Worse, the half with the light in it went to Thangam and her family, which left him in perpetual gloom. So did a larger share of the windowsill.

'We'll manage,' Nalini said, and of course they managed. The trunks were moved out—theirs, Thangam's—into the courtyard, away from the soggy ground and right up against the wall as some protection from the rain. It meant going in and out at the most inconvenient moments, and tiptoeing about for fear of disturbing Apu, who slept the brittle sleep of the old; but still, they managed.

In Thangam's half of the room Puttanna, after a day's ill-tempered effort, had succeeded in fixing a trio of hooks in the ceiling, from which they slung cloth hammocks for the babies.

This was a great boon for Puttanna, who was heartily sick of parading up and down the courtyard with a squalling infant, and who now found that merely by raising a leg he could rock his children to sleep; but Ravi, contrarily, found that the swishing of the hammocks kept him awake.

'Whatever we do is wrong,' said Thangam shrilly. 'Whatever is the matter with you? You can't get it from your wife so you have to take it out on us, is that it?'

Varma guffawed coarsely. They all knew that Ravi had to keep away from Nalini now that the birth was imminent, and Thangam had taken to making a joke of it—a silly suggestive joke that amused the others but made Ravi fume. Anything for a laugh, he thought, and Varma could certainly afford to laugh, for he had come unscathed out of Apu's re-shuffle and could spread himself in luxury in the workroom at night, sharing it only with the cripple Kumaran, who did not count. Surrounded by festoons of cloth, by buttons, bobbins and lace, with the Singer, around which all their lives revolved, brooding in one corner and Kumaran curled up in another, Varma the bachelor could stretch himself out in greater comfort than any of them with the exception of Apu, whose ossifying bones and parched body cavities prevented him taking undue advantage of it.

Chapter 21

WHEN his child was being born Ravi went outside the house and sat there the whole sixteen hours that it took. In his village it would not have been so extreme, he would only have been sent out half way through. In towns they seemed to do things differently, for at the first show Jayamma hustled him out, neglecting even to reassure him that she would send for him the moment it was over.

Here there were no fields to lose oneself in, as the men of his village had done: and as he waited he could not help remembering—stress having eaten away his defences—that there was something about the land, mortgaged though it was to the last inch, that gave one peace, a kind of inner calm, that he was acutely conscious of lacking as he gazed at the narrow, hard, bustling and indifferent street.

No fields, no friends, no relatives. Should he, he wondered in his need, buttonhole the man a few paces on who sat as idly as he, tap him on the shoulder as they did in his village and make him listen to what he had to tell? He glanced covertly at the man, but in this time of crisis he found that he had reverted, gone back to being the tongue-tied rustic in a city, so that he could not summon the necessary casual approach. It would have been easy at home, or when he had been with Damodar's crowd ... ah yes, he thought, moving around in the city had presented no difficulties then, one had felt a kind of collective strength, a jauntiness that made it easy to whistle after the girls, to jeer at the fair fat marwaris balancing ledgers on their paunches, or to pick a conversation with whoever one liked—sahibs and all, and how little *they* had liked it, especially the pompous ones with their silly solar topis and polished boots like the police wore!

The police. He shivered. Nostalgia could put a sheen on almost anything in the past, but not this thing. The police, brutes and *banchots*, men who became devils when they put on their uniforms, the bigger ones in boots that they brought down so smartly on bare flinching toes. It had happened to him once, the one time they had caught him when he was raw, new to the city ... and the pain had been excruciating, he could hardly believe anything could be so awful.

What had it taught him, that gross act of routine brutality? He could not be sure, unless it was a determination not to be caught again. But there was no mistaking the rage that had blinded him. He would have torn them to pieces with the sudden madman's strength that had come upon him only he could not see; also someone was holding his arms behind and twisting them, he did not even feel it until he saw the bruises afterwards. He had sworn then that he would get even with them, one day, somehow. He had never abjured that oath, even now he would not ... but since then Nalini had come into his life and the bitterness and the fury had been drawn off. It no longer seemed important to take revenge, to get even with 'them', all of those people who ground into the dust with a careless heel weaker men like his father and himself. Nalini, his wife, with her laughter and her sweetness. Suddenly he wanted her, he wanted to rush in and be by her side, he half got up but then he sank back. There would be a battery of women at the door, barring him, bringing up his past to account for this scandalous street-lout behaviour. He sat down again. No, he did not want that. He was not ashamed of it, he would never blame anyone who was what he had been: but nevertheless he didn't want all that thrown in his face.

'Are you always like this, brother?'

'What?'

'Talking and making faces to yourself.'

It was the man he had wanted to speak to speaking to him, confound him. 'I didn't think that I was,' he said distantly.

'Well you were.'

Suddenly the urge to talk came back.

'Actually I am a little worried,' he said. 'My wife is—is having a child . . . she has gone into labour.'

'Is that all! Ho-ho-ho!' The other's laugh resounded loud and very ugly in Ravi's ears. 'Wait till you have nine like me, then you'll think nothing of it. She won't either. Now with my wife, they just slip out like pips from a squeezed lime, the little whelps! Between you and me,' he lowered his voice, 'it's all very well for her, but there's not much pleasure for a man, all that slack I mean.'

'You shouldn't have had so many children,' Ravi found himself saying, coldly, disliking intensely this chance companion. 'It's your own fault.'

'I know, I know. They all say that. Even my wife. Now they say if I let them operate there won't be any more children . . . and they say they'll pay me so much after it's done.'

'How much?' Ravi could not resist asking. The earning of money always intrigued, even obsessed him.

'Fifteen rupees.' The other's eyes brightened over this imagined wealth. 'One could live like a rajah on that for a night or two, eh brother? The trouble is,' he said solemnly, the merrymaking glint dying in his eyes, 'one doesn't know with that kind of thing,

125

I mean supposing one couldn't? Besides it seems wrong somehow, doing that to oneself.—Why, where are you off to, brother?'

'Nowhere,' said Ravi, and stopped edging away.

'I suppose,' said the other lugubriously, 'you're happy about it . . . this child that's coming I mean.'

'Of course,' said Ravi. 'Anyone would be.'

'You wait,' said his companion. 'Wait till you've had nine like me and then see. One's easy, two's easy, three and four one can manage—but when they keep coming—sometimes I tell you, brother, I want to put my hands round their necks and squeeze until I know I'll never again have to think about feeding them, no, never again hear them whimper. Yes, you wait till you get like that, just wait that's all.'

Ravi got up and walked away. He did not want to be robbed of his elation at this momentous, precious time in his life, he was furious with this man for trying—and very nearly succeeding, for he knew all he had heard was true, ordinary people with big families and sometimes without did go to the wall—he knew it but he did not want to be reminded.'

'Ai, you! Where are you off to?'

Ravi kept silent.

'That's right, don't answer. You young fellers nowadays, you don't know how to conduct yourselves, you're all the same, mannerless monkeys with no respect for anything, not even your elders.'

Ravi turned and came back. 'Why should we respect you,' he said, nearly boiling. 'What have you done to earn our respect?'

'As elders—'

'Elders. What have they done but put up and put up and teach us the same putrid lesson, only now we've had a bellyful and we're not going to any more, do you hear?'

'Ho-ho, listen to him talking!' The man turned to the spectators gathered round them. 'Like a maharajah at least! But even they had to go in the end, didn't they? Now your trouble my friend, you know what it is? Your spleen's too large for your own good! But it'll come down to size, never you worry, when the children start then your troubles start, then see what pride you're left with!'

'When my troubles start,' Ravi shouted, 'I'll do something

about it, do you hear. Not sit by a culvert all day long twiddling my thumbs the way you middle-aged fools do! No wonder they pay no attention to you, nor to us either because you've sold us down the river as well as yourselves, you and your generation.'

He strode away, trembling with anger, with the slight sickness in the pit of his stomach that anger always brought.

'Spleen,' he heard the other shouting after him. 'But you watch it dribble away. They'll strip you naked, you'll learn to eat dust like the rest of us—'

Some distance away Ravi found a crumbling, partly-demolished wall and sat down on it. He tried to think of Nalini and after some concentrated effort managed to do so. Gradually his anger went. That man and all his generation, he thought, fools! Meek stupid fools with nothing worthwhile to leave to the young ones, not even one decent idea. He and his friends had never, would never, understand them.

Presently the bricks he was sitting on became oppressive, hot and hard under his seat. He was hungry, too, he realized, he had not eaten for how long, four or five hours at least. He wished he had a watch so that he could tell, a nice gold watch that he could strap to his wrist, shooting his cuff smartly to show it off as the clerks in government offices did—the senior ones, that is, those who possessed watches. He sighed. There was no end to his wants. . . .

Nearby was a coffee-shop. He felt in his pocket to make sure he had the necessary coins and he had—Nalini, he remembered, had put them there herself, no doubt against this very emergency. Then he thought: suppose they send down the street for me and I'm not there? He sat down again, trying to get above hunger as he and his brothers and parents had learnt to do, but that was some time past, he was no longer in training to will hunger away. Soon, to his shame, his stomach began a deep cavernous rumbling impossible to ignore.

The coffee was sweet, milky and very hot. The proprietor cooled it, cascading it skilfully from one container to another until a broad ribbon of coffee stretched between the shining brass tumblers.

'There you are.'

There was a tall head of froth, the bubbles puttered softly and broke against his lips as he drank. The coffee was satisfying, even invigorating.

'Another tumbler?'

Ravi hesitated, then refused. With a child on the way, this was no time to squander his resources. Besides he might need the money for a cup later on. . . .

'I've had enough,' he said, quickly, before he could be tempted. 'How much?'

'The best coffee in South India,' the proprietor boasted. 'The very best—'

'How much?'

'—Mysore coffee. I roast and grind the beans myself, look, here! And the final touch of excellence? You're right, it's the milk. But none of that watered stuff the milkmen bring, no indeed! Only buffalo milk, rich thick buffalo milk for me and my clients. That's why I have so many customers—high-class customers every one —eh? Yes sir, that's quite right, that's my price, I never over-charge or my customers would melt away.'

Ravi paid, briefly regretting that he had not proffered less, and returning, waited perhaps a hundred yards from the house.

It was a hot still afternoon, but neither too hot nor heavy and oppressive; the best kind of weather, he had heard (and shelved the information, not being really interested at the time) for women in labour. He hoped Nalini wasn't having a bad time. In his village women hardly ever did, even for a first child; he could remember only one occasion when a woman had screamed and screamed so that everyone in every hut could hear, and died before they could get a doctor to her. But here in town he had heard it was different, women were different; their bodies had hardened, in a kind of perversion of womanhood, from walking these hard roads and pavements with never an inch of give in them, from living in the city's hard-walled little concrete houses, so that they could not be supple and yield even when it was time for giving birth. At least that was what he had heard. He hoped Nalini was not rigid and holding out like that. But what could she, or anyone, do if that was what circumstance had done to one? No one could squirm out of a strait-jacket!

The hours went by, dissolving into a kind of timeless sea. He fell into a reverie, suspended as it were above the street's bustle, until the thread was broken by a small naked boy who came by whistling. Spotting the lone dreamy stranger the child stopped whistling and held out a wooden begging bowl which he had been cheerfully using as a drum. His face, rounded by childhood although his frame was a skeleton, grew solemn.

'No mother, no father, saar! No—'

'Beat it,' said Ravi tersely.

'Hungry saar. No food, no mother, no—'

Ravi rose threateningly. These children, they'd try it on anybody, even on those who could least afford it. Though he had to concede, from his own experience, that the rich were a lot more tight-fisted than the poor. When the boy had gone, dodging with practised skill through the crowd, Ravi realized a little to his horror that he was hungry again. He would have to dig into his pocket once more, the last thing he had intended to do.

If the thought of spending was unwelcome, the thought of food was not. He began walking briskly down the street, but at the corner there was a woman selling mangoes and curly yellow tongues of jack-fruit. Ravi stopped. He loved mangoes. It was a rarity for Jayamma, as it had been for his mother, to buy fruit for the household. Besides, he reasoned, a mango would take the edge off his appetite and be cheaper than buying a meal.

They haggled fiercely; eventually he bought, a ripe yellow fruit flecked with green. The woman, amicable again, left off cutting up the jack-fruit to slice his mango for him—in the approved manner, two thick 'cheeks', and the stone gleaming white through the succulent orange flesh for third piece.

It was a delicious mango, one of the best variety, Badami. Ravi sucked contentedly at the stone, which he had left for last. He would buy Nalini one, he resolved, later on . . . then he remembered the pale creamy mango flowers that had blown in to the roof sanctuary, in the early days of their marriage. How pleasant it had been, instead of the small stifling room they had to share with Thangam and her brood! Soon no doubt that would increase and—

'Come on, man!'

It was Thangam, sent to summon him. Ravi leapt to his feet, the mango stone slithering out of his grasp on to the roadway.

'Is it over? Is it—'

'Yes, at last. It's a boy. Come quickly.'

He ran, leaving her well behind.

The room had been emptied, the partitioning curtain taken
down. There was a steamy smell in it of hot water and wet cloth,
and the warm smell of blood. Through the half-open door he saw a
basin of discoloured water, a parcel of stained newspaper near it,
then he felt someone prodding him.

'They're both fine.' It was the midwife. 'You can go in now.'

Nalini was lying on the mat, looking spent and curiously flat
after so many months of bulging, but supremely happy. The child
was laid on a towel next to her, naked, a brown paste smeared on
its navel wound, its dark hair damp and clinging to a well-shaped
head.

'Well, isn't it a beautiful boy?' The midwife had followed him in.

Ravi grinned shyly. 'Yes,' he said. A beautiful boy. His. Theirs.
A rush of feeling almost choked him. He sat down as close as he
could to his wife and said huskily, 'Are you all right?'

'Of course she's all right, didn't I tell you so?' The midwife
answered. He wished she would go away, but she stood purpose-
fully, her red cotton sari girded about her as if she were a dancer
or an athlete about to take part in some sport.

'It's experience that counts.... I've had thirty years' experience and none of my patients has ever had cause not to be grateful
to me,' she said meaningly.

At last it dawned on Ravi. He had paid her in advance, now
she wanted a tip. His pockets were empty.

'I'll be back in a minute,' he said, acutely embarrassed. He
did not want to borrow, but what was the option?

Jayamma did not want to lend either, but something in Ravi's
pale excited face moved her, stilling her protest.

Ravi went back confidently. 'A beautiful boy,' he said jubi-
lantly, pressing the silver rupee into the midwife's hand. She
beamed at him in return. 'Blessings on you,' she said. 'Blessings
on you and your line.'

They had all been sent out: all the male members of the household except Apu, who had again exercised his privilege as its head

to stay. Now they were summoned and with varying degrees of alacrity returned to view the new infant.

Apu, the first, as usual had little to say, but something of the extreme youth and innocence of the child seemed to touch and lighten his ageing features as he bent to peer closer at the sleeping face. There had been babies before: his daughters, the twin sons of whom neither he nor his wife could bear to speak, who had been born dead, each strangled by the other's cord, so that even the midwife had raised silent horrified hands ... then there had been Thangam's babies, daughter after daughter. Now at last a male child had been born to his house, of his blood ... ah yes, he thought, he had done well by this son-in-law, there was nothing to regret in the choice. He straightened slowly and put his arm around the young man's shoulders, as he might have done to his own son, and as he had never done to his senior son-in-law, as Puttanna, relegated to the fringe of the family circle, duly observed.

Apu spoke. 'God in his mercy be thanked,' he said devoutly, 'for safe delivery of this child, and the safekeeping of his mother.' He waited until the solemn moment had passed and added, proudly, 'He is a fine boy.'

'A fine child,' echoed Puttanna, a shade too heartily, a shade too quickly, creating a dissonance that all instantly felt, though no one gave any sign. And no wonder, Ravi thought not without pity, no wonder the draught tastes bitter, to be ousted first by me, now by my son ... and then, without too much difficulty, he shrugged Puttanna off. His brother-in-law might be put out, but the others palpably were not. One had only to look at Nalini, or her doting mother, or the revitalized face of the old man, or Varma—he stopped there, for Varma, unconscious of being watched, was gazing at the child with a chill naked hopelessness and a deep yearning for what he, so obese, so perverse, could never have.

Ravi was almost shocked. He had neither known nor suspected, but now a whole host of signs crowded in on him that he could only suppose his family preoccupations had made him miss before. Varma and that cripple Kumaran. A slight shudder went through him as he turned his gaze on Kumaran; but Kumaran, temporarily, had no thought of his deformities. His sound hand cuddled the child's tiny fist, and he seemed lost in a kind of wonder that there could be such beauty, such miraculous perfection as he perceived in this whole and exquisitely formed body that lay naked in front of him.

Again, fleetingly, Ravi was moved to pity. It must be sad, he thought, to be born like that. He felt no repulsion for deformity, or for cripples: was not his friend the blacksmith hideously one-eyed? It was thinking of Varma and Kumaran in their peculiar relationship that sent uneasy ripples down his spine. Still, that was their affair, Varma's and Kumaran's, nothing to do with him. He dismissed both from his mind and turned with pleasure to contemplating his son.

Chapter 22

THEY sat on the beach, Ravi, Nalini and their son Raju who was now two years old. They did so partly because they liked the beach, partly because they could not really afford to go any-where else. Ravi would have preferred a coffee bar, one of those modern places with neon strip-lights behind the coffee machines and stools to sit on, where one could rub shoulders with people from quite other classes than one's own in a way one could not easily do elsewhere, and certainly not in a village. Ravi liked that. It gave him the sensation of living in high society, and, (in a rather more enclosed way, hardly admitting it even to himself) the notion that with a little luck he too might be like one of those carefree young men he saw, wearing cream linen shirts and enamel cuff-links and ordering platefuls of *marsala dosai* with their coffee.

Nalini would rather have gone to the cinema and sat with her legs curled under her and the fans turning slowly overhead, watching for four magical hours or more the rich, lush, romantic scenes that poured onto the silver screen. In these she could lose herself, forget there were chillies to be pounded or rice to be ground, forget the sour face of her sister, the demands of her

132

mother, the cries of her child—forget everything, in fact, that harassed her day.

Raju, however, unlike his parents loved the beach far above anything else. His podgy hands poured sand over his fat little body with the greatest of pleasure, he staggered after the small scurrying sand-crabs with endless delight; and when they paddled, one parent each side of him, cautiously advancing to the foam-edge of each wave as it broke, he had to bounce and thresh so great was his joy in water.

It frightened Ravi. He had never set eyes on the sea until he came to the city, and he could never quite overcome a slight panic as the huge white-crested rollers thundered in on the beach, retreating with a suck and drag that could easily pull a man out to sea. But Raju loved it, and so of course for his sake they came, and sat on the beach, and braved the waves. . . .

The beach they were sitting on was the one Nalini liked best. It was the respectable stretch that lay in front of the tall imposing white or tussore-silk yellow governmental and quasi-governmental buildings on the Marina. Away to their right was San Thome, where the Portuguese had first come, and then they had gone away leaving the church at Luz to remember them by. Ravi had learnt this from a teacher at school, who had learnt it from a Jesuit who taught in his school. Ravi retailed this information to Nalini, rather proud that he should know and she shouldn't, having lived in the city all her life.

'But who cares?' said Nalini, 'who comes and who goes? We remain, we Indians, and that is all that matters.'

'Still, it's interesting,' said Ravi defensively.

'Maybe.' She yawned. 'All I can say is it's the worst beach.'

This was true, for here was established a fishing colony. Here the fishermen cast their nets at first light, and furtively built their ramshackle huts on the foreshore which one exasperated authority after another tore down (without telling them where else to go) only to see them burgeon like un-beautiful flowers in the course of one night; and here the beach was as tatty as the huts, littered with driftwood and crab shells, full of fish smells and understandably unfashionable.

There was another stretch of beach, fine white sands and more convenient for them, to which Nalini would never go and Ravi could not understand why. He wondered if it was the Memorial nearby, which commemorated the fallen in wars whose aims Ravi had learnt, early in childhood, to regard as suspect. But surely not that, he thought, it was all so long ago, so long that these shunned memorials had become useful rallying points for speech-making and demonstrations.

One day he pinned her down, and learnt a part of the city's lore that he had not heard before. It was here, she said, that the British Tommies came, storming down from St. Thomas' Mount where they were stationed to maraud and rape . . . and once they had attacked a high-born Brahmin lady—Jayamma would remember her name—stripped her and tied her to a stake in the sand; and when she was rescued she had killed herself for the shame of it. Those were bad times, said Nalini, women had gone in great fear of the swaggering, lusting Tommies.

But, Ravi objected, there were no Tommies left, so why not go there now?

Because of the terrible aura such things left behind, said Nalini; and nothing he said would budge her.

Ravi gave in. It did not really matter to him which beach they went to, except that it seemed silly to come this far. . . . Still, it was a nice beach, he would not gainsay that, both popular and fashionable. If you wanted to see life you came here, and everyone else came here too. Pretty girls and young men, the fair children of the rich in the care of dark-brown ayahs, and poor children looking after one another, and long shiny limousines carrying smooth sleek people, and shabby rickshaws disgorging shabby young married couples—in fact if you wanted to see a satisfyingly democratic shake-up of society, with judges, however briefly, cheek-by-jowl with jutka-wallahs, it was to this central beach that you came.

Sometimes envy of wealth—not displayed, but *there*—overcame Ravi. The cost of just one of those motor-cars that purred along the Marina, he felt, would keep him and his family over half a lifetime. How, he wondered with a burning curiosity, did anyone ever earn so much? He never would, not if he sewed a dozen shirts in a dozen hours every day of the week for a dozen years! No wonder then that young men like himself felt the itch, as he himself had done, to get into these same cars and drive away—only most of them couldn't have got far, unless they'd had a lesson or two first from a taxi-driver!

'The rich,' said Nalini, wiping sand from Raju's mouth, 'have their problems, I daresay.'

'I daresay,' said Ravi, drily. Their big problem, as far as he could see, was to avoid sharing their wealth with the beggars who surrounded them. They shouted, and their faces grew mottled, and some had even brought servants—chokras and peons —to act as defenders, who, being vicegerents, were twice as imperious as their masters. One such scene was going on near them, where a be-ringed merchant and his plump jewelled lady sat placidly enjoying the sea-breeze, guarded by a green-belted peon. Several beggars had already been warded off, but now a young beggar-woman, bolder than the rest perhaps because of the thin blind baby she carried, evaded the servant's arm and managed to get to within a foot of the placid couple. There she stood, begging, rattling her tin, exhibiting the baby's sad little face to the couple who sat unmoving, stolidly, even patiently listening to the spate of pleas; and then, seeing they were not to be easily parted from their money, she fell at their feet, grasping the hem of their clothes. Still neither moved, neither the man nor the woman; it was the peon who, heaving and struggling, eventually managed to haul her off, sending her sprawling as he pushed her aside with his master's walking stick. She fell neatly, like an acrobat in the soft sand, her child on top of her; then she picked herself up, pouring out a stream of abuse as she gathered her rags about her and stalked away.

'These—!' Ravi swore. 'They can't even do their own dirty work!'

'Not in front of the child,' said Nalini. 'Nor would you, if you could afford someone to do it for you.'

Ravi saw the force of this. He did his own dirty work—that is to say he shouted at beggars as much as anyone else when they pestered him, which they did when there were no rich people around. But these wealthy hogs doing the same thing was somehow different, worse—or was it? He began to feel a little confused. He said, belligerently, 'They're not different clay, are they, to be treated like dogs?'

'No, but beggars are different people,' said Nalini. 'Now don't

135

say in what way, they just are that's all, in the same way that we aren't the same as they, now are we?' She gestured at the couple who, despite their demeanour must have felt their peace disrupted, for they were making preparations to go.

Ravi was silent. There were things, he felt, that his wife would never understand, and it came from never having moved from where she was born: because how, he reasoned, could one see anything but rigid patterns unless one broke the mould into which one had been cast? As he, willy-nilly, had done, although now he did not pause to consider the inevitability of his act but only its bravura.

'Shall we get some *pattani*? The man is coming.' Nalini tweaked his arm cautiously. She was not wholly unused to Ravi's silences, but they always made her a little afraid.

'Yes of course. Here you are.' He handed her a rupee, which was generous, but then, Nalini reflected, he *was* generous. So long as he had the money, he never grudged her or the child a treat, or treated himself as some men did, totally forgetting his family.

'You always think of us,' she said to her husband. 'Not like brother-in-law. He's so mean, do you know he buys himself a packet of cigarettes every week but he never thinks of getting anything for Thangam.'

'What sort of thing?'

'Well, *any* thing. Soap, or hair-oil, or even a few glass bangles, it would mean so much to her . . . but no, his smoking has to come first. Poor Thangam, she feels it such a lot.'

'Poor devil,' said Ravi. 'I doubt he scrapes together more than a few coppers each week. Thangam can't really expect him to hand over every pie just so she can prettify herself.'

Nalini wanted to say: that's right, anything to get at my sister, you're always getting at her (which would not have been entirely accurate, for Ravi more often got at her husband, the feckless Puttanna) but she did not want to ruin the evening by quarrelling, so she turned her attention to the *pattani* seller.

This man was dressed in a loin-cloth and turban, on which rested a round cloth pad, on which he was balancing a wicker trayful of *pattani*, hampered by a high wind and Raju. Raju loved *pattani*. He was too short to reach the tray, but he took hold

136

of the loin-cloth and began tugging strenuously. Nalini gave a little scream but did nothing else. She knew the tenacious strength of her son's grasp, and besides she did not really think it was proper for her to wrestle with a man's loin-cloth. It was a man's job. Ravi turned. He had been thinking about the problems of life, all of them insoluble, but here suddenly was crisis. He saw it as a crisis, for on that crazily swaying tray was ten rupees' worth of *pattani*, ten rupees or even more, and if he could not pay, and this month he certainly could not, he would be taken to the police station and—

'Hold it, you fool, hold it,' he shouted at the vendor.

'I am, can't you see!' the vendor was equally furious. With one hand he steadied his tray, taking dancing little steps to keep it level on his head; with the other he tried to fend Raju off. The child clung like a terrier. One end of the loin-cloth began to unwind.

'Hold the tray!'

'Get him off!'

'Let go!'

They were all shouting. The tray tilted, scattering a handful of *pattani*. Suddenly Ravi began hitting the child, on his back and buttocks, both fists doubled. Raju let go at once, but Ravi could not stop, he kept hitting his child and sometimes his blows fell on Nalini, who had intervened.

Then someone began punching him, hard, from behind. He fell to his knees in the sand. Around him, he realized confusedly, was a ring of muttering, hostile spectators.

'Monster! Ought to be whipped and put in a cage.'

'Not fit to have children.'

'His own son too! Here you are sonny, don't you fret any more ... that's right, hold your hands so, and I'll fill them up, yes, right up, as much *pattani* as you can hold.'

They clustered round the child, castigating the father.

Even the *pattani* man, whose stock was intact solely owing to his efforts, had turned against him, thought Ravi sullenly. He felt very much alone. They didn't understand, he thought, had they ever been taken to a police *thana* and seen what was done? He had. But it still didn't make sense, he couldn't understand himself: how could he have beaten his child like that?

137

'I don't know what came over me,' he said gruffly, staring down at his guilty hands.

'You don't know!' cried Nalini shrilly. 'I don't know either what gets into you, sometimes I think it must be the devil itself.'

She wasn't crying. If she had been, he would have comforted her, all would have been well. Now he did not know what to do.

Except for occasional convulsive gulps, Raju wasn't crying either. He had tucked himself under his mother's arm, squeezing himself against her and as far away from his father as he could, and safe in this haven was at last eating the *pattani* with which his fists were crammed.

It was getting late, across the Bay the harbour lights were twinkling. In the gathering dusk the lighthouse flashed brighter, its long searching fingers stroked the darkening water boldly.

Ravi stood up, brushing sand off his clothes. Nalini did the same, silently, impeded by Raju who was straddled across her hip. Ravi held out his arms to the child, an invitation which he normally welcomed, throwing himself with vast glee and abandon from parent to parent. Now he clung closer to his mother, eyeing his father warily and with a puzzled hurt air as if he could not really believe what had happened to him. Ravi's arms fell to his sides. Truth to tell, he could not believe it either. He cast around, and fastened at last upon the episode of the beggar. Violence always upset him, upset his balance. It was that, he concluded, that had made him do what he had done.

Usually he walked ahead carrying Raju, and Nalini trailed behind with the odds and ends—scraps of the once-handsome Binny towel, a spare jacket for Raju, a woollen cap in case the wind blew cold—that they always had to bring. Now Nalini went in front, her head held very high and stiff. Since Raju's birth she hardly ever let her hair hang down in a plait. She coiled it, as the other young matrons did, into a fat glossy bun which she fastened with hairpins and, when she went out, circled it with jasmine flowers. She had done so this evening, but in the scuffle the knot had slipped, the string of flowers dangled down her back. Ravi sorely wanted to hitch it on again, to push the holding-pins, which were half-way out, into the loosening coils, but he hadn't the courage, all these natural acts were beyond him.

138

Concrete ramps sloped gently up from beach to pavement, edged by low walls. They sat on one of these to empty sand from their chaplis and clean their feet of it, Raju protesting loudly as he was dusted. Sand, Ravi reflected, was the worst of these beach excursions. They could never get rid of all of it, and the grains that remained became a penance every step of the long trek home. On an impulse he said, 'Shall we go home by rickshaw?'

By rickshaw, thought Nalini indignantly, to make us forget his behaviour! She wanted to reject the overture, but then she saw his face and she melted.

'That would be very nice,' she said, 'if you're sure you can afford it.'

Ravi was sure that he could not, but he ran and found one. The rickshaw-wallah lowered the shafts, they clambered in, were poised for one deliciously perilous moment on the steeply inclined seat, then were off. The rickshaw ran smoothly, the puller was skilful, avoiding ruts and potholes without altering his rhythmic jog-trot. Ravi settled back in his seat. It was covered in leather cloth, quilted and buttoned, and must have been very smart at the time though now the leather was cracked and faded, and the horsehair stuffing had burst out here and there. But still it was most comfortable. Ravi closed his eyes. He could smell the oil, linseed or whatever it was, that had been rubbed into the cracks of the seat and hood; and nearer was the faintly tainted sweetness of the wilting jasmine in Nalini's hair. He leant closer towards her, and despite recurrent thoughts of the expenditure felt a blissful peace steal over him.

Chapter 23

THE sense of euphoria lasted him right through the night and into the morning. When he awoke it was with a feeling of freshness, as if there were dew on the grass instead of the grimy deposit that the morning mists left on the baked streets.

Nalini was stirring. He propped himself on an elbow to watch, and as her eyes opened he smiled down at her.

'Slept well?'

'Mmm ... beautifully. The sea air always makes me.' She stretched luxuriously and curled up again. 'I could easily go to sleep all over again.'

'Do.'

She made a small helpless gesture, implying all that stood in the way: the sounds, soon to begin, of Thangam and her family behind the flimsy partition, the sloshing and washing of the household, Jayamma wanting access to the kitchen, Raju wanting feeding, washing, attention ... the very thought made her un-curl and sit up, which Raju took as an invitation to hurl himself upon her. She cuddled him, loving his warmth, his milky baby smell, and for a few seconds he was willing to rest in her arms before struggling to break free. Ravi watched him wriggle and twist with pleasure; then—tentatively, with a sudden wrenching remembrance of yesterday—he held out his arms. He need not have worried. Raju wasted no time in harbouring grudges, al-though his back and seat were still sore from the beating he had received. He threw himself with unreserved delight at his father, who held him, thinking: I am lucky.

With Raju in his arms Ravi no longer grudged his earlier-than-usual awakening. It had given him these serene moments, set him up for whatever irritations the day might bring. Besides, it meant he would beat Thangam to the tap, for he could tell she was not yet up, her great fat figure had not yet fallen across the curtain like a shadowy giantess. He flapped his towel free of the nail on which it was hung, whispered to Nalini and made her giggle, and went out to wash.

He was sluicing water over his heels and toes, triumphantly dislodging the last fine clinging grains of sand, when a curious swishing sound, as if someone were dragging a mattress along the floor, made him turn. The sight half-paralysed him. The heavy brass *chambu* fell from his hand, thudding on to his foot al-though he felt no pain. All he was conscious of was Apu.

The old man was pulling himself along, on his stomach, slowly, with the terrible slowness of a dying animal. One arm only was working; it groped forward, the fingers opening and closing as it clawed for a hold, and the supine body followed like a carcase, huge, deadweight, with that terrible swish-h-h. ...

140

'Apu,' Ravi knelt, terrified, his throat so dry he could only whisper. 'Apu, what has happened, please speak. Apu!'

The old man raised his head. His face was grotesque, a lopsided mask half dead and half alive. Spittle dribbled down his mouth, the tight dead corner. He was struggling to speak, to say something of vital importance from the way he struggled, but only a thin stream of syllables emerged, ab-ab-b-b ... then that too ceased and he slumped forward.

They carried him to his bed. He was deeply unconscious, but breathing. Ravi ran for a doctor, even in the stress of the moment remembering to pocket a five-rupee note. He knew doctors. They were exactly like other men when it came to money, the only difference was the piety with which they pretended it didn't matter.

The doctor came. He examined Apu's heart, took his pulse and blood pressure, peered into his eyes deeply, deeply as if he would look into the brain itself. Cerebral haemorrhage, cerebral thrombosis? He could not be sure. His training was a long way away, and anyhow the best of them could not always tell.

The patient had had a stroke, he said, simplifying matters for the relatives assembled round the bed. Would he survive? That was in God's hands. What were his chances? Better in hospital, the doctor said to himself grimly, counting heads in the crowded room; but would there be a free bed, if not could they pay for a bed three weeks, four weeks, the months this calamity might take to resolve one way or the other? The doctor was a realist, he did not even ask. To the family he explained it was impossible to say, time alone would tell, but he would call again the next day. They agreed, numbly, as they would have agreed to anything he said, this god-like creature who knew what to do even at a time like this, when a human being was suddenly transformed into a gibbering hulk.

When he had gone a vast overpowering helplessness gripped them. The machine stood idle. Household tasks accumulated. The atmosphere had subdued even the children.

Jayamma sat at Apu's feet. Her eyes were heavy, dulled by shock and the *kasayam* she had drunk the night before for the gripe from which she periodically suffered. It had made her sleep soundly, too soundly... she had not heard Apu, she had not responded to his need, why else had he crawled out on his belly like that with his wife lying less than a foot from him? Apu was confused, said Varma, his plump smooth woman's hands comforting her; Apu's brain was torn, how could he know what he was doing while blood seeped into his skull? She resisted him. It was her failure, her disgrace. She beat her breast monotonously, bunched her knuckles and dug them into her temples, moaning, calling God's name. *Ishwar! Ishwar!*

How could they live through the day? None of them knew but they endured and survived. The morning wore on. Except for the children no one had eaten or drunk since the night before. Towards noon Thangam produced some rice, left over from their evening meal, and a plate of pickles. The rice was cold, shiny on the side where it had been caked to the pot, and it came out in slabs. Some ate, some couldn't. Jayamma had not moved, except to relieve herself. Nor had the cripple. He sat huddled in a corner of the workroom, his eyes anguished and afraid.

Varma, rejected by both, left the house. Puttanna wandered from room to room, uncertain and restless. He was the senior son-in-law, some decisive action, he felt, should be initiated by him. But he had neither the authority nor the money for it.

Even the doctor, he reflected, had been called in by Ravi—Ravi the shady street loafer who had inveigled himself into an old man's good graces.

Now the old man was dying. He breathed as if his wind-pipe were crushed, harsh tearing sounds that penetrated to every room in the house. Presently Puttanna could bear it no longer. He must get out or go mad. He went, noticing that no one remarked his going.

The children played together quietly, sensing convulsion in the adult world as yet beyond their comprehension. At intervals they had to be fed and watered, but beyond that they did not need adults, they formed a small sufficient company of their own.

Thangam and Nalini stayed with Apu, sharing the watch with Jayamma, ministering to the comatose figure on the bed in various pointless ways to mitigate the deep helplessness in which they were all plunged. Ravi, hovering by the door, saw them sponging the old man's forehead, smoothing the coarse sacking laid under his loins, speaking in whispers as if speech, or anything else for that matter, could distract a man making firsthand aquaintance with death. Apu, thought Ravi, had often equated his life with his grandchildren's: an old life for a new. But it had not happened in quite that way. He had not managed to die at any of the births, and Raju, the youngest, was now two years old.

Presently Ravi took courage and beckoned Nalini.

'What is it?' she tiptoed out.

'You look so tired,' he whispered. 'Come away, we'll go out for a little while.'

'And leave father? Oh no.'

'You're doing no good. No one can.'

'Nevertheless. It's my duty.'

'All night,' he said. 'Who knows how many... you won't have the strength.'

Already, he thought—though he could hardly believe it—the shock of this terrible day was receding, it must be receding for him to think ahead, away from the immediate emergency. Or was it, he asked himself with fright, that the whole responsibility for the household, its people and its acts, was already building up on his shoulders? The possibility demoralized him, as the lack of it had earlier demoralized Puttanna.

Nalini half-capitulated. She would not go out, but she would leave Apu's room. Electing, tacitly, to be without the children, they made for the workroom, which bore all the signs of the sudden, brutal halt that had been called. Here they sat, silently, among bolts of cloth, unwound bobbins, pinned and half-completed garments. Only yesterday Apu had sat here too. He had toiled late into the evening on some intricate quilting, wanting to finish it but the light had failed. The ivory satin was still held in the Singer needle. Contrary to his practice Apu had left it there, calling Ravi's attention to it as a bad habit, saying he only did it intending to resume very first thing in the morning. Suddenly it smote him, the pity, the waste. 'Poor man,' he said hoarsely, 'Poor Apu.'

Nalini had not wept so far; she had been too dazed by shock. Now her eyes slowly filled and the tears began to fall—tears more out of respect than from love of her father. Apu had not been an

143

easy man to love. He was middle-aged when his daughters were born, a remote, preoccupied figure who seldom played with or indulged them as Ravi did his child, who reserved his warmth for sons who had never been born. When the girls were no longer children he had tried, rather stiffly, to recover his loss: but by then it was too late. Nalini wept afresh, from some vague sense of chances missed although she was not very clear what, from the overpowering mortal feeling that they were all, in greater or less degree, facing finality.

From his corner Kumaran watched, crouched and unmoving. They had forgotten his presence as most people did until some obscenity of his functioning jarred on them; but now, almost simultaneously, they became aware of him, and of the glittering fear in his eyes that anyone else, thought Ravi, any decent person would at least have tried to hide. He said, roughly, 'Is this the only place for you, in here? Can't you go somewhere else?'

Kumaran rose obediently and dragged himself to the kitchen. He knew Jayamma did not like him going there, she believed he pilfered the stores, but today she was in no condition to object.

Twilight. The segment of sky that Ravi could see was purple and gold, like a shot-silk sari draped against the sky. Yesterday at twilight Apu had hurried them on, urging them to make the most of this light and the sudden flare of brightness that came at the end. It saved electricity, he was fond of saying, but besides that God's light was best. Now who was to do the pushing?—the pushing that was vital to keep this houseful fed and clothed? The question kept nagging at him, making him resentful and afraid. He was grateful when Nalini interrupted his thoughts.

'I'd better boil some rice,' she spoke wearily.

'Not yet,' he begged her. 'In a little while.'

'All right.'

She was silent for a few moments; her hands played with the fringed end of her sari, teasing the strands restlessly.

'What will happen,' she said at last, trying to remain calm but her voice catching, 'what do you think will happen?'

'To Apu?' He spoke gently, wanting to console her but knowing that he could not. 'He is in God's hands ... as the doctor said. Perhaps tomorrow it will be easier to tell.'

144

'And our livelihood,' she said, half to herself, 'What is to happen to that . . . it is true, that too rests in God's hands.'

It roused Ravi, as perhaps nothing else could have done. 'No,' he said sharply, 'it is not in God's hands, that has been said since I was so high and I am sick to death of hearing it. It is in our hands, *our* hands!'

But whose hands, actually? His? The painful cycle began again, and now it was ten times worse because although she said nothing he knew he had alienated his wife, could sense her hurt, shocked withdrawal from him.

Chapter 24

AT five o'clock on the fourth day, as if the internal alarm bell that had roused him every morning of his seventy years were working again, Apu's eyes flickered open.

Jayamma was stretched out asleep on the ground alongside, but sixth sense woke her. At first she could not believe it. She lay still and watched those eyes, so familiar, yet so terrible embedded in that stiffened face, wandering round the room, at first vacantly, then focusing, then understanding, finally meeting hers with a look of such anguished pleading and mortal fright that she flinched and cried for help, unable to bear it alone.

Instantly, it seemed, the room was full. They had all been expecting the summons, what they did not know was what it meant. Life? Death? Hope, or not? They crowded round the bed, a full circle of relatives such that a grievously stricken man might be comforted to see. But Apu's eyes still roved wildly, a string of bubbles formed on his lips, punctured by animal sounds as he strove to speak.

These signs they interpreted as favourable.

'He's awake at last.'

'Fully conscious!'

'He can even speak.'

'God be praised!'

Suddenly it was Hope. Their spirits lifted and sang praise and gratitude, injected by the hope that all would soon be well, Apu himself again, the old comfortable living resumed.

For the man on the bed it was different. For four days he had been a body without a mind. The body had suffered, but he had not known. Now his mind was there to tell him: it told him unequivocally that he was a mind without a body.

What sort of a man was he, who had a body his mind could not control? He tried to ask them this, he struggled and fought to shift the gross inert mass that impeded him but he could not. He closed his eyes at last, and tears squeezed between his tired lids and trickled down his face.

The doctor came and examined the patient. Ah, he said, the patient had regained consciousness, that was a good sign. Would he recover? Too early to say. The tears? Nothing unusual. Cases like this often reacted emotionally, you might almost say it was a reflex action.

Half the time they did not understand him.

In the days that followed they could not understand Apu either. They noted the frailty of his limbs, they interpreted the rheumy fluid that leaked from his eyes as tears of weakness, and relinquishing earlier hopes believed that now it was only a question of time. Yet to confound them Apu, lying supine and speechless on the bed, day after day fought visibly, passionately and with the tenacity of a young man for his life.

Ravi saw the effort and marvelled. In his village children lingered, but old men died easily. They had not the stamina to fight, and long before the end they had lost the will to live. What he overlooked was that Apu had become a townsman, and townsmen had not the same acceptance: they had had to contest every inch of ground in the ferocious race that town living was, and even confronted by death the habit clung.

When the initial paralysis of shock had passed the household slowly began functioning again, as it had to. For the first time in weeks Jayamma went marketing for rice and dhal to replenish the tin-lined storage boxes in the kitchen; for salt, sugar, tamarind, chillies and coriander, stocks of which had dropped to almost

146

nothing; for coconut and gingelly oil, for firewood and charcoal; and she came back ready to chivvy and harass in a way that had not been evident since Apu's illness.

The workroom, deprived of its leading worker, recovered more sluggishly. The trouble, as Ravi saw it, was that Apu was neither absent nor present. While his ghost hovered Ravi could not assume full authority, and without it work could not proceed smoothly. They wrangled over the width of a hem, the placing of a dart, the very division of labour provoked an argument. Ravi, who loathed the extensive hemming by hand that Apu insisted upon, had as one of his first actions unloaded this task on to Varma, who loathed it as much as he did. He also had less aptitude. Rather than sweat it out he simply waited his chance and, when Ravi was away, made Kumaran work the machine while he fed the material through. It was done in no time, packed in tissue paper, wrapped in muslin.

Ravi who did the outside work, collected the abuse.

He came back in a towering rage, the dress under his arm, and repeated some of the choicer language the memsahib had used.

'Minus ten rupees,' he said bitterly, 'and one good customer.'

'Wouldn't she pay?'

'Not a pie. What do you think?'

'The bitch.'

'I'll tell you this,' Ravi began in concentrated fury.

'Who are you to tell me?' The trenchant enquiry was mildly couched. Fat, favoured Varma, his position unassailable by virtue of blood ties, could afford to be mild.

'Never mind, I'll tell you anyway,' cried Ravi. 'The next lot you botch, you deliver to the customer. Is that clear?'

The workroom fell silent. Ravi never knew, sometimes it sided with him, sometimes not, he could never be sure in advance. But now Puttanna said, 'That's fair,' and in his corner Kumaran was nodding, a scarcely perceptible movement that was as far as he dared, or they allowed him to go, in making his views known.

'Next time,' Ravi repeated, bolstered by general opinion, 'You go.'

Varma looked up. 'You make me,' he said simply.

It was stalemate. Nearly all their quarrels and arguments ended in stalemate, and it did the business no good. Even the

147

women, fully occupied with house and children, became aware of the dwindling output. Thangam exhibited her empty purse in theatrical silence. Jayamma, her mouth tight and grim, began rationing their rice. In her vocal moments she flew at them, castigating them all—but Puttanna most virulently—for useless worthless loafers.

In his darkened room in his contracting world Apu lay on his bed and listened to their wrangles. Mostly it wearied him. He increased his deafness to stone pitch and retreated behind this wall. It was the one facility that came with his illness: all the rest was taking away. Sometimes their bickering gave him a strange vigour. His pulse quickened, his blood raced, he would have given anything to stalk among them as he used to, smiting here and there as merited to keep the solid business he had founded from crumbling away. But he could not. He could not move, he could not speak. The entire right half of him—face, arm, leg, bowel and side—was dead, as if some sadist had neatly sliced him in two; and the half that was not paralysed was too weak to support the dead weight of the other. The weight of it, great, dull, leaden, inert—how could they say, he pondered, that he could not feel it? Pain, cold, heat, fire, sun, a needle, the touch of a hand, all these he could not feel: but feeling had not wholly died, it persisted with a curiously subtle horror in a sensation of muted tingling as if a numb limb were coming to life. It never did, the tingling never stopped. If he knocked or jarred a part that he could not feel, or someone did in caring for him, the tingling turned to red hot needles that shot through his body. And if he screamed with the pain they stared at him, suspended whatever they were doing to his useless body with a look which said imagination, old man's imaginings for he can feel nothing in these fallen limbs.

Sometimes Apu wished they would leave him alone, not to die in peace but to conserve every scrap of strength he had to get on his feet again. Sometimes Jayamma felt she knew what he was trying to say, but she firmly rejected the thought. If she were sick would she not want to be nursed? Would she want to lie encrusted in filth, sores opening like mouths all over her back, like those feckless derelicts one often saw lying in the gutter? These sentiments helped her in caring for her husband. She

148

nursed him with an assiduity that the doctor commended, devotedly as a wife should, out of a strong sense of duty, but without love.

She had been young, he past his prime, when they married her to him. She did not love him then, she did not love him afterward, she did not even know that she didn't because she did not know what it meant. The discovery came with the birth of her children. Suddenly she knew what love was: felt the happy delirium, the joy, the anguish, felt the yearning and strain when her arms were empty, the possessive, protective passion when they were full.

None of these things lay between her and her husband.

She did not complain, neither did he. In a way they were happy. Perhaps Apu more so than she.

It was not until much later, living in the same house as the bridegroom picked for her daughter, and seeing their sated sexual faces, that she realized her other loss. She was then in the prime of her life.

She sighed. The water in the bowl beside her cooled. She called to Nalini to fetch hot water, tested it with her hand, wrung out the rag soaking in the bowl and rubbed Sunlight soap into it. Apu's body was dry, a very fine scaly grey scurf covered it patchily, like mildew. Jayamma washed, rinsed and dried, carefully, in between creases, lifting the folds and flaps of his ageing torso, spreadeagling the limbs to tend them scrupulously. The sight of his sex, limp and flopping against his thigh, moved her to a vague pity. A man's pride, its potency gone . . . well, it had gone long before, long before the stroke he had wanted nothing more of her than the luke-warmth of her hands against him.

All the time she worked Apu watched her hands. Careful, capable hands. But what did she think, what did she feel while she used them? He did not know. Communication between them had all but ceased.

Indeed communication with anyone had ceased with the loss of his speech, his prolonged illness. Sometimes Apu wondered if it was not the worst part, this silence in which he was caged. But his brain was not silent. It spoke to him continually, shrieked and raved as the frustrations built up, sank into a dark brooding. If only he could write. His left hand functioned, he could write

149

if he knew how: ah, if only, if only! The thought might never have formed but for the doctor, who in an aberrant moment, to ease the old man's struggles, had proffered pencil and pad. The blank looks of household and patient recalled him to himself, he swiftly put both away, but he could not resist a short lecture on the disadvantages of illiteracy. It bit into Apu deeply. He would have given a lot to be able to read and write: as he was now, it would have been a link with the living: but in his childhood there was no schooling.

Later, he had tried. It had not come easily, and he had given up. Should he have given up? If he had realized then what it was like now, would he have given up, could he have bludgeoned his brain till it learnt? It was all so long ago, he felt he really did not know. Apu closed his eyes and felt very tired. He wanted to turn his face to the wall, but he hadn't the strength. Presently the work-room clamour ceased, and his two sons-in-law came in to carry him to the latrine.

They came in three or four times during the day, once in the night, in an effort to keep the bed clean. Mostly, now, they succeeded, they had fallen into the way of it; but the early days, with no experience to guide them, had been disastrous. Apu had voided uncontrollably, sometimes even in sleep, and even the heavy sacking spread under him did not always spare the mattress.

Ravi's nostrils splayed wide with distaste at the memory. Not, he thought, that things were much better now. There was the hideous routine of carting the old man two, three and even four times to the latrine. He was as heavy and cumbersome as a log, they sweated getting him on to the pallet they used for carrying. He was helpless, they had to support him all through, bent double in the noisome, fly-ridden latrine, and manhandle him out again. There were the nights when they had to leave their mats and their warm sleeping wives to go through the whole thing again.

One night it rained and the rain slanted in with the gusty wind and leaked through the broken slates of the roof. The stone floor was slippery, cold under their feet; the dim light of the lantern they carried fell unevenly on its black polished wetness, on shallow dank puddles of water.

'Go carefully,' Ravi grunted, and felt his muscles straining with the darkness, with the effort of lifting. But Varma, in front, had already stumbled, his flabby arms unable to sustain the extra tension, and the old man was thrown, first Varma's end, then Ravi's, for he had not braced himself in time.

Afterwards Ravi could never totally recall how they managed to get Apu up again, to clean him and change him and return him to his bed as they must have done. All the detail was mercifully expunged although the general impression of a nauseating nightmare clung.

They took this duty in turn—all except Kumaran of course. But Puttanna was wily with escape routes, adept at excuses: it was only at night that they could pin him down. Ravi went hot when he thought of it. Here was Puttanna, unemployed, living free, dodging even this labour. He considered that if anyone's it was his privilege—his, Ravi's, since he did the lion's share of the work—to say No. But he could not. In some extraordinary way unspoken household opinion exerted a pressure upon him that made it impossible for him to do so. Why then, he asked himself morosely, did Puttanna not feel this pressure? He could not make it out, and it made for bad blood between them.

Friction, tension, the sudden halts called by Apu's necessities —how, thought Ravi with growing irritation, with all these could decent work be done? Or any work? It was all too easy, exhibiting empty purses and doling out half-spoons of rice: putting the house and workroom in order was quite another matter. And they urgently needed putting in order, for money was short.

It was at times like these, alternately vicious and dispiriting, that Ravi most missed Apu. Occasionally then he would creep into the old man's room, sit by his bed and find solace in his presence, his still being there, and come away quietened by a knowledge of his strength, his courage, his hardy qualities, and by the new serenity which, as the days went by, increasingly seemed to encompass and emanate from Apu.

They had a name for it, this luminous quality that enfolded a sick man: the twilight of the soul. It was a preparatory period, a sloughing off of the trivia of one world while the shadows of

151

another encroached. But Apu was not sinking, he was reviving. He had come to terms with himself, given up the tortured fretting that made his brain boil, and accepted for good or ill the great mutilation he had suffered. And perversely his body responded: slowly and gradually, but as the days went by with an increased momentum that surprised even the doctor.

Chapter 25

THREE months after his stroke Apu was on his feet again. His right leg dragged, but he could walk. His speech was sometimes slurred, but he could talk. And as soon as he could he took over the running of the household from its vastly relieved members.

It was not, Ravi told himself sullenly, that he could not have managed, had he been entirely alone. But there were Puttanna and Varma to reckon with, forever pulling in different directions. And was he to blame if memsahibs in the big houses preferred dealing with the older experienced tailor rather than with his apprentice?

'Why should they?' demanded Apu, grimly.

'How should I know?' retorted Ravi querulously. 'Who can possibly tell what goes on in the minds of these ladies? Only last week I had one who asked me to sew a long cane into the hem of her dress, like a hoop.'

'It is a fashion that comes and goes.' Apu softened toward his son-in-law. As a young trainee tailor, he recalled, he too had been a little taken back on his first encounter with a hoop. 'What did you say?'

'That I would try.'

'Did you?'

'Yes,' said Ravi, and hoped the matter would not be pursued.

It was. They repaired to the workroom, where the dress lay flounced on a sheet. The old man examined it, shaking his head over Ravi's handiwork.

'Best I could do,' said Ravi defensively.

Apu shook his head again, silent and disapproving. His right hand had no skill, only a slow blundering movement useless for fine tailoring, useful only for pinning or holding down; but his left hand in a sort of compensation had developed a surprising deftness. Now he set to work, contorting himself clumsily and in the oddly shaming way that the malformed Kumaran had to do, so that Ravi felt his face grow hot and could hardly bring himself to look.

'Watch me. Watch me closely, do you hear?'

The old man missed nothing—even now, with part of his brain destroyed. Ravi bent closer, and soon he no longer noticed the awkwardness, he saw only the problem being resolved.

Presently it was done. The hoop, neatly overstitched, was threaded through fine small loops in the hem. It made the dress look, thought Ravi, graceless and bulky, and far from moulding beautiful womanly curves actually hid them under a kind of tent. It was unwieldy too. Ravi foresaw a good many difficulties, not to say embarrassments, in delivering this dress.

'I would much sooner work for our Indian ladies,' he grumbled. 'One can at least understand them.'

'But they don't pay well.'

'Who does?' Ravi grumbled on. 'Europeans do when they are new here, but our Indian ladies soon teach them. You mustn't pay what they ask! they say, meaning us. Haggle with them, they expect you to, they specially put their prices up.'

'So we do,' said Apu.

'I know, but why should they act against their own people? I mean we are after all aren't we?'

'Who knows?' Apu shrugged. 'Perhaps its because they're the same—same class, same money, even coming from different countries makes no difference compared to that. It's the sameness makes them stick together.'

'If we stuck together and demanded decent money—' began Ravi.

'Get on with what you're doing,' said Apu, forbiddingly.

Once again they began going out together on their errands, but now instead of walking they took jutkas. 'My walking days are over,' said Apu, and he said it calmly, simply describing a milestone that all men in time had to pass. Ravi could not. It made him afraid, and he rebelled against it as he had rebelled all through childhood and youth against the betraying acceptances of his father and family.

'You'll walk again,' he said confidently, and with more familiarity than he usually did. 'Just make up your mind you will and you will.'

'I did,' said Apu flatly. 'I am walking. But there is a limit.'

These jutka journeys were expensive. They were only justified by the extra orders that Apu's presence drew.

'You see,' said Apu, not without triumph, 'they still trust the old man.'

It was true. Ravi found it extraordinary. Ladies—even those whose work had escaped his or his colleagues' bungling—seemed naturally to gravitate towards Apu. Ladies who had suffered, and who had given orders that neither Apu nor any of his connections was ever to be admitted to their presence again, softened and rescinded these orders when they saw the old man. He, freshly shaven, only faintly shrunken, professionally smart in high-collared white coat, soothed and reassured them, speaking in that respectful, faintly obsequious way that they approved as the mark of a good servant. No, he would not delegate any of their work to his assistant (excellent though he was). He would see to everything himself, personally. And Apu would fold his arms across his breast to hide the slackness of his right arm, or to control the convulsive and involuntary slapping movements that this limb sometimes indulged in.

Despite all this, Apu strove to present Ravi as his successor—his worthy successor, the assistant without whose help his, Apu's skill would be as nothing. Or sometimes, when a finished garment had been tried on and pronounced excellent, he would announce to the surprised owner (and in Ravi's surprised hearing) that the entire work had been done by his assistant, although always under his most scrupulous supervision. And the old man would thrust Ravi forward with a flourish, and Ravi would have to lower his eyes modestly while they favoured him briefly with their attention.

At most other times these ladies, Ravi thought, these plump and well-to-do ladies hardly seemed to see him, or if they did they did not seem to be aware of him.

154

'I mean they look at me as if I were made of wood,' said Ravi, striving to elaborate this feeling to Nalini. 'They don't seem to see me as a *man*.'

'The idea!' said Nalini, playing with her son's tassel as the midwife had shown her, so that he could achieve a strong and early virility, have no difficulty in manhood.

'They come out with next to nothing on,' continued Ravi, warmed by her sympathy.

'What, right outside?' asked Nalini, and her eyes grew round.

'No, no, not outside, up in their bedrooms,' said Ravi, 'right in front of Apu and me, and then they stand about admiring themselves in those long looking-glasses!'

'Shameless!' cried Nalini.

'Our Indian ladies are not too bad,' said Ravi, endeavouring to be fair, 'but the white ones—the things I could tell you! Why, one of them had on only a bodice and little shorts only up to here, and I had to measure her!'

'What does Apu say?' asked Nalini, to whom these details of her father's trade were largely undisclosed, and whose imagination was now producing rich and titillating pictures of half-naked bosoms and hips encircled by her husband's tape-measure.

'He is an old man, it does not affect him,' said Ravi dismissively. 'I don't think he even notices.'

Truth to tell, mostly he didn't notice either.

He was too absorbed in what he was doing, particularly with Apu ready to rap his knuckles, besides which Indian women were mostly well swathed, and they never let their saris fall below their breasts. European women were even less distracting, for with their bleached extraordinary skins (which he admired in an unattainable way, like the lotus-pink complexions of goddesses printed on calendars) they almost seemed to belong to another species. There was simply no connection: he had to remind himself to be shocked. It felt to him like a homecoming, a return with relief to what was understood and familiar, to turn from them to the rich brown chocolate of his wife. . . .

Her skin, like his son's, was brown and velvety, so firm and fine that even when she smiled her lovely wide smile no lines appeared. He liked stroking it, to see the paler colour flow in the

155

wake of his finger, and he liked seeing her angry or aroused with
the blood suffusing her skin, touching it with the russet of a
tobacco leaf at its picking peak. In the sun it was different again,
the softest burnished bronze, and her black hair had inky blue
lights in it.

'I would so like to see these ladies,' said Nalini. 'You must
take me with you one day. Raju could come too, it would be such
a treat for him.'

'What would?'

'Riding in a jutka,' said Nalini patiently. 'Two more wouldn't
make any difference.'

I don't know what Apu would say,' said Ravi cautiously.
'Besides if I took you then Thangam would come—I couldn't
bear that.'

'Poor girl, why are you always at her?' said Nalini. 'But as a
matter of fact she wouldn't even if you asked her, the jogging
makes her sick.'

'Since when?'

'Since she's been pregnant,' Nalini giggled. 'At least you can't
blame *that* on her.'

'How many months?'

'Oh, one or two, I'm not sure. Now don't go and tell her I
told you.'

'Why not? I should know soon enough!'

'All in good time,' said Nalini. 'It's her privilege deciding
when to tell her good news.'

Good news! Ravi dwelt on the cycle of screaming, suckling,
scuffling and bickering soon to break out all over again in their
room with the meagre partition, and had to bite his lip to be
silent. He thought, wildly, of leaving, of setting up somewhere
alone in peace with his wife and child; but that improbable flare
soon died, killed by a host of considerations. There was always, he
said to himself forlornly, the refuge on the roof he had built,
where he and Nalini could still find some peace; but often she was
busy, or excused herself because of their child, besides which the
shelter was no longer as snug and enclosing as it had once been,
for two years of wind and weather had taken their toll. Ravi
sometimes pictured the gaping holes as mended, and new reed
panels put in to replace those beyond repair; but he also acknow-

156

ledged it as an unreal picture, knowing he could not afford any of these things.

The cantankerous feelings Ravi had for his brother- and sister-in-law never extended to their children. So when he saw the little girls standing wistfully in the doorway, watching his family preparing for their jutka ride, he at once invited them to join. Apu did not mind. He delegated all these minor arrangements to Ravi—the jutka, who came, who didn't. He had made the effort of travelling, and only he knew what a sweated effort it was. The rest was up to Ravi. So now he sat with his legs drawn up, his back pressed against the ribs of the jutka's hood, and struggled to check his shuddering heartbeats and keep his breathing easy while maddening circles and dots darted like nimble fireflies forever just beyond the corners of his eyes.

Nalini got in next, then the children. Ravi had to lift them, their legs were too short even to reach the step let down from the jutka for mounting.

'One-two-three, up!' He swung them up and deposited them, giggling and squealing on the plump, rustling, straw-filled sacks inside on which they rolled and tumbled, small bright-eyed happy animals.

They were all in. The jutka sagged at the back, while in front the shafts rose, almost taking the thin little jutka-pony with them. The carter began to shout, first at the straining pony, then at his passengers as he marshalled them about inside to redistribute their weight. Apu's face grew cross and creased with effort, the children hugged themselves with pleasure. At last they were off, hooves clopping and harness jingling, and as Ravi sat with his head bobbing close to his wife's he felt his life was not as arid as he sometimes believed it to be.

In the big houses, carts carrying traders, servants and the like were not supposed to use the drive. It was not respectful, Apu had informed Ravi early in their association, for people like them to drive up as if they were great lords: they knew their position and must keep it. So at the gates the two of them dismounted,

157

the old man heavy and stiff as he always was now, Ravi awkward and lumbered with mull-wrapped bundles as usual. The children were supposed to wait decorously with Nalini in the jutka, but as Ravi walked up the drive he could hear them twittering, and turning saw their impish faces appear above the low compound wall.

The house they were going to was owned by Europeans. Ravi could have told just by looking, for the gravel was swept, the flower-beds neat, the clipped lawns green, giving a general air of tidiness that Indian homes lacked. Instead of a motley crew of servants there was only one peon visible, an important being in a khaki drill tunic and brass-buckled belt who sat like a guardian deity in a sentry-box next to the portico. They approached him, Apu sidling up as he had done all his life, though now he could only manage a sad copy of it.

'Is the memsahib at home?'

No anwer. The deity was asleep, although his eyes were open.

'Tell memsahib we are here.' Ravi spoke loudly—he had not the ingratiating patiences of Apu; and he poked the somnolent figure into full wakefulness.

'Yes, yes, what is it?' The peon spoke testily, rubbing his eyes from which the glacial look was only slowly departing. 'No hawkers, no hawkers allowed here.'

'We are not—' began Ravi, but Apu interrupted.

'Memsahib's clothes are ready,' he said. 'Is memsahib at home?' and at the same time he slipped a few coins into the other's palm —a procedure which Ravi resented, but which both he and Apu accepted as expenses essential to the conduct of their business, for otherwise memsahib would never be at home. They might rot in this portico until nightfall, and she still would not be.

'I'll go and see.' The peon rose stiffly and stretched his limbs. He knew—memsahib often told him—he had an easy job, but it was cramped work sitting on a stool waiting for callers from morning until the night watchman came.

Ravi and Apu waited, as they were quite used to doing, while Ravi gazed at the elaborate trellis-work along the walls that supported sheaf after sheaf of flame-coloured bougainvillea, and wondered how much it had all cost. In-between he wondered, as he often did, what memsahibs got up to while they kept them waiting one, one-and-a-half, even two hours. Bathed? Combed their hair, massaged their bodies? Somehow he could not see these activities taking up so much time, since Thangam at her worst never took longer than half an hour. The whole thing was a complete mystery to him.

Today they were lucky. Memsahib would see them at once: they were to go up. In some houses they were expected to use the back sweeper's staircase, but more frequently they used the main stairs, since most ladies disliked having their clothes trailed up the sweeper's way. Ravi greatly preferred going through the house, he enjoyed catching glimpses of the large rooms with their marble floors and rose-shaded lights, and everything somehow cushioned and quiet as if these cool still areas of space absorbed and destroyed the noise and dust, all the fretfulness of existence which other people had to live with. A sense of reality however eluded him. Did real people actually live here, like this? He had to drag Damodar in, who lived in something approaching all this, and who was certainly perfectly real, before a sense of belief would come.

The day was lucky too in the matter of fittings. The memsahib said she was satisfied, she even looked pleased. She had ordered a whole host of things—housecoats, dresses, slacks, flowered shirts to wear over them . . . far more than she needed, she reflected as she slowly tried them on, but things were so cheap here, she knew she would never be able to afford so many clothes once she left India.

Ravi watched her with the detached eye Apu's coaching had given him, and supposed that she looked what she would consider well, her flat hips and trim waist emphasised by the slacks she was trying on, her blue eyes and golden hair bright against the rich colours she had chosen. But she was not young—she must have lived at least twenty years in India, Ravi judged, for her skin to be the pale teak that it was. It was this, too, he thought crossly, that made her so adept at haggling, so sharply aware of what she ought to be charged.

They sat on the upstairs veranda overlooking the garden, she in her cane chair, they on the floor, and argued item by item.

'Seven rupees for a shirt? Preposterous!'

'So much fine work, memsahib,' Apu spoke softly, reproachfully. 'Pin tucks . . . it took the lad many hours. . . .'

159

'Not a pie over four rupees.'

'Five rupees, memsahib . . . we have to live.'

'Four-fifty.'

She beat him down. He wagged his head and looked sorrowful, finally accepting the deal. It was all part of a game which both understood. Ravi understood it perfectly too, but he had less patience and he found it less absorbing. He tried to pay attention, but his gaze kept wandering to the garden, which he could see between the veranda balusters spread out in all the colours of a Turkey carpet, and from thence to the compound wall over which the children's heads kept bobbing. There were bits of broken glass, he noticed, embedded on the top—ruby, bottle-green, dark blue; they flashed like jewels in the sun. He hoped Nalini would warn the children . . . his son's hands were so small and soft, petal-soft. . . .

'Your assistant has not heard a single word of mine. He can hardly be as interested in his job as you say.' It was the dry voice of the memsahib. She had a fashion magazine open on her lap, which she was tapping with an impatient fore-finger.

'He is, he is—it is just that the children distract him,' murmured Apu humbly, apologetically, and he snapped sharply at Ravi, 'Pay attention!'

Ravi hurriedly picked up the magazine, scanning it agonisedly for a clue as to which plate he was meant to copy, finally confessing defeat and looking to the memsahib for help. She ignored him.

'Children,' she said, and leaning on the balustrade watched the small group clustered round the jutka at the gates. 'Yours?'

'My grandchildren,' corrected Apu gently.

'Yes of course, your grandchildren,' she said. 'I didn't know you had any,' and her tone was a mixture of curiosity and disbelief, as if these people, who appeared when summoned by her servants and disappeared when she was done with them she had no idea where, had no existence in-between: cardboard figures that she found strange to think of as human beings, with lives of their own, and continuity, with children . . . she wondered whether, if they had skins like hers, they would become real to her, these people among whom she lived who were more faceless and alien than her own countrymen thousands of miles away; but it was a disturbing thought, quickly quelled, and she said briskly, 'Take them some sweets ... no, not sweets, there aren't any in the house. Fruit, then, do they like fruit? Oranges? Apples?'

Ravi swallowed. Of course they liked fruit, who didn't? When they could afford to, it was mostly country fruit that they bought: *jamblams*, mangoes in season or tongues of jack-fruit, and then it was usually only for the children. Oranges were rare, apples even more so—they would certainly be a treat. He began to feel more kindly towards the memsahib, even forgiving her for the rebuke she had earned him. Basically she was good-hearted, he thought, though perhaps a little too pernickety ... and he gazed amiably at the neat shape of her buttocks clearly outlined by the white linen slacks as she leaned over the balustrade and clapped for the peon, only desisting when he saw Apu's scandalised and disapproving eye fixed sternly on him. But then Apu's ideas, he thought, were those of another generation, unacceptable and unpalatable to his own. He treated his employers as if they were minor gods, which they would never be to him: almost another species maybe, but never little gods.

Chapter 26

THERE was a whole basketful of fruit, and because there was so much and it wouldn't keep, even by cool storage in a mud-pot, they all had some instead of just the children.

'Such delicious apples!' Thangam sighed and licked her lips for the last traces of juice. 'I only hope I don't develop a craving for them.'

'Why should you?' Jayamma spoke sharply, in a tone that should have warned Thangam.

'Well,' she said, 'I often find when I'm—' she stopped, and her eyes grew round. She knew—none better—that this was the worst possible time for another baby, with their savings eaten up by Apu's illness, and the business only just beginning to recover. She wished she had never spoken, it was that tongue of hers,

161

running away with her as usual . . . she kept her eyes lowered, and the silence grew. At last Jayamma said, flatly, 'I suppose you are pregnant again,' and Thangam nodded, drawing her sari over the lower half of her face like a penitent.

Silence closed in again. They sat petrified in the darkening room, no one daring to speak until finally Apu got up stiffly, and supported by his wife dragged himself to his bed.

That night Ravi lay on his mat with his arms crossed under his head and thought of how they would manage when the new baby came. They would of course, that went without saying, but they would have to do without this and cut down on that and feel the ring of living grow tighter round them so that what should be an occasion for rejoicing would merely become an exercise in endurance, however much eventually they loved the child.

Was it like this, he wondered, for everyone? for people like the memsahib for instance? The absurdity of the thought almost made him laugh. Of course it wouldn't be. There, it would be easy, as easy as it ought to be. He pondered on that ought-to-be with a growing malaise, a vague sense of injustice somewhere, somehow, that he could not pin down. He wished he could wake Nalini and talk it over with her, but he knew she hated this questing, rebellious side of his nature and would not understand who or what he was getting at—he hardly did himself—so what was the use? He tried to banish these thoughts and compose himself for sleep, but beyond the partitioning curtain Thangam and Puttanna had begun to quarrel in whispers, and he could not.

'Is it my fault?'

This was a question they frequently asked each other.

'Is it my fault?' Thangam repeated. 'I told you not to. Did you listen?'

'But coming out like that in front of Apu and all,' said Puttanna. 'What possessed you?'

'Well? In three months' time they would have known anyhow wouldn't they?'

'Three months is three months.'

'What difference would it make? Would you have become a millionaire by then?'

'Business would be better.'

'What business? Whose business? None of the profits will be coming your way, you can take that from me.'

On and on. Ravi wished he could be like a child again, like the children, his and theirs, who could sleep through any disturbance. Usually he could too; it was only on some nights—tonight—that it became unbearable. He sat up at last, and hissed at them sharply: 'S-sh-shh!'

There was a short silence, then the whispers began again, taking up where they had left off.

'—and then there's the child.'

'What about it?'

'What about it? You ask!' Thangam abandoned her hoarse whispering, her voice rose shrilly. 'What I'm asking is what will you do for it. Clothe it, feed it? Or is it simply a waste of breath to ask?'

'I do my best.'

'Your best! I know what that is. Nothing for the child.' Quite suddenly Thangam's voice broke. 'Not so much as a jacket, or a cap, or even a shawl to wrap him in—not one new thing to welcome his birth, only rags and leftovers.'

'This time—'

'This time will be like last time. I shall be shamed in front of my parents, in front of my sister. Have you seen the clothes she has for her son? Knitted caps, and little velveteen jackets, and—'

'I'll get you these things, only don't cry.'

'How?'

'You wait and see. I'll buy all these things for your child, so don't cry any more.'

What vain promises, Ravi thought, listening despite himself. He even felt a little sorry for Puttanna, driven by tears and nagging into making them, but sympathy soon dissolved into irritation as the noise continued. He wanted to hiss at them again, but if he did Thangam might cry even harder and wake the whole house. He held his peace, and very shortly sleep overcame him.

As Thangam had said, in three months her pregnancy was only too evident. By then they had stopped regarding it as the calamity

163

it had seemed at first, partly because with Apu around the business was improving, partly because Puttanna was making some efforts to find himself a job. Was it his fault if he did not succeed? asked Thangam loudly and defiantly. Jobs did not grow on trees for easy plucking. But in private—in what passed for privacy—she lambasted her husband.

'She ought to stop it,' said Ravi. 'Someone should seal up her mouth.'

'If she did, and he stopped trying for a job, you would be the first to complain,' said Nalini, justly, but tartly.

All these adult squabbles, however, were stilled as the festival of Deepavali approached. The children were agog, and looking into their bright expectant faces no one felt like pursuing the small personal vendettas that sputtered away the rest of the year.

There were, decreed Apu, to be no new clothes for anyone this Deepavali.

Nalini and Jayamma took this ruling philosophically, but it bore hard on Thangam, who relied on these presents to carry her family through the year. Kumaran did not mind, as he was never given new clothes anyway; it was always cast-offs for him. The children did not mind. They minded intensely about fireworks and had been promised a packet of bangers each. And a rocket? they asked their grandfather. Not just one rocket with red and gold stars?

Their eagerness touched the old man. He wished (but only briefly, he had long disciplined himself to giving vain wishes short shrift) he could cram their hands full to over-flowing with all they asked for, and more.

'Well, perhaps a rocket or two . . . I'll have to see,' he said.

It was as good as a promise, coming from their grandfather. They left him, wreathed in smiles.

How pleasing they were, he thought, asking so little, giving so much . . . why did they lose it all, grow up like, for instance, Thangam? Perhaps it was because she had troubles that she had turned mean and belligerent; it often affected people that way. Was not Ravi a prime example? The moment things weren't going his way—simply because his belly happened to be empty—he had come bursting in here, into this very house, exactly as if he were a hooligan. Was that all a thing of the past, he wondered,

164

or not? The old man stirred uneasily. Perhaps, he thought, he had been wrong to put so much faith in his son-in-law, with his disturbing beliefs and rumbling discontents, his soaring ideas that had not flown straight into disaster only because marriage had weighted his wings. After all, what did he really know about this young man, newcomer to the city? Apu pressed his knuckles to his temples and felt that he simply did not know.

Deepavali came. In the morning after bathing they went to the shrine to pray, taking coconuts and flowers as offerings. The rest of the day Apu kept them working, but the evening belonged to the children and at dusk they repaired to the maidan to watch the huge bonfire that had been lit, and to let off their own fireworks.

Apu sat on the outskirts of the crowd that had collected, his shawl wound round his head and shoulders against the night dew, the glow of the fire warm on his face, and let his mind range over past Deepavalis. How many had there been, sixty, seventy? He was never very sure, because he was never very sure about his age. Anyhow it was a good total, he could see the festivals stretching away down the years in a long sparkling line. How many more? He wrapped his shawl more closely around him, for a chilly wind had sprung up. Just a few more, he thought, please God, I don't ask for many, but just a few more.

Chapter 27

SOON after Deepavali the fire-walkers came.

Thangam brought the news, and instantly Jayamma—so it seemed to Apu's jaundiced eye—was champing to go. It was not that she had not seen the ceremony before: she had, many times, in fact almost every time it was held in this part of the city, which was once in two or three years. But still it fascinated her, drew her in a way that she could not explain herself—a way that repelled Apu, made him sharply uneasy, though he was too

165

taciturn a man to voice these feelings. Like moth to flame, was the most he ever said, and the most he ever did was to accompany her, doggedly, silently, without complaint.

He had always done so, every single time, distrusting the extreme reactions of his wife which to the others passed for a natural excitement, but which made him afraid for her safety, as if she might somehow come to harm through her emotions. He had never actually formulated this fear: it remained an old-established, ill-defined malaise of which, if only he had known how, he would gladly have rid himself. He could not, but he also refused to buy his peace by thwarting Jayamma. Why should he? She, like Thangam and to a lesser degree the other members of the household, relished fêtes, festivals, junketing of any kind: if she had the zest to enjoy them, the energy to stand immensely patient with the crowd waiting hour upon hour, who was he— and here he acknowledged the difference in their ages—to stand in her way?

Now, however, there was the dragging weakness left by his stroke to reckon with. What would he do this time? They waited, barely curbing their impatience, while Apu brooded, taking his time, and at length raised his heavy-lidded eyes to say it would be as usual, he would go with his wife.

They attempted to dissuade him. There was the long walk, the waiting, the congestion which made it impossible for jutkas to ply. Apu listened, and wished Thangam had kept the news of the event to herself which would have saved all this argument, and wondered wearily if he had made the right decision. Jayamma watched him wavering, and his weakness moved her to a sudden pity.

'Don't go,' she said gently, 'if you don't feel up to it.'

'If you go—'

'I won't. I'll stay with you.'

'You don't want to miss it.'

'No, but I can go next time.'

'This time it's going to be specially grand,' said Thangam. 'So they say.'

'Who say?'

'Why, everyone,' said Thangam loudly if vaguely. 'Everyone says you don't want to miss it.'

Jayamma thought of her daily round, of the months spent nursing an old sick man, of the living with him that lay before her, and felt her mouth grow dry with longing for all the excitements she had missed.

She thought she concealed it, she certainly tried, but Apu's perceptions, stripped and fined down, had grown to a delicate, disseminated network that picked up the smallest tremors of suppressed feeling in a way not known to his more robust days.

'I can manage,' he said. 'We'll all go.'

They were half way there before Apu noticed Puttanna was not with them, and he only did so then because Varma and Ravi were bickering over who carried whose child, and there was no sign of Puttanna to share the burden.

'Where is your husband?' Apu turned, frowning, to Thangam.

'At home.'

'Doing what?' he asked suspiciously, disliking the idea of anyone, but especially his senior son-in-law, exercising dominion over his house in his absence.

'Nothing. I don't know what. He felt too tired to come.'

Apu's frown grew deeper. Too tired, he thought, it must be from all the work he didn't do! Thangam could hear him mumbling under his breath and knew why, but paid no attention. If she let herself feel bruised every time Puttanna was picked on, she often said to herself, by now she would be pulp! She lagged behind a little, so that she no longer had to listen to the old man and in no time at all had forgotten him.

Jayamma would have liked to forget him too, to concentrate on the excitement charging the air like the winged humming of insects massing before a rainstorm, but how could she, with Apu shambling alongside her, clutching at her for very life each time someone pushed him? Why did he have to come, she thought with mounting irritation. In his condition the only sane thing was to stay at home, not attach himself like a drag-weight to her. She could not altogether withdraw from his side, but she stiffened her arm resentfully each time he reached for her. Apu was aware of the grudging help she gave him, but he said nothing; he shuffled along as fast as he could so as not to retard them, making as few demands on Jayamma as he could.

Varma and Ravi walked behind, a child at each hip, followed by Kumaran, who could get along quite fast despite his pronounced limp. The children were nodding, three-quarters asleep, the younger ones bare-bottomed so that they could easily be held over gutters if they wetted, the older clad in their best warm jackets for whose splendour, sadly, they had by now ceased to care.

'Is there much further to go?' Apu could feel his body sweating, although it was a cool evening.

'Not far—the end of this street.' Thangam answered him— Thangam who always knew where things happened, even if they never happened twice in the same place.

But by now one didn't have to know: one simply went with the crowd, packed shoulder to shoulder in a slow-moving mass.

The end of the street was a cross-roads, a junction of four streets each of which had been turned into a cul-de-sac by bullock-carts, man-handled into place without their animals, that blocked each exit. In this arbitrary space the fire had been laid, a long low bed of coals perhaps twenty paces long and fifteen across, resting on piled firewood and kindling saturated in kerosene and ghee. On either side were the drummers, seven, eight of them, one taking up where another fell silent, filling the air with a steady, gentle rataplan.

'It's already begun,' Jayamma whispered, the prick of disappointment in her voice.

'Only just.' Apu closed his eyes against the thick white smoke billowing up from the kindling, but the heavy acrid smell of burning—burning oil, wood, ghee, and the tar and kerosene-soaked rags of blazing torches held by the fire lighters—excoriated his throat and nostrils, he felt if he put up his hand his fingers would encounter raw surfaces instead of lining membranes. How long did it last—three hours, four? That was about how long funeral pyres took—the essential business of it, the reduction of a still-recognisable individual into impersonal charred fragments—although the embers continued to glow for a long time afterwards. Apu found himself swaying and opened his eyes. Nowadays he found that closing his eyes affected his balance. Not, he reflected wryly, that he would fall far in this crush, but the dizziness was unpleasant, it reminded him how easily control might slip from him and the reminder was frightening.

Ravi, wedged with the children some distance away, saw the old man falter and wondered with a mixture of annoyance and guilt if he could be expected to fight this throng to go to his aid. But before he could decide Apu had recovered, and his annoyance turned to admiration. Brave old man, he thought fleetingly, venturing out in this simply because of some funny notion lodged in his head! Then there was a roar, people echoing the fire as the wood burst into flame, and he forgot everything else.

The fires, and the drumming that had risen to the strength of heart-beats, began to take possession of whom, of what? their spirits, the night? Apu wracked his beleaguered mind but he could not be sure. Beside him Jayamma stood stockstill. Her eyes were burning, they reflected the fire in leaping, blazing pinpoints of light around her jet-black pupils. Her lips were dry—with heat, with fever? Apu felt the questions jostling him again, he shook his head to try and clear it but he could not, even this simple answer seemed to be beyond his power.

'When they die, *then*,' said Jayamma. Her eyes grew dull as the rearing flames checked and began to shorten. 'When they die down *that* is the time.'

'What did you say?' Apu asked confusedly. Jayamma stared at him, seeming not to understand. 'When they die, *that* is the time,' she repeated, and now it was what the crowd was saying too, she intoned in unison with them.

> When they die, then is the time.
> The time is when the flames die down.

The chanting rose as the fires dipped and sank. The sound was a wave, a torrent lashed by the frenetic tattoo of the drums, on which they were swept along, swimming, sinking, rising to strike out again. In the arena the coals glowed brightly, a vivid bed five layers deep that rumbled and shook itself down, layer by layer, each subsidence adding an ashen edge to the glow until at last the grey and the orange were equal.

Now, *now!* The plea rose simultaneously, in a hoarse, strained whisper as if the crowd were poised, unbearably, on the trembling brink of climax. In answer there was a movement in the shadows, a dozen men came out of the night into the full glow of the fire-bed. They were naked, except for loin-cloths; their bodies oiled, their feet bare: the firewalkers. There was a gasp, the mass holding-in of breath before release. If the leader of the firewalkers heard, he gave no sign. He stood still, in a terrible lone stillness, head bent, his eyes brooding on the burning coal, and at length stooping gathered up a handful of ashes and smeared both feet. Then at last he raised his head and said, clearly, 'The power is thine, O God, not mine,' and at once with no further hesitation he stepped on to the coals and ran lightly over the glowing bed.

In his wake came his followers, invoking God's power as he had done, treading the same path as lightly as if those red-hot coals were flowers under their feet.

And now the invocation rang out from the crowd, again and again, all but drowning the thundering beat of the drums.

The power is thine, O God, not mine but thine.

With the cry an undulating movement in the packed mass began. Cracks appeared, spread and widened as gangways were created, down which came those with the faith and the will to follow—a thin stream, of whom perhaps a half did not turn back.

Not mine, O Lord, not mine, not mine . . .

Ravi, with Raju half asleep on his shoulders, watched with a deep, half-recoiling interest. This part of the ceremony fascinated him the most, seeing ordinary people like himself touched by the power of God . . . and then he thought No, not people like himself, he and they could never bring themselves to put so much trust in God, such things were for those of another generation. Briefly he experienced a vague sense of loss, as if his life as it was now had one depth the less, but the feeling soon left him, for he had never had much patience with these soulful hankerings.

Twenty paces on Apu kept close watch on his wife—as close as he could with his smoke-filled eyes streaming with tears—and wondered how far faith and emotion would carry her this time, now that the drums were calling, now that the time was close. He kept his hand on her shoulder, only partly for support, and suddenly felt a tremor pass through her, and another and another until it was a sustained quivering. He tightened his grip, knowing that the moment had come, the moment he always dreaded when his control over her was as if it had never been, not in all the years of their marriage, and her control over herself was so attenuated that he could not tell whether it would hold or break. It was a double-edged fear: for if her surrender was complete she might come through the ordeal safely, but if through him a vestige of control remained... Apu trembled, and clung convulsively to her arm.

If Jayamma felt it she gave no sign, she did not even seem aware of the dense crush about her. Her eyes, enormous and brilliant, seemed concentrated on some inner cataclysm, her voice was harsh and unlike her own as, once more, she cried out the invocation. Then she began to move towards the burning coal.

Apu went with her. His grip was not very strong, but somehow he managed to keep his hold and felt himself being hauled along in her wake, buffeted, half-blinded by the surging crowds until they were at the head of a lane that opened for followers of the fire. Here Jayamma paused, gazing fixedly at the coals that glowed golden a few yards from them. Perhaps she would go, Apu thought in brief respite, or perhaps not. But if she went he knew he would go with her, for here on the very edge of truth he recognised its face, acknowledged that if she went it was because of the long hungers in her that he had failed to satisfy. He was not afraid for himself—an old man, so near death, was he to nurture a fear that God might not uphold him? His great fear was for her, because her motives for treading this path whether she knew it or not were wrong and impure.

Ravi, from his stance further back, noticed their progress and was appalled. He knew nothing of the obliquities that led them, scorned such faith in God's power as they might have, saw nothing but a devil's brew of illness, suffering, doctor's bills and disaster attending their efforts. Madwoman, he thought, and the memory of her blows across his shoulders revived a pain and anger he had believed forgotten. *Madwoman!* Shouting to Raju to hold tightly, hitching Thangam's child closer to him, he began to struggle forward, thrusting savagely with his shoulders, until at last he was there, beside Jayamma, and seeing her he began shaking her violently with his one free hand.

He was never quite sure afterwards of the sequence of the

171

events that followed. He heard Raju whimper, heard Apu's shout, felt the child slide from his hip and in attempting to retrieve it lost his balance and fell, awkwardly, with Raju still on his shoulders. Then it seemed to him as if people were falling everywhere, beside them, on top of them, in a stifling sickening mass that pinned him down, and he screamed as loudly as he could with the air still left in his lungs, his screams joining the muffled, diminishing cries of the two children. Then as suddenly as it had begun the nightmare ended. He did not realize it and went on screaming until the cool night air fell on his face and he saw the anxious crowds pressed back to make space for the fallen, hands held out to help them to their feet and steady them. He looked round for the children, with a slight return of his earlier panic when he could not immediately see them, but then someone pointed and he saw them safe in Jayamma's arms.

'Are you hurt?' she asked—without, he thought, much interest in his fate.

'No,' he said, 'Are you?'

She shook her head. She looked very tired, the energy that had coursed so strongly seemed to have drained away.

'Let us go home,' said Apu. His thin voice seemed to come from very far away, but the determination that had brought him here and kept him on his feet all evening still functioned, and with his slow dragging steps he began to lead the way homewards.

Behind them the coals were dying, quite quickly now. Some still emitted a faint glow, an occasional spark fleetingly enlivened the ashes and cinders, but already the near reaches were dark as night closed in.

Chapter 28

THE days that followed were calm and placid, an orderly succession of mornings and nights without incident which even Ravi, ordinarily given to harping on their dulness, found pleasing—especially by sharp contrast with what had come to be called firewalking night. It was too recent to be a memory, its sting drawn and its edges smoothed by time: the mere mention of it was sufficient to turn them all haggard, each for a different reason. Now, gratefully, they returned to their old routines, women to house and children, men to the business of earning.

Apu took to his bed, suffering a delayed reaction that they realized was natural, but which made them anxious to the point of debating whether to send for a doctor, although in the end financial reasons deterred them. Apu, however, was up within the week, declaring himself a new man for the rest, setting with renewed zest to putting his workroom to rights.

The whole of that first day, almost from the moment he left his bed, Apu kept them hard at it. At midday he allowed them a break, but half an hour later, when they were blissfully imagining he had worn himself out, he was back, urging them to get on. Their backs aching, their eyes strained, it seemed to them that day that dusk would never fall. But at last it was twilight, at last it grew dark. In the courtyard beyond the workroom the women were filling the lamps and lighting them—the electricity had failed again. The smell of kerosene wafted in and presently Nalini entered carrying a lantern.

'Will you be working much longer?'

She did not directly address her husband or his overlord but left it between them for either to answer.

'No, no, we have finished for the day.' Apu uncrossed his legs, using his hand to straighten and stretch the weakened right limb. 'Here, help me up.'

Once on his feet he could manage, but for several moments he stood still, adjusting to his upright stance before attempting to walk, and surveying his workroom with deep, close satisfaction. A good day's work, he thought, everyone had laboured hard, even Varma, even Puttanna ... but he did not say anything, it was not his practice.

When Apu had gone they began clearing away, meticulously as the old man insisted, although they were all dog-tired. Nalini helped, folding, smoothing and putting away with neat quick movements so that they should be done the sooner. Now and then she brushed against Ravi; he could smell the lingering sweetness of the sandalwood paste she used and he wanted to put

173

his arm around her but the presence of the others restrained him.

At last it was done. Ravi picked up the Singer's oil-cloth cover—the shrouding of the machine had acquired ritualistic significance, symbolic of the close of the working day, and was always left till last. He was about to slip it on—the cover was poised aloft in his hands—when from the living quarters came a loud cry, a sound of panic and rage that trailed away into an incoherent whimper of loss.

Ravi stood petrified, not even lowering his hands. Apu had had a stroke, he thought—they all thought. But before anyone could move, speak, enter or leave there was a frenzied shuffling outside and a thud against the door.

'Open it.' Apu's voice, harsh and stern. So it could not have been a stroke, or his voice would have gone.

'Open the door!'

Ravi obeyed. Apu limped in, and behind him in shadow were the frightened faces of Thangam and Jayamma. He was carrying something—a bundle, a child? In the wavering glow of the lantern they could not be sure.

'Turn up the light.'

Nalini raised the wick with shaking fingers. The flame grew brighter and steadied, they could see each other clearly now, could see that what the old man carried, incredibly, was his pillow, the small, hard pillow he slept on at night, or sometimes settled against the small of his back when he leant against the workroom wall.

'Which of you has done it?' Apu held up the pillow as if it were an exhibit, revolving slowly so that all could see.

Done what, to a pillow? He must be raving, Ravi told himself, but he felt a little uneasy too, a little frightened because of a quality in the old man's voice far from madness, an implacability of tone that his brain coldly and precisely placed: policeman's power, policeman's implacability. He shivered. He had not meant to call up those memories.

'Look. You, Ravi, look at this, look at me.'

His eyes had wandered, the sharp command brought his gaze back to the pillow. It was old, patched, worn, grey with age, so familiar one hardly noticed it. What was he supposed to see? He

174

looked in bewilderment at the old man, met his accusing eyes and thought angrily: Why pick on me? Is my past still on my back? But before he could burst out the old man had passed on with his questioning and scrutiny.

He did it coldly and methodically, commanding Jayamma to bring extra lanterns, holding up the pillow for each of the men in turn to see. And now Ravi thought he detected something, and he peered closer at the patches that covered almost the whole surface of the pillow. They were beautifully executed, the stripes of ticking and patch meeting invisibly, the neat tiny stitches hardly showing—all except one, that had quite clearly been sewn in by another hand. Here, too, the stitches were neat and small: whoever had made them had laboured to copy Apu, but Apu's skill, product of a lifetime, was after all beyond any of them.

'It shows when you look, does it not.' Apu's finger traced the outlines of the small square patch. 'Did you think I would not see it—the old man, the fool, too far gone to notice that the stitches were no longer his . . . but you were right, whichever one of you it was, because I am old, and my old eyes did not at once notice what had been done.' There was a long pause while Apu gathered his strength, for his speech had begun to slip. When he resumed again his voice was higher, stronger.

'Every pie has gone, my entire life's savings, the money upon which we all depended, and it is one of you that has done it, one of you in this house, in this room.'

There was a silence, hushed, tense, broken by a sudden piercing cry from Jayamma which at a glance from her husband she quickly smothered, clapping her hand over her still open mouth. Then no one moved or spoke or dared to look up, and Ravi could feel his guts twist with nervous fear, although he knew he was innocent.

'One of you here,' the words fell like cold pebbles, 'with patience and great cunning . . . but there is no hand that does not leave an imprint, no work to which I cannot put a name for the letters are clear to me in every stitch.'

Apu stopped, and in the oppressive quiet Ravi felt himself accused, felt the walls closing in around him and knew again the old panic urge for flight; but when at last he raised his eyes he

175

saw that Apu was not looking at him at all but past him, his gaze rested on Puttanna.

Puttanna stood quite still, except for a slight twitching of his hands which he appeared unable to control although he had locked them together. His face was oddly discoloured, as if the flow of blood had become uncontrolled too: a curious mottling of the skin like clay imperfectly baked in a damp kiln. He said not a word, of defence or admission or exculpation. Why can't he deny it? Ravi asked himself frenziedly, why can't he? But he did not, and Apu, his forebodings of firewalking night hardening into certainty, knew that he could not.

'Fed you, sheltered you . . . forgave your follies, asked for no return. . . .'

Ravi listened to the bitter declamation and in it was not only the anguish of betrayal but the rancour of all those long parasitical years and he thought to himself: I would not have borne it, I would have kicked him out whatever people said, no man should go under because of his sponging relatives; and he even tried to despise Apu for adhering to these out-dated beliefs but he could not, for now in his anger Apu was not despicable, he had a strength and command that Ravi in his heart knew none of them could equal.

' . . . no longer of this house . . . go from here in shame.'

They heard him out in silence and at the end it was only Thangam who cried out merciless, *merciless*, her anguish overcoming even her awe of the old man; but he gave no sign of having heard as he turned and went slowly from the room.

Puttanna left in the morning, taking with him his sleeping mat and bedding roll and the secret of what he had done with the money. Thangam remained, haggard and strained, done with weeping after the first stricken night. No edict bound her, but she knew—they all knew—that where a man went there his wife must go, and with her would go her children.

The only question was when.

Thangam did not speak of it. What she did speak of—what seemed to harrow her the most—was the preventable nature of what had happened. 'If only,' she said, forlornly, over and over

176

again, 'if only I had not left him that night ... he was weak, the temptation was too much for him ... but how could I know this would happen?'

'Nobody knew,' said Nalini, attempting to console her sister. 'Nobody knew about the money, otherwise we would all have been more careful. He only found out by chance.'

'By evil chance,' said Thangam, hollow-eyed, husky-voiced.

Nalini wept for her sister, the more violently when Ravi, as he thought, tried to put the matter in perspective. 'At least he's got a nice bit of capital now,' he said, 'and really you know the fault was hers as much as his, always nagging the poor man for bonnets and saris and heaven knows what so in the end he just took all he could lay his hands on.'

Nalini raised her blotched angry face. 'You blame *her*,' she shrieked at him, 'what about him, *stealing*, taking what wasn't his, is there no such thing as right and wrong, what's the matter with you that you can't see it?'

He fell silent, he was so taken aback by her fury. Certainly he regretted the loss of the money, it was a serious matter; money was serious, something one legitimately snatched and fought over, thought of and dreamed about, because without it all one was left with was to stretch out and die. But he had no sense of moral outrage, no feeling of inner damage, or damage to some abstract standard that she seemed to hold, and which the elders of his village had been so fond of brandishing at him and his friends. Who had been the sinners, though: those who kept their standards and sacrificed their families, or those who went out to grab what they could? Ravi felt he knew the answer, he had never had any doubt from the moment he had shaken the dust of the village from his feet and even before. Marriage had painted a few streaks of respectability on his back, it had insidiously revived the old values in him, so that he once again lauded the superiority of work over loafing: but he would not go back on what the soundings and observations of his life had taught him, would never give up the new values he had deliberately built up for himself for the old, patently useless values bequeathed him by his father's generation.

Puttanna needed capital: he took it: that was the end of it. If anyone was to blame, thought Ravi, it was Apu, hoarding his savings up in an old pillow like that. Why, it was the first place he would have looked in, if he had had a mind to it! Pillow and mattress, a tin trunk under the bed, or inside a mud statuette of Govinda, these as he and the city crowd well knew were favoured hiding places. But all these matters of course he kept from Nalini, and, indeed, he had not thought about them himself for some considerable time.

About a month after Puttanna's departure Thangam began making preparations to leave. No one knew precisely how it had been arranged between husband and wife, but Puttanna had been seen in the street outside, although he had been forbidden to cross the threshold and indeed never did so again, and there were occasions when Thangam vanished, leaving her children in Nalini's care. She never said where she went, nor would she answer their questions, and Ravi concluded it was done to foil any attempt to regain the money. In fact, however, Apu was too shocked to be capable of doing so, and the rest of the family saw it as a family disgrace, best confined to its members.

After his initial savage outburst, no one knew what Apu felt or thought. He was remote and unapproachable, even more so than usual, saying very little and that straight to the purpose, driving himself along at a young man's pace as if to make up for his loss.

How much had it been? At least two thousand rupees, whispered Varma, but as Ravi argued it, how did he know? No one knew. The old man had always been very close about his money affairs, there were no books or ledgers that they could look at, he carried it all in his head. Even when handing over to Ravi this was one compartment that he still kept locked, torn in two between the urge to act before it was too late, and the hoarding, gloating, jealous desire to keep it all to himself. So no one— apart from loser and taker, and the loser was not too sure in his own mind because he was aware it sometimes wobbled—no one knew how much money had gone.

But for the money Jayamma would have been kinder to Thangam. Her daughter had suffered a good many years—ever since her ill-starred marriage to that good-for-nothing husband— as well she knew, for it had gone on under her roof. Thangam had nagged, cried, bullied, and in the end put a bold cheerful face

178

on it: what else could she do? but the hurt was plain to see, especially when she had to mend and make-do for the children while the children of more provident fathers ate better, dressed better, spoke of their parents with pride. Jayamma sighed; it was a hard thing for a mother. Nevertheless, she felt the loss of the money as a personal blow. It would have come to her, it was hers, only the slenderest threads bound Apu to this earth. And she would have found it sweet, having all her life had to manage on what her husband doled out to her. Of course they had never starved or anything like that. Her husband was a respectable craftsman, they lived respectably, but still there were all the small luxuries that she had gone without, like say Margo or Vinolia soap as a treat instead of forever bar soap, and Mysore coffee beans instead of the mixed lot she had to settle for in the bazaar. For a few short months she had tasted nectar when Ravi became a member of the household, and there were cinemas and cool drinks ... but now he had his family responsibilities there was nothing, no small pleasures. Over the years it added up to a lot.

When these thoughts came her mood would harden, turn her against Thangam; and Thangam, conscious of her mother's harshness, would rush to her children—who were weathering the storm with their customary sturdy good sense—and enfold them in a mutely accusing demonstration of what mother-love should be. The message was not lost on Jayamma. She found it acutely provoking, and was less sympathetic to her daughter than she really wanted to be.

Finally, a month to the day after her husband's departure, Thangam packed her belongings. By this time she seemed to have reconciled herself to the move, and spoke cheerfully of some employment her husband had in mind. Privately Ravi discounted this. Perhaps they all did, but no one had the heart to say so. Nor could they indulge, in the stony, forbidding presence of Apu, in the theatrical leave-taking that would have delighted Thangam's heart. She went, perforce, quietly, her small subdued children trailing behind, each carrying a cloth-wrapped bundle, and the hapless Puttanna hovering ineffectually round the nearest corner.

When they had gone Ravi took down the sari curtain that had partitioned their room so long and so irksomely. He felt festive about it, but was deterred from any overt exultation by

the pale, set face of his wife. Nevertheless he felt as if his life was
at last opening up, that he could breathe again after the cramped,
ill-borne conditions of the years that had passed.

Chapter 29

THEY were going, that particular morning, to the house of the
lady of the apples. Raju had begged to be taken, Nalini had flown
about the house finishing her work, and the two of them were
now triumphantly ensconced in the jutka.

Raju had the coveted seat next to the carter, Ravi sat opposite
Nalini, and beside her was Apu. The old man had difficulty in
keeping his balance as the pony cantered along, and the wooden
wheels encountered the ruts and bumps of the uneven streets.
Now and then he leaned against her, momentarily, before regain-
ing his upright stance. They had got so used to this sideways
lurch that they hardly noticed when he fell against her rather
more heavily, and it was only when his weight grew leaden
against her shoulder that Nalini realised he had not moved for
some moments and that something was wrong. In her alarm,
without thinking, she shifted her position slightly, and as she did
so Apu fell forward between them. When they raised him up
they knew he was dying.

For some time they simply kept on going, impelled by the
momentum of what they had set in motion, the actions of the
living. Then Ravi pulled himself together and tapped the carter's
shoulder.

'Turn back,' he said hoarsely. 'Take us home.'

All the way back, on that never-ending ride, the carter kept
slapping his breast in sombre melancholy. Black, black day, he
intoned, what evil star had possessed him to carry a man so near
death? What misfortunes might not befall his family should the
stranger die upon his hands! At each cry Nalini flinched and
cowered and Ravi wanted to protect her from this chilling dirge
but there was no way. He sat stiffly, his arm held across Apu's

chest to stop him toppling forward. They had propped him up between them, because the way he had fallen they thought he would suffocate, but it made no difference to his loud, terrible breathing. It was not a satisfactory arrangement, for at every jolt the old man slipped forward, and they had to fight to get him up again, and when they had him up his head lolled and swung, hideously, with the motion of the cart.

'What's happened to grandfather?'

Again and again Raju turned to them with his question.

'He's not well.'

'Is he going to die?'

They did not answer him, and Raju knew that he was. Death would not have worried him, he had seen a fair number of dead animals and dead people, but this was not death but dying. It frightened him to see his grandfather like this, making these awful sounds, bumping and swaying in his seat like a lumpy ragdoll. His fear grew and made him tremble, and presently he began to whimper. Nalini heard her child and wanted to take him in her arms, draw her sari over his eyes and keep him from distress but she could not, she had to attend her father, wipe the froth accumulating on his black swollen lips and support him as well as she could.

At last they were home, and they lifted the mattress off Apu's bed and laid him on it on the floor. Ravi would have fetched the doctor but Jayamma restrained him, she knew the signs and so for that matter did he. Neither saw any point in incurring unnecessary bills.

By noon the following day it was over, and the women covered their heads. Ravi tried to feel, but there was nothing except emptiness. He stared at the old man, lying there like a dry, discoloured husk, and presently in a last gesture touched the closed lids, gently, feeling the skin cold and papery under his fingers. Then he went away, leaving the body to the women.

Jayamma washed her husband as she had done when he was ill, but it was the woman they had sent for who laid him out. She did it neatly and professionally, straightening the limbs, girding loins and jaw, placing betel-leaf in the mouth, and touching each

181

of the orifices of the body with camphor before wrapping it in the winding sheet she had brought. All the time she worked she crooned, a low lament that spoke of the fragility of life, the impermanence of all things.

Ravi listened, sitting alone in the workroom, listlessly fingering the silent Singer: and the emptiness in him enlarged and expanded, and somehow he was one with it, no longer an identity but part of this vast time and space that was in him and all around him, in which he floated and into which he was absorbed, so that beyond this state nothing mattered. Then the low monody stopped, and he was jerked back into himself, as abruptly as if the halter binding him to the earth had been roughly pulled. He turned, and there was the woman standing in the doorway, waiting to be paid by the head of the household. He, Ravi, the head of the household. He rose, wearily, already feeling his burdens, and the fringe of the infinity he had seemed to enter curled away and was as nothing he could even begin to understand—less than nothing, a mockery, a savage delusion. Well, he thought, he had always said it was claptrap, brought on, taught and used by old men—a conspiracy of old men to keep young men content with their lot, because they wanted no rebels in their midst.

And Apu? Yes, even Apu, he thought, lacking the courage to grab what he could in this world and compensating by wallowing in thoughts of the next. But hiding it. Disguising it all by calling it prudence. What kind of prudence was it that took whatever the world thought fit to give? The thoughts came crowding in—all the thinking that Apu's presence had checked, released by his death.

Someone was summoning him again, insistently: Jayamma this time, it had been Nalini before. Thangam was there too, with her children, but she had not brought her husband. Ravi roused himself at last. Other duties devolved upon him that he had all but forgotten. The wake. The burning ground. He got up and went in to Apu to begin his vigil, sitting cross-legged at the head of the bier where joss-sticks smouldered, their vapours blue and thin in the dim light of oil-soaked wicks burning in earthen lampions.

182

Chapter 30

A HANDFUL of ashes, people said . . . but it had been more than that, several handfuls, Ravi thought, staring down at the river upon whose waters Apu's ashes had been cast. He had done it himself, he and his son who were the heirs: body to fire, ashes to water. Yet after all these months he still found it difficult to believe that Apu was no longer there. His presence clung, in a way that sometimes impelled Ravi to physical movement as if to be rid of actual weights placed on his back. The illusion he could have endured, but unbearably irksome was the knowledge that he was inhibited by an old dead man, kept from the daring and innovation, the raising of his labour to a dignified level of just return upon which he had set his heart.

No one understood him.

If he put up his prices, said Varma, business would fall away. Ravi paid no attention. Why should he? Varma was a parasite, although since Apu's death he had shed some fractional part of his habitual indolence. He might know the artifices and wiles of parasitical existence, what did he know about running a business? Ravi dismissed his views, contemptuously but not too brusquely, for fear of being left single-handed.

Nalini, taking courage, said the same thing. He shouted at her. If he didn't ask for more how were they to eat? All Apu's savings had gone. Business had already declined. Were they then to live hand to mouth like those down-and-outs who cluttered up the streets? Nalini crept away, her eyes bright with tears; he had not been as rough as this with her before.

Ravi brooded on the dilemma, for dilemma it was. Should he raise his prices and risk losing customers? If he did not how could they manage, with orders nearly halved? The answer of course was to get more customers, more orders—but how? He almost laughed, thinking of Apu's efforts to secure his succession—the fawning, the patience, the ingratiatory attentions, the bribes and the inducements.

With all this, it was more than he could do even to hold on

183

to those customers he already had. A smouldering anger rose in him against the rich uncaring inmates of homes they had served cheaply and well year after year, turning away so casually now. Bitches, he thought, nothing mattered in their eyes, not death itself could match the importance of a dress being ready on time. A few days late, and you were out. It had happened to him more than once, and the first time had been the worst since it was the lady of the apples, an important customer, upon whose humanity, because of the apples, he had relied. But she had eyed him coldly, after keeping him waiting for an hour.

'The gown was promised for Monday last week,' she reminded him, 'not Monday this week.'

'My father-in-law died,' said Ravi simply. To him it was an adequate explanation, he even prided himself that the delay had only been a week, with most other people it would have been longer, they would not have come out until the mourning period was over.

The memsahib did not soften. These people, she thought, with their innumerable uncles and aunts and cousins who seemed to be forever dying—really they were quite impossible, impossible people inhabiting an impossible country. But if this cocksure young man imagined that she, who had lived so long in India, could be taken in so easily, he was very wrong. She said, shortly, 'Rather sudden, wasn't it? Besides I don't see why it should have stopped you working.'

Ravi was aghast. Work? How could he? Did this woman realise how they lived? the duties and ceremonies that fell upon the head of the house? In her community did they simply carry straight on after a death as if nothing had happened? As for suddenly—she must have been blind, he thought, less than human, more fool he to have imagined otherwise.

'It was not sudden,' he said, with a coldness to match her own, pulverizing the prudent image of Apu that formed in his mind. 'My father-in-law had been dying on his feet for several months.'

The memsahib felt uncomfortable. Now that he mentioned it she did remember the old man had been doddery for some time. Then she recalled her own ills. The dress had been wanted for a Saturday reception. Knowing India she had deliberately allowed a leeway of five days, but despite every caution and injunction he

184

had let her down, she had had to wear the same flowery frock she had worn at least half a dozen times before. But what did all this matter to this impudent lazy oaf impenitently squatting on her veranda? Obviously nothing, she thought, and now she came to think of it she did not like his tone either. It was part of something that was new, new attitudes of people in a changing country to which she never intended to be reconciled. Impertinence, she thought, and she said, frostily, commandingly, 'That will be all.'

Ravi went away. The words in themselves seemed senseless to him, an extraordinary phrase that memsahibs were fond of: but that it meant his services were no longer required was perfectly clear to him.

At least she paid him in full. The Indian memsahib didn't even do that. She was an important customer too, although she paid so poorly, haggling expertly until she had beaten him down to a level which few Europeans ever reached. Still, one could be sure of work there, for she had a large family of three boys and three girls who seemed to be constantly needing clothes. It was in cutting out a blouse for the eldest girl that he had slipped up. He had had to hurry, the garment being overdue, besides which he had never been very good at cutting. That was Apu's special skill, the foundation of his success as a tailor. He had striven to pass it on, but the craftsmanship of years could not be easily acquired, and though Ravi did his best both men acknowledged in their hearts that some skills could not be learnt. So was it his fault, Ravi asked himself morosely, staring at the ill-fitting back that ballooned so alarmingly at waist level, if garments did not turn out as well as they had done in Apu's hands? He tried to remedy the damage by putting in a few darts, but even he could see it did not really help. If it had been cotton or even silk, he would have gone out and bought a length and made it up to placate memsahib; but it was not, it was costly material, cloth-of-gold interlined with silk organza of hibiscus red.

The memsahib was angry. She shouted at him over her daughter's head, tweaking at the blouse where it did not fit.

'Fool! Wretch! Call yourself a tailor? A barber would have done better.' She advanced a few steps and would have buffeted him with the pattern book she held but he retreated. This infuriated

185

her further. 'Rogue!' she cried, 'You have ruined it completely, such expensive material, do you know how much it cost? Fifty rupees a yard, fifty, do you hear?'

He heard, and an anger grew in him to equal hers. Fifty rupees for one little jacket for one little girl, while of late they had not even been able to afford a few vegetables for the evening stew. He subdued his feelings then, but on his way home, after his dismissal, with his pockets empty, it lay like gall in his throat.

They could afford it, he thought bitterly, and other things too, for instance anger . . . they never had to swallow it as he did, they could show it, shouting as this one had done, or coldly with a sharp sarcasm like the English mem—and why not, since they had money and money was power. Money, he thought, with a craving that crawled like a disease in the bones and marrow of his body, if only, if only . . . and in his mind it took on the shape of a dark flame over which men crouched like opium-eaters to taste the savours of life.

Although there was nothing wrong with him, he ached physically as he lay down beside his wife that night. With Thangam's departure they had the whole room to themselves, he could talk to her as he had not been able to do since the early days of his marriage; but now there were no eager plans he could share with her, no visions, he thought with a pang, of new shiny bicycles with gleaming spokes, or soft beds laid over thick springy mattresses. All he had now were problems, which he wanted to load on to her without delay since he felt their weight so intolerably. So he retailed the day's events, dwelling on the injustice, on the humiliations heaped upon the poor by the rich that they were expected not to feel, and he spoke with the subconscious hope that she would be one with him, take his side and comfort him.

But Nalini was full of fears for the child she was carrying, she could think only of the money that was lost and what it would mean to them, and her preoccupations kept her silent.

'Well?' Ravi raised himself on an elbow and looked down at her. 'Haven't you anything to say?'

'What?'

'Anything at all.'

Under his probing, hostile gaze Nalini grew flustered. Her mind refused to lift itself out of the groove she had worn for it, she could think only of her fears and placatory words would not come.

'Should I have fallen at their feet?'

Still the words would not come. She lay rigid, suddenly afraid of her husband, unable to meet his eyes.

'Grovelled in the dust for their custom?'

He watched in a furious contempt—those eyes, scudding wildly like a terrified animal's.

'Look at me.' He could see her cringing and he compelled her, pinning her down by the shoulders, increasing the pressure on the thin bones until he saw her flinch and her eyes dilate and felt pleasure rising in him in a thick stream, felt the power that filled and flushed his body like a coming consummation. 'Now tell me.'

At last she managed to meet his eyes, and her face seemed to break, ravaged by ugly furrows where smooth flesh had been.

'No,' she sobbed. 'No, no, no,' on an ascending note that seemed to pierce his brain. He began to slap her then, sharply, blow after blow across her face.

Chapter 31

HE could not face his wife the next day, nor the one after. He buried himself in the workroom and from here he watched her covertly, noticing the extensive bruising he had caused, her downcast looks, the heavy way she moved about the house, and was eaten up by his misery. Work held no enticement; but he kept the Singer buzzing ferociously in an effort to work it out of his system only to concede defeat in the end.

He felt very much alone, estranged even from his son, for Raju had woken frightened in the night and in the morning had seen the results of what his father had done to his mother. He loved his mother, he loved her almost unbearably now that he saw her so cruelly hurt and he clung to her, not allowing even Ravi's shadow to fall across his path.

'Cheer up, man,' said Varma jovially, slapping Ravi's back. 'Everyone has these little quarrels, it'll blow over in no time.'

The cripple Kumaran said nothing; but it was he who went out and gathered the tender leaves of the *vadamadikay* tree, pounded it to a green paste and applied the poultice to the worst bruises under Nalini's eyes.

Jayamma at first was concerned for her daughter, but when she realized there were no real injuries she held her peace. In all the years of their married life Apu had never once raised his hand to her, but then, she thought, with the faint contempt she still bore her husband, which even his death had not expunged, in that way Apu had never been much of a man. She shivered a little thinking of Ravi's masculinity; and there was even the seed of a thought in her mind, though she would not let it grow, that in her daughter's place she would have welcomed her wounds.

In Nalini there was no room for anything but heartache—a dull pain, occasionally lit by flashes of fear. What had turned him into a violent stranger? From now on was it always to be like this? She wanted to break the silence, pull down the bleak wall that had come between them, but she was too nervous, too unsure of herself and afraid of his reactions. She could not even speak to him of her fears for herself, of the abnormal behaviour her body had developed and which she desperately hoped would cure itself through the sheer fervency of her wishes, so that it was not until Ravi, closeted in the workroom but more concerned with what went on outside, saw the blood trickling down her legs that he realized something was wrong.

He rushed out of the room. Whatever had tied his tongue dissolved, the words burst out. 'Nalini, what's wrong—the baby, are you—?'

Nalini was stooping down, furtively wiping drops of blood from the floor. She straightened up, startled, looked at him miserably and began to cry. 'I don't know,' she said, choking, 'I don't know what's happening. It's been like this off and on but it's worse now, it won't stop at all.'

He put his arm around her and supported her into their room, noticing how clumsily she walked holding her wet legs wide apart.

Someone to wash and clean her up, he thought, and he shouted loudly for Jayamma until he remembered she had gone out, escorted by Varma, to goggle at one of those accursed processions.

Rapidly he spread their sleeping-mat and pillow, aware that Raju had come in and was watching him in implacable silence, accusing him of this further ill to his mother.

'Go away,' he said roughly, unnerved by the child's hostility, 'Go and play with your cousins.'

'They've gone away,' said Raju flatly, but he left the room without argument.

They'd been gone a long time, Ravi thought, whatever had made him say that? Then Nalini claimed his attention. She was lying with her knees drawn up; her eyes were closed and she was moaning slightly; all the colour and strength seemed to him to have ebbed away, and he sprinted for the doctor.

The doctor said it was a hospital case.

The hospital kept her for a week. They stopped the flooding, stitched her up, and even managed to save the child. The doctor who told them appeared delighted. Her face was wreathed in smiles as she gave them the news and, more humane than any doctors they had ever known, she even found time despite her busy round to treat them like human beings. Ravi warmed to her; and she in turn thought what a pleasant couple they were, the girl as gentle as a doe but with a vast endurance, the man so civil and smart in his neat white high-collared coat. They could be symbolic of the new India, she thought, and sighed, because there were so many who clearly were not and would never be.

Ravi sailed home riding smooth on her euphoria. Nalini was out of danger: she would soon be home. In a matter of months their child would be born and was it to be said that a smart young man like himself could not support his family? He squared his shoulders and held his head high, his pride revived by the admiration he had seen in the doctor's eyes.

It was only afterwards, months later, after Nalini had come home, that it occurred to him to wonder if the disaster so narrowly averted would not in fact have been a blessing. It was a brief thought, flickering pale and evil through his mind before he stamped on it; but it left behind a turmoil, a sick self-hatred that made him savagely question his fitness to be assigned the dignity of a human being.

By now the bills had come in: the doctor's, the hospital's. Medicine was free, and there was no surgeon's fee, but because he earned, and was above what they classed as a low-wage earner, there was an in-patient charge. Ten rupees! he thought, staring at the pink slip of paper in surly disbelief; what did they feed her on, Nilgiri fruit and purest butter? In his exasperation he even asked Nalini, brutally, and was offended when she said, timidly, 'I couldn't help it.'

'Who said you could?' He turned on her. 'I asked you something quite different; did I say it was your fault?'

She made no reply. She had answered the implication rather than his actual words, and he resented it.

But he knew better than not to pay. He knew several poor unfortunates in his village, who had taken this simple line, and had just been bodily thrown out of their homes and left to wail in the fields. He shivered as these boyhood memories welled up, though it had not happened to his family because they had never had a home or anything to take, only a mud-hut. It was different now; having possessions had made him vulnerable. Not that they had very much, he thought, but what they had they could not afford to lose. So in the end he paid both bills, drawing heavily on the fund put by for current bribery expenditure.

When he had done so he experienced a huge relief that brought home to him how far he had come—or should it be declined, he asked himself—since his time with Damodar. In those carefree days, he thought grimly, he would never have allowed a minor thing like debt to sink its talons into his back. He would simply have flitted, as they knew to a fine art how to do, rejoicing that the rich had been bilked to the advantage of the poor.

But there was some cheer for him too, in that a buyer appeared for Apu's bed. He had coveted it for years, this bed with springs instead of strings across its frame, on which he had slept with his wife on their marriage night and for ten nights afterwards before Apu reclaimed it for his old bones. Now the desire for it was dead in him; it had been squashed down too often to survive. Besides,

190

with business dwindling there had to be sacrifices, the sale of whatever could be spared.

The buyer was deliberately offhand. He had heard of this bed; he did not really want one, but he thought he would take a look. Then he asked, delicately, about the last occupant, who he had been told had died. Ravi reassured him. The old man had, according to custom, been laid on the floor when he was dying; he had expired there. The mattress had been burnt; being an old man's you understand . . . The buyer did, in fact he and Ravi understood each other perfectly. For an hour or so they argued about the price—amicably, for each could see the other came from the same harassed class, although temporarily one was up and the other down.

In the end Ravi was eight rupees the richer. He nursed the coins between his palms with covert pleasure, feeling almost rich because the money was unexpected bounty, in the sense that it was not already accounted for, mortgaged to vanishing point even before its receipt. What should he do with it? Replenish the bribery coffers, he thought, already low because of sickness bills. But this thought brought forth such gloom that he pushed it out of his mind while he dwelt, harmlessly and idly, or so he thought, on what he would have liked to do. There were a good many things, and he thought about them all on his way to the Catholic Convent to deliver a finished batch of stiff white aprons.

He was on his way back when suddenly a thirst assailed him. He was surprised. He had not touched liquor for a long time, and although on occasions in the past he had drunk heavily, it had not left any permanent craving. But now he felt he needed a drink—a sociable one if possible, but anyhow a drink. After all had he not just concluded a satisfactory business deal, and was it perpetually to be nose to the grindstone for him? These belligerent thoughts helped, but not much. He licked his lips and felt guilty, while he wondered where to go.

Presently he made his way to a small cafe-bar that had once been one of his haunts.

There was no one there that he knew, even the proprietor had changed; but the familiarity of the place was soothing, like meeting old friends.

The bar proper was behind the cafe, you went to it through

swing doors that had coloured glass panes. It was a very small room, with two or three round iron tables from which the paint had long peeled, a bench, a few stools, yellowing pictures cut from old calendars pin-tacked to the walls. Ravi sat by himself with his drink—it was his third glass, for his thirst had increased since coming in. The gin was raw and burned his throat, for he had grown out of the habit of it, but it spread a warm sensation of well-being in him. Life wasn't all that bad, he thought, the important thing was not to let it get on top of you; and he hummed a little tune to show that he for one never intended to.

Next to him in a group sat three young men. They had been chattering noisily, taking no notice of him, but when he began singing they fell silent.

'Come on, sing,' he invited them warmly.

'Don't know it,' one of them answered, and he realised then that the tune came from an eight-year-old film hit, which he could date from his courtship of Nalini. The thought was deflating, for he had seen himself as a contemporary of these young men, whereas in fact he was nothing of the sort. These were gay carefree youngsters, eighteen or nineteen, and he was—why, he thought, with a seniority of less than a decade he might almost belong to another generation, and he could see they regarded him as such. What, he wondered, had happened to those years? the freedoms he had grabbed with such effort, that he now saw personified in these young men? Free men. Not only years lay between them: something more—much more—a whole attitude of mind, a wholesale shift of axis on which one's world revolved.

He rose abruptly, paid for his liquor and walked out. The effect of the gin was wearing off rather more quickly than he would have wished, but the smell hung on his breath. Nalini would spot it at once, he knew. She always did—he could tell from her face that she had—no matter how much he gargled or ate cloves. The very smell of cloves, even eaten without motive, was enough to raise suspicion. Not that he was afraid of her: it was the look on her face he could not bear. What should he do? He began to walk aimlessly and must have ranged far for presently he found himself outside the fashionable shop—miles from any place his sort might frequent—whose plaster models were sometimes dressed in clothes of their manufacture, though rarely now that Apu was gone.

He stood looking in through the large well-lit plate-glass windows, admiring the tall graceful models with their waxy pink skins, their huge eyes and long curled lashes of real hair. Near these motionless figures, casually disposed on little carved tables and stands, was a whole array of luxurious accessories. His trained eye took them in with professional keenness: the beaded waistcoat jackets, the little velvet boleros, the long graceful stoles with fringed. and embroidered ends, the large monogrammed hand-stitched bags. All of the finest workmanship, all of the finest material, the costliest silks and brocades and velvets.

And all, he thought, for other women, always for *their* women.

They expected it of one. Took it for granted that people like himself were without feelings; that they could be surrounded by riches like this without ever seeking to possess a part; could handle the rich cloths, work on them and fashion them into beauty, and then hand them over dumbly, as if one had no desires, no yearning ever to lavish something of this opulence upon one's own women—as if one were some kind of eunuch. And they never questioned this expectation, never once to his knowledge had anyone done so. Why should they? To them it was the natural order.

He began to walk away, rapidly, driven by the whips of suppressed anger. Before he had gone far it seeped away, he became more concerned about his gin-smelling breath and the effect it would have on Nalini. She wouldn't say anything, he knew that. Sometimes he wished she would, then he could bawl her out. She would be silent, and refuse to meet his eyes, and this would make him want to hit her. Perhaps he had, he thought confusedly; his head began to fill with a curious buzzing and he had to sit down.

Beaten her, he thought above the buzzing that blurred his thinking but not sufficiently. Taken it out on her, not many times but more than once, certainly more than once. How many more? He crushed his head between his fists, doubled his hands and dug the knuckles into his temples, but he could not extract the information he wanted. It was there somewhere, buried in his head, but it stubbornly refused to come out. All he could remember was the feel of her body, flinching under his blows, and the sight of her puffy tear-stained face; the rest ran together indistinguishably. At last he rose, unsteadily. I love her, he thought, but I beat her. Is it her? Is it me? What is wrong?

When he reached home the door was locked. His wife, the bitch, he thought, but no, it was not like her. He rattled the snake-handle again, vigorously, and this time heard the bolts being lengthily withdrawn.

Jayamma was waiting for him inside. He could just make out her plump form in the darkness, standing grimly arms akimbo and blocking his further ingress.

'So it's you at last.' She spoke shrilly, in the domineering tone she had not dared to use since widowhood had lopped her status. 'Loafing about half the night, can't even keep your family but—'

'Let me pass.' He kept his arms clamped to his side, afraid of what he might do to her once he started.

'—what do you care, so long as you can drink we can starve, only what one expects from a street arab—'

'Let me pass I said.'

Now she was silenced, her hands flew to her mouth. He saw the sudden movement, the way she shrank against the wall, and it gave him a venomous pleasure. Roughly he strode past her to his room.

Nalini was asleep. She had fallen asleep waiting for him for the hurricane lantern was still alight, though from the strong smell of kerosene in the room he could tell the oil was running out. He bent to lower the wick—it tended to grow ragged and char if allowed to burn dry; then he stopped, held by the sight of his wife. She was lying, almost sprawling, on her back, her legs flung wide and abandoned in the unconscious effort to relieve her heavy late pregnancy. It was to be twins, they had been told . . . she was carrying them high, her belly huge and swollen under the disordered folds of her sari. Her limbs, by contrast, seemed childlike and thin, like sticks. . . . How did women stand the strain, he wondered, the waiting, the discomfort? Nalini never complained. He had seen her fighting for breath, or covertly rubbing oil into the livid stretch marks on her abdomen, or arching her back for relief against the cold granite grinding-stone, but he had never heard her complain.

Neither of the ills of her pregnancy, nor of him.

He did not want to think about that. He unbuttoned his high-collared white coat, dragged on a flimsy half-sleeve shirt and lowered the wick whose flame had begun to putter wildly.

But he felt sodden and heavy as he stretched himself out on the sleeping mat beside Nalini.

Chapter 32

BECAUSE of complications during labour Nalini had to be taken to hospital. To avoid the hefty bill he had been confronted with before, Ravi brought her and the babies back as soon as he decently could and the doctors would agree, which was thirty-six hours after the birth. Nalini didn't seem to mind. She got up obediently, knotted her few things together in a cloth, and they came back through the dark maze of streets that was the city at night carrying the swaddled babies, both girls, one apiece.

Afterwards she took up her household tasks without fuss. She looked ill and strained, but it did not seem to affect her capacity for work, for coping with house and husband and the imperative demands of the twins and Raju, and things were more or less as they had been.

Sometimes Ravi noticed that she did not look too well and it troubled him, but he had evolved a method of staving off his worries by promising himself to think about it later, and into this uneasy slot he dropped Nalini. Mostly he did not even notice. It was a relief to have his wife around and about again and available, and he did not often go beyond this simple feeling.

To both of them the twins were an endless delight, and at least for the first year of life sealed off from all other anxieties and preoccupations. They were dimpled, bonny little babies and, after

195

three months of howling at the universe, extraordinarily amenable. Ravi found them enchanting. He played with them by the hour, since there were many hours which he could not fill with work; and was flattered to ecstasy by the rich response he evoked, their blissful wriggling when he bent over them, the wide smiles with which they greeted him. Sometimes through them he remembered Nalini, who had borne them, and at these times he was gentle with her, as gentle as he had been in the early days of their marriage. At these times too the old feeling crept over him—the feeling he had wrapped himself in for consolation when confronted and crushed by Damodar's wealth—that this was what life was about, not the riches and luxuries upon which he had once, long ago, set his heart. But it came rarely, and was not always convincing.

These brief interludes with his family were the cherished part of Ravi's life that he used like a blunderbuss to annihilate the other, ominous part that was concerned with the harsh business of earning. Sometimes he succeeded, refusing to think about it until it had slipped beyond the edge of his consciousness. Increasingly, as the months went by, he found that he could not. In self-defence he got into the habit of saying: I'll think about it later, but the cumulative effect of deferred thinking was a little worse than immediate encounter might have been, so that he added a vain regret to his worries.

For things were not going well. They had not gone well since Apu's death, but now the downward incline had become a steep slope down which they were slipping with increasing momentum. At nights, especially, the image took on a terrifying near-reality. Again and again, vividly, he pictured them all hurtling downward, always downward, toward destruction.

How could he halt the slide? Ravi did not know. One notion that presented itself was of putting everyone on starvation rations until he had paid off the loan—taken out on the security of the Singer—and accumulated a bribery fund; but he knew if he did there would be sickness bills. Besides he could not risk Nalini going dry, and having to buy milk for the babies, and the household was too close-knit for selective rationing.

It was a real hardship, having to find the money each month to repay interest on the loan. And it was a real hardship not

196

having the money to sweeten his way past the watch-dogs of compound wall and bungalow into the memsahib's presence.

The old man's palm-greasing made abundant sense now, although how much, he reflected, he had resented it at the time! Still, resentments grew ancient and faded, ideals had to be felled. What troubled him now was not having to bribe, but not being able to do so. Yet his mood was not one of final resignation, there were moments when he rebelled fiercely, quarrelling bitterly with those whose pockets he knew had been well lined in the past. Once they came to blows, he and the supercilious chokra who denied him entrance, refusing to allow him to show the memsahib the swatch of samples he had brought in the hope of securing an order.

Their loud altercations brought the other servants running—the cook, the mali, the peon, the ayah. It even penetrated the house, forcing its master to abandon the sybaritic silences of his air-conditioned cell and emerge into the enervating heat of high noon.

'What is the matter?' He spoke irritably.

'He won't let me in.' Ravi was trembling. 'I have samples for memsahib but this—this *banchot*—'

The eyebrows went up. Ravi controlled himself. '—this servant of yours won't let me see memsahib.'

'Memsahib resting, sahib.'

'I told him I would wait! He wouldn't let me, he—'

'Is a no-good man, sahib.' The chokra's voice rose; he had retrieved his turban and held out the uncoiling evidence. 'He knocked it from my head, sahib!'

'It fell off! I—'

'—hit me, sahib.'

'—began shoving me, that's why!'

'—lie sahib. He hit me, then I—'

'He hit me first. I told him to take his dirty hands off me.—'

'No sahib, he first, ask mali, ask—'

'I haven't time to listen to servants' squabbles.' The master shouted above them all. 'If you want to quarrel get out, get outside the compound and quarrel there do you hear?'

He stalked away. The servants began hustling Ravi out. He went; what chance had he now, if he had ever had any?

This was not the only hazard. A greater loss was the encroachment on his preserves, on customers who had been served for decades by the old man and would probably have been content to go along with his heir but that competitors presented themselves, or were enticingly presented by interested servants. It would never have happened in Apu's day. Each among the older craftsmen had his own territory, houses and areas over which after long years he had carved his name and which the others scrupulously respected. This was the old tradition: muscling in was new.

Apart from any of this, the old man had too firm a grip on the situation: he would have out-classed and undercut, ruthlessly, and destroyed any rival. Ravi could do neither. He could not see them all living on finer margins of profit, and a handful of years' experience could not match up to the skills acquired in a lifetime.

What price now, Ravi thought bleakly, the old man's efforts to get his successor recognized? The plotting and planning, the ingratiatory introductions, the well-timed shove to bring him to the attention of memsahib? Poor Apu had miscalculated. To the memsahibs all working men looked alike, and even if they recognized a face—familiar, old and faithful as Apu in some sentimental ferment had imagined it—they did not give a damn.

In his heart of hearts Ravi did not blame them, or those brash new men who hung around the big houses hour after hour hoping to steal his customers. It was the way life was: a jungle, as he and his kind knew all along the line from birth to burning ghat. In this jungle one had to fight, fiercely, with whatever weapons one had. Or go under.

These were old thoughts, reviving from long ago, dredging up others with them. There was the waterfront warehouse. A night raid, some of those fancy materials the memsahibs craved and still couldn't get, and Ravi knew he would instantly be reinstated in all but a few of the houses he had lost. There were spiked deterrents. If he were caught—his skill diminished, his contacts lost—he would be gaoled, and then what of his children? They would be worse off, he thought bitterly, if such a thing were possible, than ever his father had left him.

What price then his pledge to his unborn children, sworn even before he had turned his back on his village hut, that he would bequeath them something better than the pious hopes and the suspect morality that old men had offered the young, sending them fleeing from their villages in droves?

More frightening even than gaol was the thought of being caught by the thieves from whom he was thieving. They were merciless: they had to be if their rigorously organized society was to survive. He recognized this, but it made him shiver, even now so many years after his last criminal flights.

There was one other deterrent: his silent promise to Nalini, long before she became his wife and at spasmodic intervals thereafter, to give up his old life and be worthy of her. But this was a pale watery thought, hardly alive, which passed almost before he could take it into consideration.

So what should he do? The curve of his thinking came round to the start and clicked, full circle.

He tried putting it another way. What should he do that he had not done? This was easy, the answer was nothing. He worked hard, he rolled every delicate hem and hand-stitched them, he delivered garments on time or as much on time as he could. What had he done that he shouldn't? Here the ground was more perilous. Sometimes he thought, perhaps I priced myself too high. At other times he furiously endorsed all he had done and would do again, for was there no such thing as equity, the dignity of the labouring man, a price worthy of his hire? But he never said any of this audibly, for he was wary of the sardonic Varma, who would certainly ask him where he had learnt these high-sounding phrases.

Chapter 33

No one, neither his wife, nor his mother-in-law, nor the two whom he dominated in the workroom, endorsed the truths and beliefs that Ravi had grafted on to his life, and to which he still desperately clung. Let them look askance, be silent, turn away—

they were blind unthinking rats, who could not see the end of the alley down which they were scurrying.

Still, time went on, and as month after month their resources dwindled the grafts that had taken so well and upheld him so strongly grew stunted and feeble. He seldom, now, proclaimed the inviolable rights of human beings as he had once done, nor spoke of the retribution they were entitled to exact if these were violated; he felt rather less passionate over them, and accepted passively much that he knew he should have forcibly rejected.

It diminished him. He knew that too but felt too beaten to reach for the justice and dignity that had once given him stature. Only occasionally a slavish suggestion, or more often some pert observation of the sardonic Varma, raised a flash of his old spirit.

'You're losing your grip brother, you know that?'

'What in hell do you mean?' Ravi rounded on Varma. His reactions to family needling were still fairly healthy.

'Not so high-horse,' Varma elaborated. 'Fat's melting down, as they say. It's the rich fat globules in the body turns to pride in the head. The condition was well marked in you, brother.'

'And so it ought to be,' said Ravi, allowing his eyes to travel scornfully up and down Varma's flabby body, 'in anyone who calls himself a man.'

He spoke out of conviction and felt the better for it, but the exhilaration that followed this exchange soon gave way to a deep depression, and he stroked his thin arms and wondered if men were indeed meant to be humbled, bit by bit, body and spirit together? At length he rose. It was still far from dusk but he put away the work he was doing, sheeted the Singer, and went to his family quarters.

Nalini was suckling the babies, one at each breast. He spread a mat and sat opposite her, and presently felt a slight pressure and realized that Raju had come in and was sitting close up against him. He would hardly have noticed the child except for his mood: but now, his perceptions spun fine and nervous, he glimpsed a disturbance in the boy akin to his own.

'Are you all right, Raju?' he roused himself to say.

'Oh yes, father.' Raju answered as if he were a little surprised to be asked.

He was a sturdy, self-sufficient little boy, making few demands

200

upon any of them; and yet, Ravi thought, it must be difficult for him, left with only a receding memory of the girl-cousins who had played with and cosseted him, now forced to yield his beloved mother to voracious strangers who grabbed such unfair slices of his parents' attention. It happened to all children of course; nevertheless it moved Ravi to see the small forlorn figure sitting so patiently by his side, and on an impulse he swung the child on to his lap, cuddling him as he had done in his baby days.

'There! More comfortable than the floor isn't it?' he said with a forced, robust joviality.

Raju nodded, but warily, for he did not often see his father in this gentle mood. Presently he said shyly, earnestly looking up, 'Do you still like me?'

'Of course I do.'

'Why?'

'Why?' Because you're such a rascal, Ravi was about to say, pushing his joviality along, but then he saw how still and anxious Raju was and he answered seriously. 'Because you're my first-born child. Because you're my only son.' He felt the child cling to him, but by now his other preoccupations were crowding him and he had no further time for Raju. Loosening his hold he set the boy down, turning his attention to other things.

As Nalini retreated into silence, so Jayamma's loquacity grew. Most of it concerned the past, long rhapsodies of the life she had known, the balconied house of her parents, the good living that had been hers with Apu, before the children came, before he grew ill and Ravi took over.

'Never less than two kinds of vegetables per day,' she said to her daughter. 'You remember, don't you? Curds or buttermilk every evening. A tumblerful of coffee in the mornings, with rich thick milk and—'

'Don't,' said Nalini.

'Why not, child? No harm in thinking of nicer things is there? I used to make such things for you at Pongal and Deepavali, *ladus* and *hulvas* and—'

Nalini was winnowing rice, which nowadays she found so full

201

of stones and chaff. She made the grains swish and rattle vigorously up and down on the winnowing tray to try and kill what her mother was saying. But the damage was done, her mind flew to her babies, who cried after every feed for the milk she could no longer give them, turning speechlessly away from the boiled-rice mush she offered instead.

She would, she thought, have to buy more than the ollock of milk sanctioned by Ravi which they all had to share, though it was not really enough for five of them. It would mean asking him for extra money, and perhaps he would shout at her, she thought, take her by the shoulders and shake her while he shouted as he often did; and it made her feel afraid and a little sick. She frequently felt this way, and she wondered, a little bleakly, what it would be like to have no fears at all, like a memsahib say, who could not possibly have any fears about milk or money or the future, or the heavy hand of a moody husband.

'Nalini, are you listening or not?'

'I'm listening.'

'Perhaps I wronged him,' said Jayamma, staring queerly at her daughter. 'He was a good man, your father ... perhaps I did him wrong ... but he was an old man you know, he seemed old to me even when we married. . . No matter, it is over.'

Though it was over she worried the subject, dwelling on his goodness to her and suppressing her part in the affair. Their present privations lent a glow, comparative and exaggerated, to' her easy living before Apu died. How well they had fared, such good food, such nice clothes—her voice penetrated the workroom, rousing a wry amusement in Varma, who had even longer experience than Ravi of the old man's parsimony.

Ravi and Varma shared, warily, this cynical view of Jayamma. They were more warmly united in their opinion of Puttanna, who from being called that worthless good-for-nothing was now invariably referred to as that absconding scoundrel.

'If only I could lay my hands on him,' growled Varma, 'I'd make him disgorge—never mind how, I'd make him.'

When eventually, however, news trickled in of his return to the town, they discovered him living in a penury a good deal harsher than their own, having gone through most of the old man's life-savings, and with little to show for his long absence beyond two additional babies. It did not matter. They had let him go: had baulked at ugly measures, and not known how else to make him disgorge. The old man himself had not known. Now there was little left. So no matter, no matter.

The discovery of Puttanna, and a sight of the one room he rented crawling with babies and flies, put a seal upon their knowledge that there was no going back to easier times for any of them. If anyone had nursed the prospect of sponging on Puttanna, it died swiftly now: and the Ravi household became as exercised to keep out the Puttanna brood as Puttanna was to be allowed to eat through on his own what little was left of the old man's money. The family code that Apu had broken, booting a relative into the street, remained broken: and whatever half-hearted steps they might have taken to mend it, circumstance prevented them taking.

Jayamma spoke occasionally, not too convincingly, of the tragedy of a family split as hers was. 'That I should live to see it!' she would cry—a periodic exclamation that they suffered with equanimity, knowing full well the slender regard she had for her elder daughter and her husband, as well as her own robust love of life.

But even Jayamma, for all her vigour, and for all the faith she increasingly lavished on charms and amulets, had no great hopes for the future now. Nevertheless she still went off alone, and came back with little secret packets, and they still strung round their necks the tiny metal cylinders she had procured for them which contained the written incantations that would change their luck; but her original fervour was lacking. Perhaps it was only something to do: a small positive action to thumb defiance at the fate that was forcing them to their knees.

It was a relentless process. Ravi looked on, and when the sight grew too nauseous diverted his gaze to the thought which he kept embedded in his mind like a valuable pearl: that there was always Damodar. When he could no longer manage he would go to Damodar, work for him as he had done before, and all would be well.

Chapter 34

ONE day, mulling over household finances, Ravi decided to keep accounts in the hope of managing better on what he earned. Apu had never done so; he could not read or write and besides, as he had been fond of saying, he could carry it all in his head. Ravi had no such facility, and the laborious work was not to his liking. He settled to it only because of the speed with which his hard-earned money seemed to vanish, and to confront his wife and mother-in-law with evidence of what he had convinced himself was their bad housekeeping. But his figure-work was shaky, never having advanced beyond the elementary level at which only his father had marvelled (and this bitter truth too Ravi now swallowed). He could never tell for certain where the money had gone —there were always wide gaps between income and expenditure totals—and anyhow knowing where it went was no help. And Nalini, for once stubbornly standing by her rights, refused to accept the charges of extravagance or bad management he flung at her. This was how his money had been spent, she told him, and she took him through the list item by item, having inherited the ability from her father for this exercise. So much on rice, so much for milk, this for the extra milk, this for dhal, chillies, vegetables, soap, oil, charcoal, firewood. . .

Ravi listened in exasperation. All this proliferation, just to keep alive. He was angry too, that his wife should challenge him, and at one point in the recital he stopped her.

'Twenty rupees for rice? Last month it was eighteen!'

'The price has gone up.'

'The month before it was seventeen rupees, here, look!'

'I know.' Nalini was trembling. She had twisted her hands together and he could see that they were shaking. She kept her gaze fixed on the book he had thrust under her nose.

'You know! Can you explain it?' He flipped the book up, so that it caught her across the face. 'In heaven's name we don't eat any better do we?'

'No, we don't do any better because, because—' Nalini was

gasping a little from the blow—' the price goes up and up, you see, it goes up all the time, they say it's because of the bad harvest—'

Bad harvest. It was the echo of a knell, sounding away down the years, part of a pervading consciousness—his own, his father's and his grandfather's. Ravi felt very tired. He thought he had cut clear of all that, very simply by walking out; now here was the slimy tentacle reaching out from the sodden paddy-fields of endless abject villages to clutch at him in the middle of a town.

'They don't even give you good measure.' Her husband's silence emboldened Nalini to continue.

'What?'

'So many stones,' she said, and he saw she had cupped her hands and filled them with rice, and all among the long white grains were small black stones, freely sprinkled in like mustard-seed. One paid for this corruption, he thought, staring dully at the speckled grain. You asked for food, and they gave you stones. Suddenly he swept aside Nalini's outstretched hands, violently spattering rice on the floor.

'You buy this rubbish,' he cried, 'with my money. What's the matter with you, is it that you think I'm made of money, or have I really married a cretin?'

'I try, I do try.' She was crying, great ugly tears rolling down her face. 'But it's the same everywhere, I swear to you—' She had muffled her voice, at any rate it came to him from some vast distance which ate up the words, he could hear only the whine.

All day long, whine, whine, whine.

He walked away from the noise, and became aware of a round accusing face that was Jayamma's, and the smaller accusing face of his son, and a disapproving, gnarled nut of a face—why, he thought, even that little runt thinks I'm a bastard, and for a moment he felt like laughing but then swivelled round abruptly and seized the narrow crippled shoulder.

'Get out,' he said distinctly. 'I'm done with feeding and keeping you for nothing. Thought you had a safe berth didn't you? Well, it's over. You can get out and stay out.'

The words had a familiar ring, which he placed afterwards. It was how memsahibs spoke. Power-conscious memsahibs. 'That will be all,' or 'You can go now'. Well, he thought, Varma had

been wrong. If he could talk like that he was not yet crushed, the
fat globules still rode high in his blood and he could still show
them who was master of the household. Master of his own house,
if nowhere else. But this taste of power, he knew, would have
been sweeter, as sweet as the memsahibs found it, if he could
have exercised it on someone or something less puny than
Kumaran; and this nagging ferment soon turned the honey into
gall.

In the nights Ravi walked the city alone.

He walked the streets that had once been as familiar to him as
the back of his hand, and felt a strange harsh freedom in the
anonymity into which he was once again swallowed. Here in
these narrow twisting lanes and alleys the night pressed close, no
longer fended off by the blue-vapour lamps of the thoroughfares,
and he was no more than a shadow, one of many that merged
away into the deeper shadows thrown by the clustering houses
and jutting derelict walls.

Who was he here? He did not know, he did not care, no one
cared. He walked silently, in his bare feet like a padding cat
guided by instinct and memory, and the darkness was a soft pall
except where it was rent by the sudden flare of a match lighting
up a beedi or the swinging radiance of a lantern slung from a
pole in a recessed doorway.

'On your own, brother?'

'But not friendless.' He answered automatically, it was the
familiar challenge unaltered over the years; and passed on unmolested, knowing again the camaraderie of the outsider: not the
vagrant hulk washed up by society, but the unbroken rebelling
outsider who had opted to come out. Yes, he thought, that was
what he would do: come out against them, the forces that grudged
him a living, denying him the status of breadwinner and householder and shrinking him in the eyes of the family. That was the
answer, to declare war as Damodar had done, to go out and take
what a man owed it to himself to have.

What were those things? He laughed derisively, thinking of
the pretty fancies of his youth. Bougainvillaea swarming up
whitewashed walls. Sprung beds. Shiny spokes on a new bicycle.

No, what he wanted now was embracing and fundamental. Pride. The power that earning conferred on a man. The decency of a fair reward for his work. These were the preoccupations of a man, not those tinpot triflings of his youth.

Where, for that matter, was his youth? Gone, he thought, walking softly in the darkness that pressed down like a pall; gone very quietly and beyond recall. When he looked at himself now, propping the cracked glass upon the window ledge to do so, it was a middle-aged man that he saw with sagging contours and downward-scored lines on each half of the face lopsidedly presented by the cracked mirror. How old in fact was he? He did not really know, but going by the confused memories of his long-dead mother he guessed getting on for thirty. As things were that was more than half way through. And then blackness and silence like this. Or would he be re-born, as he had been taught, and believed he would in his less depressed states? But not like this, he did not want to be re-born into what he was now. Something better, he thought, his mind beginning to wander. Perhaps as a priest, well-fed, housed and cared for by his flock whether Hindu or Christian. Or a sahib. Or a police inspector—

A powerful hand fell on his shoulder.

Speak of the devil, he said to himself softly, and at the same time he ducked, wrenching his shoulder round to free himself. But the hand was experienced, not out of practice as he was. He found himself held.

'You. What's your name?'

'Ravi. Ravishankar.' He answered at once, obediently.

'What are you up to here?'

'Nothing. I'm just walking.'

'It's a criminal pastime.'

He wanted to laugh, but he controlled himself; that big boot would hurt, landing on his toes or square on the base of his spine. He said, civilly, 'What is a man to do, turned out of his own house? That old hag of a mother-in-law insists on it every time—seems a child can't be born without its father doing penance.'

It was an inspired lie, but he knew it sounded true. That was something these last years had done for him: given him the accents of a respectable man.

'You live here then?' The grip relaxed fractionally.

'Not far.'

'Where?'

He named a street at random, thanking his gods he knew the area well enough to do so.

'Where in the street?'

'At the second cross-roads, first house.'

He was free, the hand dropped from his shoulder. He could have run, but he no longer wanted to; it was the powerful accusing grip that had earlier impelled him to panic and flight. Strange, he thought, that the old fears should ride so strong... or had they revived since his alignment with Damodar? Was he so aligned, beyond the point when thinking stopped, was he prepared actively and finally to commit himself? Not yet, he thought, padding lightly through the blackness; not quite yet, but the time was coming.

In the mornings there were the threadbare students. He saw them aimlessly pacing the streets as he himself did, looking for a job, for often now his mornings gaped open, empty of work. Thin young men—younger than he was, with bony wrists and raw knuckles to their hands, who dressed neatly in faded drill and clipped pencil and pen to the breastpockets of their clean frayed shirts, and hung around the government offices and the municipal offices and the revenue offices with the same look on their faces that he saw on his own in the morning. The look of no work: the common look.

Sometimes he despised them, these refined young men who were having their education slapped back in their faces and seemed not to know what had hit them. Mostly he identified, joined in the common bewilderment, knew what it felt like, how it was to wait and at the end of the day to go home wanting. It amused him now —a slight wry amusement—to think that once he had thought he could compete with them: he with his elementary school smatterings of this and that, pitted against men fresh from the colleges, bearing the seal of these great institutes of learning. And these young men waged as fierce a competition as any he had known. He had seen the queues that every vacancy produced, the long waiting lines, the fine-drawn patience that suddenly snapped, turning these mild, well-bred men into screaming agitators. Well, he thought, why not? They were only human beings like himself after all, though they came from a class different to his own and belonged to a world far removed from it. They had the same human feelings.... To them too the city was a jungle, he had witnessed their violent assaults upon it too often to doubt that. A man-made jungle, as full of snares and traps and unkept promises for them as for him and his like. No wonder they fought, he and they. But the battle had never yet been waged as a joint one, and until it was the day of reckoning would not dawn.

When he plied the Singer alone, or, worse still, returned from his solitary night walks, the whole house seemed to Ravi to be unnaturally silent and empty, peopled though it was by his wife, himself, his three children, his raucous complaining mother-in-law. At one time it had sheltered Puttanna and his brood, but they, and Apu, had long been gone. Perhaps, he thought, it was Varma's company that he missed, that made him feel like this — fat easy going Varma with his indolent hands and his sharp ready quips, his emollient blandishments of Jayamma, who had heaved himself up from a life seat of sloth and gone the same day as his strange paramour.

He did not know where they had gone, though he suspected that Nalini did; but when he questioned her she was evasive.

'I suppose you think it was a crime to throw him out,' he challenged her one day.

'Varma can manage,' she answered, with what he considered a maddening obliquity.

'The other,' he said impatiently. 'You know I meant the other.'

She did not reply. He shouted at her and she appeared to shrink, seemed actually to become smaller, shrivelling like an old woman in a way that nauseated him.

Often now he took refuge, when he could, in his children. They did not always allow him such refuge, preferring to go to their mother, whose love was constant and serene where his was volatile, subject to disconcerting spurts and quirks. Raju, especially, seemed not to know how to take his father. He approached

209

him uncertainly, ready to return his smiles and affection, equally prepared to withdraw if rebuffed, but never any more with that triumphant confidence with which he had once joyously hurled himself into Ravi's arms. Such a warm, loving child, Ravi thought with an evanescent regret; it was a pity he had to change. Perhaps it was natural: they did say boys turned to their mothers. And it did not occur to him to look into himself.

The girls were different. They ran to their mother most, but if he wanted and really tried they would come to him too, eagerly, climb on to his lap and chatter to him. They were pretty little girls, he thought, taking after Nalini and as pretty as she had been when he first knew her. Two-and-a-half now, they toddled sturdily around the house, flashing the heart-shaped silver pubic shields girdling their loins that their grandmother had seen fit to buy them. Their grandmother: not their father. Interfering bitch, thought Ravi; as if he could not have done as much for his own daughters! Eighteen months old, the incident still rankled. He had meant to buy the shields—Nalini had already spoken to him about them. But that month he had paid the bill for electricity, and the next there was the house repair account to be settled, and the one after his earnings were down—and while he was trying to get round to it there was Jayamma, saying how unseemly it was, once girl-babies began to walk, for them to go about as these two were doing, sounding off with her parrot-cry of shame-shame two and three times a day until he savagely shut her up. It was then that she went off silently, her lips tightly pursed, and bought the shields, out of her own small secret hoard of money saved from Apu's day, so that he could not even accuse her of wasting the housekeeping money. Ravi knew he could not afford gestures; otherwise he would have torn them from his babies' and flung them in the gutter.

His babies were now little girls, with soft brown bodies almost as chubby and dimpled as when they had been infants. How long would it last, he wondered in those sick stretches of his unemployed time ... children folded so quickly, one drought had been enough to produce a whole pack of skeletons, and the burning-ground fires were hardly ever out. But those were bad days, his village days. It would never come to that here, he thought, and felt his thin arms for reassurance. Thin, but not skeletal. The twins chubby, rice in the store-room. That old, grim kind of suffering was out, and in a cold sweat he swore he would see to it that that was where it stayed.

Chapter 35

WHEN Ravi sheeted the sewing-machine on the evening he was going to Damodar he felt little secret spurts of pleasure inside him, as if he were jumping off the treadmill that he worked every day of his life to begin a journey piquant with possibilities.

Damodar was a big name now, as Ravi soon discovered. The men who told him laughed when he claimed acquaintanceship, and for long cool moments he saw himself through their amused eyes: an insignificant shabby-respectable figure with stooping shoulders and the red-rimmed, near-sighted eyes of an overworked tailor. Once he would have winced. Now he no longer cared; a man could not help what he looked like, nor the odd shapes into which his work forced him, whether tailor, blacksmith or beggar. What mattered was to remain unchanged within, and after the most stringent scrutiny Ravi felt that he, the real he, the man within the shell, was not the abject little tailor he saw reflected in their cruel gaze.

Damodar knew it too: the thought rejuvenated Ravi. Otherwise would he have picked him, trained him, maintained links which, however tenuous, he had never finally broken? Even now, long after the time when his allegiance might conceivably have been useful, Damodar acknowledged the pull. He had sent for him, the summons came within a few days of Ravi's first fruitless efforts to make contact. It was only then that he knew where to go, for suddenly, or so it seemed to Ravi, the world to which he imagined he had instant entry by reason of his past—this world sealed itself off from him. Closed mouths, bland eyes, stone walls met all his enquiries, until he cursed the respectability he had donned which had grown into a second skin, barring him contacts vital for him to make.

211

No second skin masked Damodar. He was as he had been, save that the attributes which had always been there were now ingrained, a conscious endorsement in his later years of values and attitudes which he had early developed as best befit ing the society in which he lived. Ravi admired him. He too had known, quite early, what he was up against, the stand that he had to take to prevent himself going under. But he had vacillated: had allowed his strength to be shorn from him while he mooned over pretty pictures of a cosy peaceful living which in the end had proved a delusion.

So here he was, ten years late, sitting at Damodar's feet on the wide tiled veranda of his house, waiting to be told what to do.

Unlike many who had grown rich as he had, Damodar had not felt impelled to move to more salubrious districts. He stayed where he had made his money, among the corn and grain merchants, the distillers and importers, preferring the pungent air of these turbid streets to what he might have breathed in the rarefied casuarina and hibiscus areas. But his new house was no less imposing. It stood on the site of a dozen tenements, which Damodar had bought and torn down, scattering its dazed inmates without qualm. Built to dominate, several storeys higher than any of its neighbours, with a wide frontage on to the teeming street, the edifice had been planned as a bold salute to success; and the price per square foot of the land on which it stood mocked that of any snob building in the classy areas.

This last factor had been as strong as any in influencing Damodar's decision to stay.

Ravi wondered in passing how Damodar's ownership of what was almost a landmark could have remained unknown to him. It could only have been, he thought, because he had no contact any more with those who would have known; and also, despite his faith in Damodar, he had somehow not connected him with quite this magnificence. It awed him. Since being summoned he had passed and re-passed the house several times, hardly able to believe that Damodar owned it, and was waiting for him inside. Now he said, warmly:

'It's a splendid house. It must have cost a lot.'

'It did.'

'I can imagine.'

212

'Can you? Really?'

'Well, it's not difficult to *imagine* things, is it?'

'I wouldn't have said it was your long suit.'

'Oh well,' said Ravi, 'what's the use? I used to imagine lots of things, I suppose I had a pretty good imagination once . . . now it just seems a waste of time.'

'Dreams?'

'Or anything else . . . just a bleeding waste.'

Damodar leant against the bolsters on the low divan and drew on his hookah. The liquid bubbling notes seemed to Ravi to symbolize the cool repose awaiting the steadfast man, the man who kept his course unswayed by the weak babblings of myth and conscience that poured into his ear. He said: 'I shouldn't have pulled out.'

'No.'

'I didn't think it would come to this . . . I mean if one works one ought to be able to live, it isn't too much to expect, is it?'

Damodar said nothing, allowing the younger man to come to his own tortured conclusion. Ravi knew what he thought. One-eyed peasant. Credulous fool, believing any kind of crap.

He said: 'It's not that I don't make a living, I do . . . only it's not really living, one just goes along and all the time there's something or other building up that you know is going to topple sooner or later and hit you hard but—'

'Debts?'

'Well of course,' said Ravi, 'but I wasn't meaning only that, it's the whole atmosphere, the uncertainty, the—'

'Many debts?'

'Yes, but—'

'How many?'

'Well,' said Ravi, 'I've borrowed on the sewing-machine, I have to keep up the interest payments . . . and the rent is mounting up . . . and the light bill . . . and there's no water, the sewers have cut the water—' He stopped. He had not meant to say any of these things, it had just spilled out. He said, stiffly, 'I don't know why I'm going into all this. It won't interest you.'

'It does interest me.' Damodar's voice was level, void of any inflection that might have been a guide to his mood, and without

213

it Ravi found it impossible to continue. He sat quietly tracing with one bare toe the design along the tiled veranda floor, a pattern of swastikas to signify well-being, neat, shiny black swastikas like little running men showing their heels. Outside in the street, three storeys below, a string of bullock carts went creaking by, rear lanterns swaying in flickering arcs, the bullock's eyes a luminous green in the darkness.

Damodar said, abruptly: 'What are you going to do?'

'What shall I do?'

'Go back.'

'Where to?'

'Go back to your village. It's more your size, you're not fit for anything else.'

Ravi flinched; his face began to burn, as if Damodar had deliberately struck him. Well, he thought, now he knew what the mood was going to be, the cold deliberate flaying which Damodar was so skilled at, and his anger rose, surmounting even his awe of Damodar, these imposing moneyed surroundings.

'The village,' he said, 'what do you know about it? It's not fit for cattle, not even the sort of cattle you think I am. I know, I was born there, I tell you anyone who survives it is *twice* the man you are, yes, even a man like you that's climbed to the top. You know *nothing.*'

'Maybe not.' Damodar's face was taut, his light eyes ugly slits in a mask of anger. 'But I know what a city's like. I've been scavenging in it since I was so high, ever since they found me crawling on a garbage heap and threw me right back onto it. Well, I've got by. It drags the bloody entrails out of you before you do but I've done it. Now I'm at the top, and I don't want any little runt like you telling me what the slime round the bottom's like.'

They were both dark with anger, trembling, each with the memory of his own scalding experience to match against the other. Then it was over. The locked combat ended without either giving ground, more by a slackening of the high tension which had held them; and in the quiet, suddenly, briefly, they were equals.

Damodar said: 'We've both been through the mill.'

'Yes.'

'Different kinds of mill.'

214

'Yes. No. The grinding down is the same.'

'Maybe. One comes out of it differently though.'

'I suppose so.'

They were silent: Damodar, whom success had underwritten, and Ravi, whose dangling feet were nudging rock bottom. Both of them brooding, looking down the long sunless vistas of their past. At last Ravi said: 'I didn't know . . . about your being an orphan.'

'I don't know that I was.' Damodar spoke grimly. 'But if my parents were alive they were pretty good at keeping out of the way, God curse them.'

Ravi was shocked. He had never felt like this about his parents; contempt for his father certainly, but never this jagged hate. He said, awkwardly: 'It was a rough deal.'

'Forget it. I didn't mean to tell you.'

'Perhaps they couldn't help—'

'I said forget it.'

Ravi closed his mouth and sat waiting until presently Damodar said: 'It didn't make much difference to me, in the end. Nor to you.'

'No.' Ravi half smiled. 'Except when I wanted a nice wife, then my father was a great help, he—' He stopped, stiff with dismay, remembering too late Damodar's women: the succession of sleazy mistresses coquetting in yashmaks and veils whom one never more then half-glimpsed, shadowy figures lounging behind curtains that closed off the private rooms, or mounting or descending from rickshaws.

The silence dragged on, like barbed wire stretching between them until abruptly Damodar leaned forward and snapped it.

'So he helped you to your nice wife.' He spoke briskly, his thin lips curled in sarcasm. 'Splendid. How is the good woman?'

'My wife?'

'You haven't two fires to poke, have you?'

'You know quite well,' Ravi spoke in a low voice, striving to control the humiliation that was tightening his throat, 'I can't even support one.'

'One plus three?'

'Three children and my mother-in-law,' said Ravi. 'And another child on the way.'

'What are you going to do?'

'I don't know,' he said. His face was beginning to work and he rose and leant over the parapet, the tang of the street below sharp in his nostrils. 'I don't know,' he said again, harshly, and turned to Damodar. 'All I know is I'm through with what I'm doing, through with toeing the line, through with getting kicked in the teeth for my pains. I want something better. I'll do anything to get it.'

'You've said that before: ten years ago. You didn't mean it.'

'I mean it now. Ten years is a long time.'

Damodar clapped for the bearer and the man came up with a load of bottles and tumblers. There had been nothing before: no sherbet, not even a jug of iced water. On a tray with the drinks were betel leaves and twists of tobacco. Joss sticks glowed in the window embrasures.

Ravi drank, and the anger that burned his belly raw died away, the knotted muscles of his limbs and aching throat relaxed in a soothing golden warmth. The struggle was over, he thought, help was at hand, soon he too would be sipping the sweet care-free life. He cradled the feeling to him, lost in the voluptuous foretaste, and somewhere through the warm haze heard Damodar's words like the sound of a harsh insistent drum.

'... corner the grain market ... not all that difficult ... people have to eat, lakhs to be made ...'

'What did you say?' He stumbled back from euphoric distances, hearing the high wild notes of frenzy of his own voice.

'I said I needed men to handle the distribution. I've bought to the hilt, the lorries are ready to move in ... we can start pushing up the prices the moment they've unloaded. Job's made for you, there isn't a dump in the city you don't know—'

Ravi rose unsteadily. He felt like retching but he controlled the spasms and went down to the street. Somewhere inside him he could feel the shrill seeds of hysteria sprouting and he knew he could contain them for the moment. But only for the moment.

216

Chapter 36

DAYS, weeks, a month. Ravi lay sluggishly on his mat, thinking.

Should he go in? He owed them nothing. He owed nothing to anyone. He was alone in the jungle, and in the jungle one fought. Or died. The knowledge was an incandescent light at the core of his being like the single eye set in the forehead of a demon. Lying, sleeping, waking, even in his frenzied acts of love its beam scorched and excoriated him.

What held him back? Had respectability entered his soul, smirched it with the shoddy morality of a hypocritical society? Slough it off, join hands with Damodar. But they were dirty hands, hands that grew rich by squeezing people's throats. People like him. People like his wife who stood two hours each day in a line outside the grain shops, a line that lengthened daily as the shortage grew. When the lines were really long the money would come rolling in. Not peanuts, Damodar wasn't interested in peanuts: real money. All he had to do was to get in on Damodar's side, before the government pegs came down, while the money was still totting up. Get rich and get out.

He could not do it.

If he didn't he perpetuated the rottenness, this vicious living that had pared them down to one meal a day. One good meal, his mother would have said, clasping pious hands together thankfully, indicating the rice, the dhal, the vegetables, the thin chilli-water brew. One good meal, and he had to watch his children sucking their fingers, grown silent and anxious, long before the next one was due. This one good meal was not enough for him. He wanted more. It was his right, his children's right. In the heavy ferment of the close hot nights he swore in their name he would see that they got it.

And all the time upright or supine the invisible tether jerked and writhed, making him sweat as if he were jigging in some hell. As if he were still tied to the land. As if the frayed bleeding cord still held, still pulsed although he had hacked at it so long, prohibiting him from tampering with its fruit. The grain. Rice. Pale brown secret kernel. Hard labour, sweet life. Anything else, he said to himself. Anything else. Each cry was a soft muffled explosion that marked, but did not end, the long dialogue in his brain.

'Won't you try and eat a little?' Nalini stood by his mat, her drooping eyes going over and past him, never once looking him square in the face.

'There's never more than a little, is there?' He grunted at her, irritated by her constant attentions, these solicitous wifely attitudes.

'I don't think we do too badly,' Nalini said, and the bright false note jarred his nerves.

'Well said.' He sneered at her .'But you don't really think that do you, you think what your mother thinks, that it was never like this when your father was alive.'

Nalini bit her lip; the skin was pale where the sharp white edge of her teeth cut down. She said: 'It's the heat wave. I've never known it as hot as this. It pulls us all down.'

'Yes, the heat,' he muttered, turning on his side, feeling his sweat-drenched shirt shifting its clammy suction to fresh patches of his body as he moved. The heat, he repeated to himself with a sense of unreality. What was he then, a memsahib accustomed to spending the hot weather in the hills?

'Here, put this on, you're soaking wet.'

Nalini handed him a shirt, a soft thin threadbare mull, clean and freshly ironed. He had seen her wielding the iron, packing the heavy casing with burning charcoal taken from the *sigri* and as carefully replaced. Well, charcoal was expensive, not to be lavished on ironing their own clothes; why did she want to bother with it anyway? Nevertheless he liked the smooth cloth next to his skin and he sat up, stripped, dropped the shirt he had taken off in a sodden heap on the floor and slipped into the clean one.

Nalini squatted beside him. She produced a fan and began to fan him, sending stale waves of air drifting past his face. It wasn't, he noticed, the old palmyra fan that Jayamma used over the cooking fire, blackened with smoke and the handle burnt

218

where the flames had licked up. No, it was another, a fancy one of pleated silk with a peacock painted on it and a flowing silky tassel.

'That fan,' he said, 'where did you get it?'

'Apu gave it to me a long time ago. I came across it the other day.'

She was a bad liar; her skin went patchy when she lied. It was uneven now, dark and pale in places. He grasped her hand, his heart thudding with his mad suspicions.

'Who gave it to you?'

'I told you, Apu.'

He gripped her wrist, and the single thin glass bangle she wore broke. His blood, hers, scarlet, spurted and seeped between them, but he did not let her go, and the fan was still in her hand.

'You're lying.' He shook her wrist until the fan dropped. 'Who gave it to you—one of your admirers?'

Her mouth was working, but she did not reply. Her breath came in short, high, frightened gasps.

'You bitch,' he said. He picked up the fan and crushed it; the fragile bamboo ribs splintered between his fingers, poking through the silk like thin white bones. He threw the broken mess down.

Nalini bent over it. She was crying, her tears fell on the pale silk. 'It was so pretty,' she said. 'No one gave it to me, I bought it. I don't know why, I knew it was wrong when money's so short. But it was so pretty. Why did you have to destroy it?'

He did not answer. He would not even look at her.

'You go out,' she said, crying, 'at night, for hours. They say you meet this man. He's vicious. Everyone knows he's vicious.'

He was doing something to her, he could feel her soft twisting flesh, but he could not make her stop.

'Now its you too. I've tried not to believe it, but I can't any more. You've changed, he's changed you.'

He let her go.

Somewhere in the ether their voices reverberated.

I can't go on, I can't.

Get out. Get out!

Round faces, startled eyes. Tears, and the long grey furrows they wore down cheeks. Children snuffling. The raspberry sounds, the fluids of grief. What did he care? All he asked for was silence, ah yes, silence. He went out into the teeming street to welcome it.

When he came back it was dark and the house was quiet. In his room the blood and shattered glass, the mangled fan, had all been cleared away. The mats were neatly laid, the lantern filled and lit. There was no sign of his wife or children. Jayamma was in the kitchen, not doing anything until she heard his step and then she began stirring a half-empty pot.

'Where is she?'

'How should I know? You told her to get out.'

'She was here when I left.'

'When I came in she had gone. That's all I know.'

That broad back, turned on him. How much it could say! He left her and went to the courtyard, opened the tap and put his head under it, forgetting that the water had been cut until he heard the hollow gurgle. But the *hunda* was full. Nalini, or some-one, must have gone to the municipal tap down the street to fill it. He washed, pouring beakerfuls over his head. The water was cold, not stale and warm as it came from the taps in daytime; it seemed to clear his head a little.

What should he do now, go after her? Think first. Think clearly. what he should do and say, otherwise it would only be another shambles. It would be easier if he could think it out on his own, alone, without his mother-in-law brooding like a buddha in the kitchen.

By himself, alone.

There was the sanctuary, built on the roof it seemed in another age, by him for himself and his wife.

The rope-ladder was still there, looped over a hook in the wall and forgotten, clogged with dust, cobwebs stretched between the rungs. He tested it first; it held, and he climbed up and gained the roof. It was not as dark here as it had been in the house. A sliver of pale moon lit up the gables, laid a faint sheen on the floor. Still lashed to the supports was the thatched shelter he had built for Nalini, nothing now but torn fronds that flapped rasp-ingly in the wind. The khus-khus blind was completely gone, not

220

a shred left to show where he had hung it, that blistering day, to protect them from the glare, he and his pregnant wife. She had appreciated him then, had liked all he did for her, had been kind and loving and they had been happy together, here in this very spot they had been happy.

And today she had left him. Gone off, not a word, leaving him with his troubles. Forgetting the duties she owed him, the duties of a wife to her husband. This was where she should be now—here, beside him when he wanted her, not where her fancy took her. Where was she now? Bitch, he said, bitch. He climbed down quickly, his breath coming faster.

Jayamma was locking up; he could hear the bolts being rammed home. He came up behind and gripped her shoulders.

'Where is she?'

'How should I know?'

'You do.'

'I've told you I don't know. Now take your hands off me.'

'No,' he said and laughed at her. 'Why should I? You've wanted it for months, for years. All the time you lay with your husband. Every time you looked at me.'

'Ruffian. Thug.'

She was struggling. He held her and his excitement grew with her movements; her arms and breasts were soft and pulpy under his hands.

'You like it,' he said, his mouth rough on her nipples, bringing them up hard and erect. 'Do you think your body doesn't give you away? Do you think I don't know how you have been starved?'

'Guttersnipe.'

But her face was luminous in the moonlight, her eyes wide and brilliant, the whites showing, closing, and he was lost, in soft enveloping flesh that tossed away past and future, wiping out pain and unhappiness, and all his waking and sleeping terrors.

Chapter 37

In the morning she was gone and he was glad. He did not want to face her, to admit his carnal knowledge by daylight; he did not even know how he would conduct himself. All he felt was a wild revulsion for the incestuous lust that had overwhelmed him, a sense of uncleanness almost physical that drove him to strip and scrub down without perceptible amelioration.

The empty house made it worse. He trailed through the quiet rooms, his mind disquieted, feeling the stillness like a criminal accusation. Had he, then, driven them all out of it? He, Ravi, who had worked and supported them, and seen his own ambitions wither in the sustained blast of earning a joint family living— could he be responsible? Yet they had gone one by one: the cripple, whose deadweight he had refused to carry, and Varma who had followed him, and Nalini who had not even left him his children—

He would get her back. If he had to scour every street in the city he would do it. It might not come to that. The neighbours would know, the neighbours always knew. Some wouldn't talk, but some would be only too happy. . . . He pulled on his shirt in nervous haste, camouflaged the Singer against a surprise sortie by his creditors by laying it on its side and burying it under the bedding, and was looking round for other portable possessions that needed concealing when he heard the door open.

Nalini, he thought, and his heart began to hammer. But it was Jayamma returning from the early morning marketing, following her usual routine while he, magnifying her wrong, imagined she had gone for good.

'Where are you going?' She put down her basket, regarding him direct and unabashed. As if nothing had happened. As if passion was unknown to her. The difference, between day and night! He said: 'I'm going for Nalini. The neighbours will know where she is even if you don't.'

'Neighbours,' she said shrilly. 'Haven't you created enough scandal without that? Are you out of your mind?'

'I must have been,' he said, imagining she could only be thinking of the one thing, his sin of the night bearing harshly on him. 'Forgive me.'

'What for—last night?' she said, and stared at him. 'Do you think I care about that? Who cares what goes on between four walls? It's the public scandal that breaks one in two, you roaming all night, and creditors at the door every day.' She wiped her eyes. 'It's the scandal.'

He made to go, but she stopped him.

'Nalini,' she whispered. 'Don't go round asking. She's gone to her sister, anyone except you would have guessed. Where else could she go—' her voice began to rise shrilly again, '—with three children and not a pie on her? Not even the housekeeping money—even that you didn't give her this month.'

He went away, the loud voice trailing him, through the door and out into the street. She cared for this. The sin that stained and discoloured him was nothing to her. Invisible, so long as she was not seen committing it. No sight, no sin. Respectability, he thought, the sense of betrayal like alum on his tongue: so low, a piddling little wall fit only to be kicked down.

Puttanna and his family lived in one room and one veranda. Ravi did not know which room and which veranda, he had never visited them before and had only vaguely listened to Varma's descriptions. But the whole tenement knew, and a dozen tenants came out to guide him, fingers pointing dizzily past tier upon tier of rooms and verandas to an eighth floor of the block. She's there, they said to him, gazing at him with sympathy, with frank bold curiosity. What had she done? What had he done? And they shook their heads and clicked their tongues, and some ran along the passage with him to show him the courtyard where the stairs began, and some accompanied him up the stairs. At the third floor there were five of them; at the sixth, two, both out of breath. When he reached the eighth he was alone.

Eighth floor, turn right, go round the corner, it's a back room. He followed their directions, walking softly in his bare feet, and rounding the corner caught sight of her through the open doors of the room.

She did not see him. She was sitting on a string-bed, her head in her hands, her unkempt hair falling over them. Black thick hair, wavy from constant plaiting, with silver strands in it. Her wrists bare of bangles, bare like a widow's, and a thin row of scabs where the glass had drawn blood. On the floor beside her Kumaran, the cripple: gravitated to this shelter, such as it was.

—He beats me. Her soft voice.

He beats me, I don't know why. For nothing at all.

—Don't fret. Kumaran, his tenderness that was like a woman's. Don't fret any more. It was a bad moment, it is over now.

—But all the time: why does it go on all the time? Is it me? What have I done? What have I not done?

Her bewilderment, her pain, spilling out.

—I try and try, I swear to you I try but it makes no difference. He's angry with me. All the time, I don't know why. I can't bear it any more.

—Because you're tired. Worn out, unhappy. Stay here, rest here, you and your children. Your own blood sister, you have nothing to worry about any more. When you have rested it will not be so bad.

—If only that were true.

—It is true.

—If only it was like it used to be. In the beginning. We were happy then.

—It is a passing thing . . . who can hold happiness?

—But still . . . just to hold it once, only for a little while, just to feel what it was like. . . .

He did not want to hear any more. He went and stood in the doorway, his shadow falling across the room, but it was Thangam who saw him first, Thangam who sat in a far corner attending to the children, his and hers, her sharp eyes ready for misdemeanours, her tone as sharp as he remembered it.

'So you want her back, do you. You're like all men, you think—'

'She's my wife,' he said clearly, and ignoring them all—Kumaran and Puttanna, Thangam, the children—not really seeing them at all, his vision narrowed down to one—he turned to Nalini.

'Come,' he said, and she rose at once obediently.

224

Chapter 38

IT was, for a while, like being back at the beginning: so much so that Ravi felt a profound, disproportionate sense of relief as if he and Nalini were really starting anew instead of settling for an uncertain and wavering copy of what had once been theirs. But the balance was precarious. He had to be scrupulous, where once he could have been carefree, and the light squabbling which had given their marriage tart piquant flavours had now to be measured arguing for fear of ugly splits. Still, by comparison it was happiness. For both of them a kind of happiness.

Ravi found a new job, hemming sheets for a hospital. It was a poorly paid job, but it was a new hospital and there was plenty of work. He brought home bolt after bolt of unbleached calico, and took back, five miles each way, heavy piles of cut, washed, neatly hemmed sheets.

With these additional earnings he managed to keep pace with house rent and food bills, although the backlog of debts and arrears remained as heavy as ever. Even here he thought he saw daylight. A little more pinching and scraping, another twist of the screw, and he could begin paying off capital and interest which made such heavy inroads into his earnings.

In the evenings, now, he sat with pencil and paper working out economies. It absorbed him, as if he were engaged in some complicated game of skill which required him to pit his wits against an invisible, merciless adversary: and it blotted out the rank malaise he had known, lying on his mat totting up in barbed anguish what his rejection of Damodar's offer had cost him.

'We can pay off ten rupees a month, I reckon,' he said to Nalini, and sucked his pencil. 'That is if we can manage as we are doing.'

'Of course,' Nalini agreed, and thought of the coming baby.

'Ten rupees a month,' Ravi went on, 'that means we shall be clear in two years, say three at the most, and then—'

Nalini listened to the optimistic recital and hated him for it. She knew the pit into which he would cast himself when these

225

dreams fell to dust, dragging them all through hell with him. She said: 'Of course, it all depends.'

'What do you mean?'

He knew very well the two imponderables that straddled most lives: whether one would earn, whether what one earned would keep pace with rising prices. But still he had to ask, and resented it when she answered.

'If things remain stable,' she said. 'Rice—'

'I know.' He cut her short. He did not want to talk about it, he did not want to be reminded. He would have resisted all knowledge of the vicious manipulations that were squeezing grain prices up, submerging Damodar's confidences in the darkest pools of his mind, but for the fact that his money bought less and less.

Insidiously, week by week, the price crept up. Then one month it shot skyward.

That month he knew that whatever he did there would be no surplus. He also knew that if he did not run he would slip back, and it was a prospect he could not endure. Not now, not after so much. So he went day after day to the hospital, bringing home the heavy bolts of calico, taking back the finished sheets, working late into the night because of his driving fear that cheaper, quicker labour than he could offer might be found.

While he worked Jayamma sat yawning in a corner of the room, waiting for him to finish so that she could sleep. She slept in the workroom now, for the monsoon had wrecked a fair section of roof over her room, dislodging several tiles and cracking as many more. Ravi had carried out some sketchy repairs, as much as he could afford, but more was needed. When it rained the water came through, the walls were weeping with damp. Jayamma dragged the trunk containing her saris and jackets into the centre of the room, complaining bitterly that her clothes were never dry, refusing downright to sleep in the room until the roof had been properly sealed. Her joints were swollen with rheumatism, which she shrilly blamed on the damp; and the occasional help she had given Ravi with the machining, or trips to collect and deliver work, ceased wholly.

'Haven't you done yet?'

'No.'

Jayamma sighed impatiently and cracked the swollen knuckles of her hands. She could not sleep, she said, until the Singer stopped clacking; he could hear her mumbling peevishly all the time he worked.

'How much longer will you be?' she asked again.

'I don't know.'

'I'm tired.'

'So am I,' he said, 'so am I.'

At midnight he stopped. Jayamma was asleep in the corner, slumped over her bedroll. He woke her, so that she could not complain next morning of having sat up all night, put out the lantern and went to his room.

All he wanted was sleep; it was his one vast yawning desire, to fall on his mat and black out. But Nalini was awake, kneeling up and arranging the cover over Raju, filling the room with furtive rustlings that set his teeth on edge.

'What is the matter?' he said to her tersely.

'Raju,' she whispered. 'I think he has fever. He had earache all evening.'

'Don't fuss over him,' he whispered back, 'for heaven's sake go to sleep.'

She lay very still and in a few moments he was sound asleep.

Raju's whimpering woke him in the morning.

'What is it?' He sat up, rubbing the sleep from his eyes, looking round for Nalini to take this chore of sick nurse off his hands and then realizing she was in the courtyard coping with the twins.

'My ear hurts,' said Raju, snuffling again. 'My head too—here, and here.'

Ravi glanced at his son, his mind on other things.

'Well, have an Aspro,' he said, 'Tell your mother I said you could.'

Raju brightened. Aspros were something of a treat. They were doled out very sparingly and only when the pain was really bad, and they usually made you better.

Ravi had a quick sluice, drank his coffee and went on his way.

He was anxious to deliver this last batch of sheets and be paid for it, for rent day was near, he wanted to count his earnings and see where he stood.

He had not done this in Apu's lifetime, still less before; he had simply earned and spent. But now it had become an obsession with him, figuring out these sums which showed if he were standing still, or how far down he had slipped.

He was ending his calculations that evening, full of anxieties, when Nalini came in. It was rare for her to interrupt.

'Raju's earache is worse,' she said. 'Perhaps we should send for the doctor.'

'It won't work out,' he said, looking at her owlishly. 'We shall have to cut down on something. I don't know what.'

'Raju,' she said again. 'He keeps bringing up. He won't even let me touch him, he screams. I don't know what's wrong with him.'

Ravi put away pencil and paper, switching his mind to her problems with difficulty. 'Earache is always painful,' he said. 'Give him some more Aspros, he'll be better in the morning.'

They all slept badly. Raju moaned fitfully throughout the night, and Ravi had also to contend with the little sums that grew magnified in the darkness and taunted him. He woke feeling muzzy, and was not appeased by the anxiety on Nalini's face.

'He's no better,' she said worriedly, indicating the sleeping child. 'I think a doctor—'

'A doctor,' he cried, 'What are we, memsahibs or something to send for a doctor for every ache and pain? Will you pay his bill? Five rupees before he even steps out of his house!'

'I know,' Nalini's lips began trembling in a way he knew so well and hated, 'but it may be serious. I—'

'We'll see when he wakes,' said Ravi. 'Don't drive me to distraction. I've said, we'll see when he wakes,' and he flung out of the house.

In fact Raju never woke properly again.

In a way they were glad, because he suffered so much pain.

The doctor came and examined the child. He questioned them. Treating meningitis with Aspros, he thought, my God, these peasants. He rebuked them, sharply, for not calling him earlier,

228

pondered on whether to move the child to hospital but decided against it, wrote out a prescription and left.

Ravi kept watch by his son.

Nalini had to think of her other children, she could not let go. Ravi had no such lifeline to hold him. All of him, his whole being, was concentrated upon his sick child. His earlier obsessions —work, earnings, the equations that never worked out, the leaking roof and the empty water-taps, all had dwindled away to remote distances: their light reached him, but only to kindle a glimmer of pale astonishment that these things should once have concerned him.

Two days and three nights. He was aware of darkness and light alternating, but with no pattern that he could discern, time sometimes telescoped, and at others hideously expanding. Somewhere in the middle Raju opened his eyes and said, echoing some distant memory of childish heartache, 'Do you still like me?'

'Of course, my son. I always have, I always will. Do you have to ask?'

No answer.

'Why do you have to ask? Answer me.'

No answer, only those hazy eyes, slowly closing. How deeply sunk they were, dark hollows, the face was too young for such deep hollows, too young to take them.

'Why do you like me?' The eyes had opened again. Child's eyes, look into them and feel your heart break. So dull with fever, with pain. What kind of a being could inflict suffering on a child?

'Because,' he said huskily, his throat raw, 'you're my son. My first-born, my only son.'

When had he last said these words? Long ago, in another age, thinking of something else he had absentmindedly proffered them. And Raju had clutched at them and been comforted, grateful for these crumbs of his father's affection. All he could offer: a few crumbs. My God, my God, Ravi cried to himself, and he bent close and said again, 'Because you're my son! My beloved son!'

But Raju could not hear. He had withdrawn, his mind dispossessed, his body jerking in convulsion. Terror was beating at

229

Ravi, paralysing wings, but he fought it off and gathered his child to him and held him tightly, feeling the kicking muscles and nerves as if they were joined to his own tortured body, not putting him down until they ceased.

Then the convulsions came more frequently, exhausting him, but he did not move until presently Nalini came in and he turned to her, blindly, but felt only a stiffness, she had nothing to offer him except her stiffness. Then he went out, into the loneliness of the courtyard, and prostrating himself on the ground begged for his son's life until Jayamma's voice halted him.

'Yes, pray,' she said, harshly. 'Pray for him, not for yourself.'

'What did you say?' He raised his haggard face.

'Pray for him to be taken,' she said. 'Have you no pity?'

He stumbled back to Raju and sank down beside him. Hold fast, just for a little while my son, all will be well. Small body, racked. Fingers curled into closed fists, tightly. How much they had done, these hands: a hundred lively skilful things although they were so small. And the mind that had directed them, where was it now, bright, sturdy, suffering, wandering? He did not know. How did one tell?

Raju lay quietly in between spasms; but as darkness gathered in the room he began to scream, short sharp cries, and a quivering wait for the membrane of silence to rupture again. Then at last Ravi prayed, not for himself but for his child to die; and towards dawn there was a last convulsion. Ravi held his son in his arms, tightly, crooning to him to take the terror away, until it was over. He would have gone on holding him but Nalini touched him, and turning saw the tears rolling down her face and then he knew, and laid his child down.

'My son,' he said gently, 'my son.' His face was wet. He wiped it with his hands so that Raju should not see before he bent and drew up the covers. He hoped Raju could not hear him cry: it was unfitting for a man, which was what he had wanted his son to be; but whatever he did he could not check the hoarse sobs that rose in his throat.

Chapter 39

SOMETIMES, after Raju's death, he wondered if his mind were affected from the erratic way his memory worked, scoring certain events deeply into his mind, clouding others over.

Very clear was what the doctor said, and his smart young assistant agreeing with him. That because you had two already and one on the way the loss was less. And going on: that because you had a dozen, and because you were poor, you could not care that much for one. How wrong they were, how wrong. Saying so much, knowing so little: not even that a child is a child whatever.

And Nalini, with her stony passive rejection of him, their precious new beginning already ended; and a confused memory of saying to her: Did I—? Was it my—? and her silence. And saying to her, with a queer obstinate clarity: I don't blame myself for not getting the doctor. I blame them. *Them.* Society. Guilty of casual murder.

And the man in the white coat, cutting him off because hospitals could not wait for overdue work. Telling him: I have a wife and two little girls and my wife is pregnant. And hearing him say: I'm sorry, but I have a hospital to run, and we have no more work for you.

And the woman's anger; throwing back in his lap his botched work, commanding him to go. Telling her: I have a wife and two little daughters—and she cutting him short: I have heard all these stories before, excuses, excuses!

The ferment rose and boiled and reduced itself down to one thing, and he knew what he must do. Go to Damodar, do his bidding.

No more blocks and restraints. No more loyalties and responsibilities for he had none. Neither to the land nor to people nor to their society nor to society's betraying ramshackle codes. Only one thing: to renew the oath he had taken on the lives of his children to gain them their rights; and this time to keep it.

231

'I've come,' he said simply to Damodar. 'And this time it's anything.'

'Anything,' said Damodar. 'Are you fit for anything?'

'I beg you,' said Ravi. (Where was his pride? All of it gone?) 'I beg you, do not desert me now. Whatever you say, anything. The grain shops—'

'That's over,' said Damodar. 'You're too late. I've pulled out. I pulled out a long time ago.'

Voice and face, both were neutral. What had he expected—a flicker of pity, acknowledgment of an old allegiance? Ravi did not know. But he had to find out: he could not go away now, like this, carrying despair like a dead foetus inside his body.

'There must be something else,' he said, and his voice was thin, like a reed. 'A man like you . . . there must be.'

'There is,' agreed Damodar. 'Only—not for you.'

'I'm no different,' said Ravi, trembling. 'I'm what I was when you wanted to use me. The same man.'

'Are you?' Damodar reached out and chucked him under the chin as if he were a woman, an ageing harlot unused to any but the most derisory attention. 'Well, look again, I don't know what you'll see but—'

'The same, the same,' said Ravi, and his teeth were chattering. 'The same.'

'—I see nothing,' said Damodar. 'You're empty. No heart, no spleen, no lights, no guts. Something's been at them.' He began to laugh, a high sharp ugly laughter. 'What was it, termites?'

Chapter 40

IN the afternoon there was a crowd. It formed slowly. Ravi was sitting by the gutter outside his house, throwing stones into the viscid stream, and he watched, desultorily. Presently someone hailed him and he got up and joined the fringes of the assembly although he did not know where it was going or what it was angry about. Its numbers swelled as the day wore on; periphery became the nucleus, and he was the centre of a seething mass.

It moved, this mass: in an unwieldy shapeless amoebic way, but with a strong purpose. When he was joined to it and breathing with it Ravi learnt where it was going and what it meant to do and he acquiesced. Not incandescently, as the crowd did, but in some pale corner of his mind he acquiesced.

In the market-place they stopped. There were loudspeakers here, a quartet of them clamped to a standard in the middle of the square. A voice issued from it: a strident indistinct voice that ordered them to disperse, alternately cajoling and threatening until silenced in mid-sentence as the wires were cut.

A hush fell; and in it people could be heard shuffling their feet, and coughing and clearing their throats, and these were the last small ordinary sounds before the concourse fused, and became an entity of its own over and above the individuals who formed it; and with an ascending roar of triumph it wheeled away from the square and began converging on the grain shops.

Ravi felt the force, he could feel himself being sucked into it, but part of him was still benumbed, he could not quicken as a young man would, he could not manage the act of surrender. But he went with them, marching alongside students and workmen, and petty craftsmen like himself with the same fires burning their bellies.

Only his, having burned longer, was dying.

'Rice today, *rice*. Rice today, *rice!*'

A lone jubilant voice rose, and was taken up at once and swelled to a pace-setting chant that stepped up its frenetic beat until within sight of the objective they were jog-trotting, shoulder to shoulder, their feet pounding the earth in rhythmic unison.

But word had gone before them, spreading along an expensively cultivated grape-vine and alerting traders and merchants. The grilles were down. Iron grilles, steel shutters.

The concourse halted, baulked, demoralized; then in its extremity threw up a leader.

'To the godowns! Make for the godowns. This way!'

Chaos retreated. The crowd re-formed and followed and Ravi was borne along with it. He did not know where he was going; so long as he was with it it did not seem to matter; but presently old memories stirred, disjoined conversations overheard while he walked the city numbed, and then he knew. The godowns were

233

those closed echoing sheds in the congeries behind the docks where rice was stored.

By the government some said, as famine reserves.

By hoarders and price-fixers, whispered others, a curse upon them, death to those who crucified the living.

It did not much matter which; that was where they were going, to those secret dumps whose secret rumour had breached; and as word filtered down a tension grew, as if screws were being tightened all along the invisible cords that connected them together.

Ravi knew the area well. He had served a strenuous apprenticeship in it, it lay like a map in his mind. He could have led them to exactly where they wanted to go, only he was no leader. Would never be a leader, now, did not want to be. He followed.

When the godowns were reached the crowd halted again, puzzled, suspicious.

No steel shutters here, no iron grilles.

No guards, no police, only a wavering line of frightened watchmen.

Had the owners relied upon the secrecy of their enterprise, the anonymity of their sheds, to protect their stores?

Or had they beaten the grape-vine, surprised the police, by the speed of their advance?

Was it a trap, about to be sprung?

The seconds ticked by, loaded, heavy, and suddenly began to race as a loud cry fell like a whip on a bare back.

'*What are you waiting for? Forward!*'

With an answering roar the crowd obeyed, bearing down upon the shed with its full massed weight. Ravi felt himself hurtled along by the impetus, yet falling behind like flotsam too water-logged to be carried far. From his position at the rear he saw the watchmen go down, shrieking as they were overwhelmed. Then the surging advance phalanx reached the shed, laying it open as if it were a sodden cardboard box. Revealed within was a vast granary, stacked high with pile upon pile of gunny-bags. Upon this the mob cast itself, plucking, tearing, stabbing at the bulging sacks until the grain began to flow.

Ravi heard the long triumphant howl, he knew what it meant, he almost believed he could hear the rustling of the grain as it poured from the sacks although he was too far behind to see. He ought to be there, he thought, out in front, taking his share before the place was picked clean. It was his right, his children's right. He began to fight his way forward, but he was not as agile or powerful as these young men any more, or perhaps there was something missing, he thought tiredly, something vital like heart or spirit. . . . He tried to redouble his efforts, and then, above the tumult and the outcry, above his own panting breath, he heard the voice of Kannan the blacksmith, roaring at him in a mixture of rage and astonishment.

'Ravi! Ravi you fool! Keep away, this is nothing to do with you, this crime, none of your business, work of madmen. . . .'

It stopped him, momentarily, it was so unexpected. He turned, digging his heels in to keep his balance against the tide, and saw Kannan, trapped, his forge overrun, clutching desperately at a terrified jutka pony that was already on its knees.

'Ravi, keep out!' Kannan cried again. 'The rice is for all, this way is wrong, this way the innocent suffer!'

Then Ravi found his voice and shouted as loudly as he could, his lungs near to bursting. 'They have already suffered!' and he lunged forward again, this time going with the tide.

By now the first shed and a second were sacked, and a third smashed open. Men were swarming up the piled gunny-bags, frenziedly, holding out baskets, sacks, their shirts, their dhotis, whatever they could find to receive the rice like women in the paddy-fields at the end of a harvesting.

This time, Ravi said to himself as he struggled to reach the grain, this time at least, and he clenched his empty hands and watched with frantic eyes as the rich heap dwindled, and the empty sacks flopped and sagged and were snatched up and filled or humped away full on shoulders that could bear them. All around him were men driven by the same fear, screaming and fighting in the contaminating rice-frenzy, until suddenly there was a shrilling of police whistles, the squeal of braking trucks, a confused shouting, and the thudding of heavy boots.

Ravi began to run as the crowd broke up. On all sides men were running and he ran with them, wildly, crossing his arms above his head to shield his skull from the baton blows that came raining down. One blow caught his thin shoulders, spinning him round, but he recovered his balance and went on, whimpering, dizzy with pain. Bastards! Police bastards! Then he fell again, this time so spent that he lay where he was, hardly realizing what had tripped him until the steamy smell reached his nostrils, and he saw it was the terrified little nag Kannan had been holding. It was half dead now, crushed and mangled in the stampede, but it still kicked feebly and he thought, poor beast, working himself close to its protective flanks. Then he forgot it, concentrating only on keeping himself alive.

When the pounding had stopped he raised himself slowly. The main body of the crowd had vanished, leaving only a few stragglers who were limping away from the scene of the action. The ground was littered, strewn with shreds of sacking, sticks, stones, broken glass bottles and other implements of battle. Rice lay everywhere, scattered like chicken-feed. Already beggars were edging in, prepared to sift the dust for the grain.

Ravi got to his feet, surprised to find that he could both stand and walk. Others, not so fortunate, lay in crumpled heaps, moaning and moving weakly, some not moving at all. There were policemen among them and he thought, it's a bad business when policemen are hurt, there'll be trouble, a whole heap of trouble . . . and he pulled his tattered clothes round him and began to run, hearing the sirens go as he drew clear.

He ran without stopping, his torn shirt flapping against his breast, until he judged he was out of police range, but as he sat gasping for breath he heard whistles shrilling again and he started up but it was only a gang of police-baiting youths. When they had passed another band came swinging by, and yet another, and this one was an older company, youths and men armed with staves and clubs.

'What is it, brother,' he called to one of them. 'What is happening?'

'We're evening up the score,' the other answered. 'The whole city's astir. Aren't you coming?'

'Where are you going,' he cried, 'Which way?'

'Where the nobs go,' a jeering voice replied. 'We're going *their* way.'

'I'm coming, I'm coming,' he cried. He didn't understand what was meant but he lurched to his feet and a new strength, a new courage flowed in and steadied him as he fell in among them.

They had come to the end of their road now. To Nabobs' Row, to the gilt and glass, and the sensuous sumptuous unthinking display of wealth for the unthinkably wealthy.

'But there's nothing here,' he cried bewildered as the first stones began to fall. 'No rice, no grain, only what the nobs want.'

'What difference does that make, you fool,' a rough voice answered. 'We want what the nobs want'!

'What the nobs want!' shouted Ravi. The name EVE floated in front of his eyes, he saw the golden letters for a full clear second before they disintegrated into shining splinters, crashing down with the remainder of the façade. Inside the elegant disdainful models still stood, pale pink wax, exposed, vulnerable without their glass.

'We'll get them yet,' a hoarse voice beside him exulted. 'Your turn, brother!'

Ravi took aim, poising the jagged brick level at his shoulder. But suddenly he could not. The strength that had inflamed him, the strength of a suppressed, laminated anger, ebbed as quickly as it had risen. His hand dropped.

'Go on, brother, go on! What is the matter with you?'

'I don't feel in the mood today,' he answered, a great weariness settling upon him. 'But tomorrow, yes, tomorrow. . . .'

MULK RAJ ANAND

Across the Black Waters	175.00
A Pair of Mustachios & Other Stories	95.00
Lajwanti & Other Stories	95.00
Things Have A Way of Working Out & Other Stories	95.00

"Anand writes about the Indians much as Chekhov writes about the Russians, or Sean O'Faolain or Frank O'Conner write about the Irish... He has, most of all, the touch, the power that makes the writer great — he can give human weakness a dignity of its own."

Elizabeth Bowen *in Tatler*

"With great deftness, Anand pictures India ... He impresses with his profound knowledge of Indian religion and culture."

Books Abroad, USA

"Mulk Raj Anand stands out as the most wide-ranging and prolific ... a figure of towering humanity whose works guide us through the multitudinous complexity of India in this century with more verve than any other prose writer of his time."

Alistair Niven *in The Hindu*

Dear Reader,

Welcome to the world of **Orient Paperbacks**—India's largest selling paperbacks in English. We hope you have enjoyed reading this book and would want to know more about **Orient Paperbacks.**

There are more than 400 **Orient Paperbacks** on a variety of subjects to entertain and inform you. The list of authors published in **Orient Paperbacks** includes, amongst others, distinguished and well-known names as Dr. S. Radhakrishnan, R.K. Narayan, Raja Rao, Manohar Malgonkar, Khushwant Singh, Anita Desai, Kamla Das, Dr. O.P. Jaggi, Norman Vincent Peale, Sasthi Brata and Dr. Promilla Kapur. **Orient Paperbacks** truly represent the best of Indian writing in English today.

We would be happy to keep you continuously informed of the new titles and programmes of **Orient Paperbacks** through our monthly newsletter, **Orient Literary Review.** Send in your name and full address to us today. We will start sending you **Orient Literary Review** *completely free of cost.*

Available at all bookshops or by VPP

ORIENT
PAPERBACKS

Madarsa Rd, Kashmere Gate
Delhi - 110 006. India